Tracey Chapman is a British novelist who has loved to write since a young child. Her career began with obtaining an HND in business studies. She has worked as a forestry insurance claims coordinator, business administrator, a fancy dress shop sales assistant, and a childminder, among many other things. She lives in Milton Keynes in Buckinghamshire with her husband Steve and their dog Flossie. They have two grown children and a granddaughter. Tracey grew up in Chinnor at the foot of the Chiltern Hills where her family continue to reside.

Tracey Chapman

THE HENSLEY LEGACY

AUSTIN MACAULEY PUBLISHERS™

LONDON ∗ CAMBRIDGE ∗ NEW YORK ∗ SHARJAH

A CIP catalogue record for this title is available from the British Library.

ISBN 9781035863990 (Paperback)
ISBN 9781035864003 (Hardback)
ISBN 9781035864027 (ePub e-book)
ISBN 9781035864010 (Audiobook)

www.austinmacauley.com

First Published 2024
Austin Macauley Publishers Ltd®
1 Canada Square
Canary Wharf
London
E14 5AA

With heartfelt thanks to: Steve, Emily and Oakleigh. Without your support and encouragement, this would still just be an idea in my head.

Chris and Lisa Splitlog, for inspiring me with the idea behind the legacy.

Lee Philpott, for the stunning photograph of a beautiful Maltese beach.

Noreen Cadle, for your help and assistance.

Chapter One

Stretching into the morning sunlight, Ava lifted her head from the pillow and raised up onto one elbow. She loved this time of day, the peacefulness enveloped her and made her smile. Ricco, her beloved cat, lay curled like a cushion of plush fur at the bottom of her bed. He had nestled into the covers and was purring contentedly. Ava wriggled free from the soft cotton sheets and moved over to the door of her balcony. She opened the door and stepped out onto the little platform which hung above the streets below. The balcony was small, encased in pots of sweet-smelling herbs, lavender and roses. The smell at this time of day was divine and Ava, in her white cotton nightshirt, inhaled and then sat on the wooden bench that ran along the wall. Ricco came out from the bedroom to join her, jumped onto her lap and stretched his paws up onto her shoulders, his face pressing against her own.

Bliss.

Looking down the street to the beachfront, Ava could see the owner of the corner coffee shop just opening up, pulling down the sunshade and fetching the small tables and chairs out onto the pavement. He had done this a thousand times before, and the position of each chair and table almost locked into place as though there were grooves in the pavement where they belonged. He raised a hand and waved at Ava when he noticed her watching and made a 'C' shape with his hand as though to indicate he was making her a coffee. Ava gave him a thumbs up and waved back. She went back into her bedroom, found her t-shirt and shorts which she had cast aside the night before, along with her flip-flops, and took them with her into the bathroom.

Ricco had settled onto the bench on the balcony; he would stay there now until he heard Ava prepare his food. He had found a perfect owner in Ava. He had trawled the streets for several years, scratching at doors hoping for a morsel of fish from the dinner table of the occupier and for some time he had been successful. But a bad case of fleas and constant scratching at the offending mites had made him less welcome and his scrawny frame soon became noticeable to the locals. Ava would see him every morning at the coffee shop and when she noticed the fleas, she bought a little comb and with a lot of encouragement, mostly with crumbs from her morning apple-filled pastizzi, she would begin to groom him and rid him of the fleas. It took many days and lots of combing, together with lots of pastry crumbs, before his trust in Ava was complete. Following her home and settling in was the easy part. Ava looked at his little round face sitting by her front door. She opened the door wide and Ricco found his new home. That was a few years ago and the two of them enjoyed the gentle lull of life that now surrounded them.

Down at the corner coffee shop, the owner, Indri, was back inside brewing up the first pot of the day when Ava knocked on the window. The cafe was not open yet so he went over and dropped the latch to let Ava in and handed over her morning espresso. She lifted the smooth velvety blackness to her face to breathe in the aromatics.

"Pastizzi?" Indri asked.

Though why he would ask her each day if she wanted her favourite pastry alongside her favourite coffee, she didn't know but she welcomed the most minimal of exchange at this early hour. She took her coffee and pastry and went over to the windows facing the beach, folded back the large glass panels and opened up the coffee shop to the gentle sea breeze and faint hum of the waves. In the kitchen behind her, she could hear Indri singing to himself—the occasional high-pitched note which he really couldn't make, made her chuckle as she sipped her coffee and soaked in the morning warmth before her shift in the shop began.

Ava knew how lucky she was. She immersed herself in her life here on the coast and embraced every day. She had lived here now for more than six years having visited mainland Malta several times on holiday since a young child and always felt a strange sense of 'being home'. It was the usual relationship break-up—time to move on to pastures new scenario—which had brought her here and she hadn't looked back since. Whilst she'd had a good childhood, she had never truly felt that Gozo was right for her. Ava was an only child to older parents. Her green eyes were so bright they glistened like peridot gemstones and were truly enhanced by her pale features, despite her long dark straight hair.

She questioned her pale complexion around the age of eleven when her school friends asked if she was adopted. Horrified, she ran home to her mother and begged her to tell the truth. To Ava, her mother was a strong woman not prone to emotion but that day her eyes glistened as she looked into her daughter's young face.

"My young child," she began, "God saw the path for you and brought you to my heart. You are my light. The desire for a daughter overwhelmed my existence. Your father assured me that one day my prayers would be answered and when you arrived, I knew that my life had been fulfilled. Yes, you bear the look of your ancestors so unlike those of your father and I, but remember this, no child was ever desired more than you were. God gave me the blessing of a daughter and I nurtured you from the first breath you laid upon my shoulder. No, my love, my sweet child, you are not adopted."

These were words that Ava cherished, she knew how loved she was, and the bond between her and her mother was very strong. To this day, now in her mid-thirties, Ava would telephone her mother weekly, keep her up to date with her life, check on her mother's state of health and listen to her soft nagging about finding a husband.

Ava, having finished her coffee, took her cup into the kitchen and found her apron. Indri was already setting out the morning pastries for the customers on to large white plates. The smell of fresh coffee and pastries drew the morning patrons in and Ava found this her favourite part of the day.

The minute hand almost seemed to hover over the hour of nine waiting for the first of the customers and today was no exception. The four mechanics from the nearby garage could be heard in the street before they entered the shop. Ava knew their order by heart; two kafè latte with their equal mixture of hot milk and coffee, one kafè iswed, her favourite espresso but with extra hot water, and for Joe, the quietest one of the group, a te aħdar, a green tea with a thin slice of lemon.

On hearing their voices, she began their order, called out to Indri that they were arriving. He dusted down his apron and came out from the kitchen to greet them. Indri's enthusiasm for his customers was contagious—everyone was special, everyone was valued and everyone was welcome. The four men pushed open the door and called out their 'good mornings' to Indri and Ava. Mikiel was the owner of the garage and he would buy his men their morning coffee and breakfast every day—baskets of fresh sliced bread, ġbejna, a traditional Maltese sheep cheese, and ham which Indri bought in whole and sliced himself so the slices were good and thick—and this, alongside their coffee, set them up for the morning.

Today, Joe put down his tea and walked over to the counter where Ava was busy stacking small plates and sorting out the cutlery, clean from the kitchen, into little baskets. Ava looked up and Joe smiled.

"There was someone here asking questions about you yesterday," he said, "tall man, slight build, dark rimmed glasses...?"

The upward inflection at the end of the sentence made the question stand for itself but it was a tone which put her on edge. She had never liked this trend but it was more and more popular and like most changes in life she knew she would probably accept it at some point. Her ex-boyfriend used it all the time and that was another reason why it grated on her but it was so reminiscent of Australian soaps from the 1980s, something which she despised. To be truthful, she despised all soaps on the television—dumbed-down drama being the way she described them. Ava looked up from placing the tiny coffee spoons into their basket and raised a quizzical eyebrow at Joe.

"Really? I can't think who that was, are you sure he was asking about me?"

Joe shuffled his feet a little and was looking slightly embarrassed.

"Well, err, um," he stammered, "he was asking if I knew of a lady with dark hair and bright green eyes. Most local people around here have dark eyes." As he mentioned her eyes, he stared directly at hers, a little too intently for Ava's liking but it felt as though he was reassuring himself that hers were green.

"How odd," she said, "no, he doesn't ring any bells with me."

Joe seemed ever more embarrassed and slightly nodded his head as he stepped away from the counter, as though a servant backing away from his master. *Poor man,* thought Ava and in a motherly way, she wanted to give him a hug. Her imagination took over and as she hugged him, his face took fright and he ran back over to his colleagues! Ava smiled inwardly to herself, not sure why her imagination took on these little snippets, but it was like her own private film footage which, from time to time, played out the 'what if's' of life.

By half past nine, the café was empty again and Ava cleared the table where the guys had been sitting. They never made a mess, but Ava ran an extremely clean café and not a crumb would be left in sight. Old Ġorġ was next in; he popped in a couple of times a week on his way back from picking up his fresh fish from the harbour. Ġorġ couldn't hear well at all and his eyesight was diminishing rapidly but he managed to manoeuvre his way around the tables with ease. As a rule, he only ever put his head around the door, not wanting to bring his fish inside the café. Not that it smelt at all, it was so fresh off the fishing trawlers that morning, that the faint aroma was pleasant, and wrapped tightly in yesterday's newspaper you would never know he was carrying it, but it was his way. If it was raining, Ava would see him scuttle past the windows. She would call out to him, but whether it was his poor hearing or whether he was in a hurry to get home out of the rain, he would barely raise his head towards her.

"Good morning, Ġorġ, the usual?" Ava called out rather loudly, but necessary, nonetheless.

Ġorġ acknowledged her with what always sounded like "Yup!" but Ava was never sure what word he did use, but it was enough for her. She flicked the hot water boiler tap on and filled a large white tea pot full to the brim. Inside were already two English breakfast tea bags and the pot soon began to give off its slightly sweet smell of musky tea. She took a large green mug down from the shelf behind her, put it on a tray with a small jug of milk and several white sugar cubes on to a saucer. The café only served white china on the whole, but Ġorġ liked his large green mug—he had brought it in the first day she worked there and placed it on the counter in front of her like a trophy he was presenting.

"I'll take my tea in this please," he had said, "your china is a bit too fancy for me, frightened I might break it, you see?" and with that, he walked back outside and sat down with his bag of fish.

Ġorġ was holding his face towards the sun when Ava took the tray out to him, his eyes so tightly closed, she wondered if he had fallen asleep. Laying the tray in front of him, she went to walk back inside when he gave her thanks for his morning tea. She raised her hand in acknowledgment and went back into the café. Indri had come out from the kitchen having washed the plates and cups from the breakfasts earlier and nodded at Ava.

"Is that Ġorġ out there?" Ava smiled and affirmed. "I'll make him some toast to go with that tea, it will give him the strength to get back up the hill." Indri disappeared back into the kitchen and Ava heard him singing away to himself again.

The morning sun was now high in the sky and Ava could feel the heat of the day beginning to warm the front of the café a little too much now. She went to the front and pulled down the sunshade facing the beach, staring momentarily at the waves gently lapping the sand. It took her back to her childhood days on holiday where she played happily at the water's edge. She remembered many other children around her, squealing with delight as the cool water frothed over their toes. Ava would scour the beach for shells and plop each one into a little red plastic bucket. One time, one of the smallest shells had a tiny crab inside and she sat down staring into the bucket watching it climb over the other shells, walking in circles. She gently took the shell and lifted it out, held it in her hand briefly to watch it, but it had tickled and she quickly brushed it off onto the sandy beach once more.

There was always a hubbub of children's chatter around her but she was able to isolate from it, and being quite content to amuse herself, would wander along the beach for what seemed to her young mind, like hours. She was probably about seven when they started to visit Għajn Tuffieħa in the northern region of Malta. With its beautiful beach and the lovely village of Manikata, her parents would talk of the lack of tourists with great pleasure, and together with the couple of fantastic restaurants serving fresh fish and traditional Maltese cuisine, they simply loved the quietness and tranquillity. Before this time, Ava could not recall much about holidays with her parents. She had vague recollections of being amongst young children, but that was all. Whether they were family friends she could not recall but those days on the beaches were the precious moments of her childhood which she remembered fondly to this day.

Indri called to her, "Another espresso, Ava?"

"Mmm, yes please," she called back from outside.

There was always a quiet lull in trade just before midday—the locals had been for the morning breakfasts or coffee but it was generally the business people from the village that would appear for lunch. Both Ava and Indri would take ten minutes or so between these times to chat about the day so far. By this time in the day, both of them were more ready for conversation.

They worked so well together and had done so from day one when Ava came and asked if he needed help of any kind—she was happy to wash dishes, clean floors, anything to earn just enough to keep her in rent and food. Honestly, he didn't believe that he needed any help, but she looked so earnest and had offered to work a week for him with no pay to show him how hard she could work, that he couldn't refuse. The end of the week came and Indri gave her a week's wages, she tried to refuse him but he insisted. He had finished each day that week without a sore back and without falling asleep the moment he sat in his favourite armchair in the evening. He hadn't believed it necessary but it had taken just one week for him to realise that he was getting older and needed a helping hand. Ava had appeared at just the right time and Indri was completely grateful.

As Ava and Indri sat sipping their coffee before the lunchtime rush, Indri mentioned the man that Joe had referred to earlier. He told her that this man had not been seen around these parts before the last couple of days but the gossip from the ladies who came and took tea in the afternoon on a Wednesday each week, was that he was a journalist over from Canada investigating siblings for an article he was writing over there. May, the 'leader' of their little group, had said that he asked her lots of questions about people living in these parts and wrote everything she had said into a small brown leather book that he kept tucked under his arm.

It was not unusual for May and the other ladies to fill Indri in on any latest gossip they had acquired. This week's gossip could be next week's scandal or more usually just forgotten tittle tattle but it kept them chatting longer and having fun before going back to their mostly solitary lives. Indri would shower the ladies with compliments, not for any other reason than he enjoyed seeing the pleasure it would bring them when he admired their latest hair style, new scarf or perhaps even a new shade of lipstick. The majority of the group were in their late sixties or early seventies, retired in the most part although Francisca, the youngest of the group at just sixty-three, was still working part time in a little boutique that sold baby clothes.

Each week, they would gather at Indri's café with their knitting needles or fabric and sewing supplies, and chat away whilst making baby clothes for the shop. It kept the dexterity in their hands and just getting together and chatting over tea with, naturally, the occasional slice of cake, kept their minds active and gave them something to look forward to each week. May had been involved in organising so much during her younger years, from petitions to sponsored events and certainly didn't shy away from rallying people round to a good cause. The group was her idea having met Francisca in the baby boutique. She had commented on the need for better quality goods and preferably those sewn or knitted with love.

"These imported, factory produced garments are cold," she had said. "What you need is garments that give off the love that has gone into making them."

Francisca had always enjoyed crochet and sewing so she was very open to the idea of handmade or hand-crafted goods for the shop. After discussions with the owner, she approached May and between them they decided to see who else might be interested in creating baby clothing for the shop. Before long, May had organised a small group of ladies from all over the island and between them they added to the stock of beautiful baby garments available. They didn't make that much money for their time and skills, but it was the pleasure that it brought them, that they received the most fulfilment from. After the first six months of their weekly meetings, they had heard that people were travelling from miles around to the shop and they had become local celebrities to an extent, even featuring in the local magazine and having their photographs taken. Their renewed sense of purpose was a wonderful boost and since many of them were now widows, it also gave them company and common purpose.

Ava was really surprised that a man all the way from Canada would be seeking her out. *How odd,* she thought to herself, but just shrugged and didn't dwell on the matter any further.

Chapter Two

The sunken bunker of a basement seemed to jeer at him as he approached it. The natural daylight was fading, replaced by the dull yellow of the street lighting which seemed to add a dingy aura to the already dismal stone surround. Stopping by the top of the steps and looking down towards the doorway, Mark Wheeler hesitated. He really could not face another evening in this shabby place. He fumbled through his jacket pocket for the key and took the stairs, two at a time, to the door. The musty dampness hit him immediately and, as each time before when he went through the door, he retched slightly. He left the door open to let the smell waft out into the streets above—he truly believed something or someone must have died down there.

Taking the suitcase down from the top of the small brown wardrobe that was tucked behind the door, he began to fill it with his clothes and limited possessions. As he packed, he noticed the musty smell had permeated his clothes. Mentally adding a note to his 'to-do list', tomorrow would be about finding a launderette and shaking off this grungy place with a good hot wash.

The basement dwelling where he had been staying for the past few weeks was right on the edge of the little town. It was part of what looked like a dilapidated building that had seen so very much in its lifetime. He had been told that Maltese people hid in cave like dwellings which they'd carved out of rock to protect themselves from the constant bombardment from enemy bombs during World War Two. Whilst his room was not quite that of a bomb shelter, it felt damp and had echoes of poverty and squalor.

Back up on street level, Mark already felt a sense of relief. His company had paid for his 'accommodation' if that is what it could be called, but frankly whatever the cost to him now, getting out of that place and finding somewhere warm and welcoming was all he cared about. With his suitcase on its little plastic wheels behind him, rattling over the bumpy pavements, his suit bag over his shoulder and his laptop case in hand, he strode towards the centre of town. The lighting from the shop windows, many of which still welcoming the evening customers, gave off a beautiful glow. He could hear the chatter of voices ahead and almost like a warm shower of water washing over him, he sighed with pleasure. There were a few hotels in the area, as far as he had learnt from chatting with some people earlier that day. One hotel, right in the centre of town, came highly recommended but all Mark wanted was to find a room with daylight, dry walls and fresh bedding. For a while, he stood still, slightly weighed down by his luggage, but enjoying the feeling of life around him.

Setting off again, he took a left turn into another street and at the far end saw the main entrance to the Solaqua hotel. It looked like paradise to him after his recent experiences. A pretty, dark-haired young girl sat behind a small glass counter. She had a telephone held to her ear but looked up and smiled at him as he pushed open the door. Mark approached the desk and waited whilst the young girl finished her conversation. She replaced the receiver and apologised for keeping him waiting.

"Do you have any vacancies for tonight?" he asked her hopefully. "I would like to stay for a few weeks, but a dry room and bed for the night is all that I am looking for." Mark looked at her with hope in his eyes.

"We have three rooms currently, two double rooms and one large single room with a view over Il Bajja."

He looked at her quizzically.

"The Bay," she added with a smile.

"That sounds perfect to me, can I take it for two weeks with a view to extend it if possible?" he enquired.

The young girl nodded in confirmation, turned, took a small silver key from a wooden rack behind her, and requested that he follow her up the stairs. The landing was small and thickly carpeted in shades of bright blues and yellows. It had a faint smell of lemons and was lit by small overhead dimpled glass bowls which dappled the floor delicately. At the end of the landing, the young girl unlocked a large door and took him into the room. She was quite correct, it was large for a single room, a low level bed sat in the centre of one wall, a glass topped desk flanked the opposite wall and a sumptuous looking armchair was positioned by the window, which in turn looked out over the bay. A small door led to a bathroom which had a deep semi-sunken bath and separate shower.

Mark stood shaking his head, it was so much more than he could have hoped for and he was amazed at the little gem he had found. Grinning from ear to ear, he told her he was most happy with the room.

This wasn't the first time he had been sent to the other side of the Atlantic for work. He had visited Scotland a few years back and had never enjoyed a business trip so much as that one. He had stayed in a small croft in a place called Auchendrean. The croft, an old and often tumble-down stone cottage was the epitome of rural Scotland and, to Mark, it was just what he needed to really connect with the place. The wind whistled into the building through many cracks, crevices and actual openings that it felt as though, at times, he was in a wind tunnel. Luckily, the weather had been favourable and, to him, it was pure joy.

He was certain, however, that to have been there through the cold Scottish winter, he would have felt completely different no matter how authentic or traditional the croft was. Although brought up in Banff, Canada, where the winters were extremely cold, he was softened by the comforts of a middle-class home where fires roared in every fireplace and radiators pumped out enough heat at times to mean that the wearing of winter jumpers were never required indoors. His mother, Vera, was of Mediterranean origin and despised feeling cold. To go outside in winter took her a considerable amount of time, layering her clothing to such an extent that she appeared several dress sizes bigger than she actually was. The layers would contain at least one of Cashmere and one of fur. She did not shy away from the wearing of real fur and embraced its softness against her skin whenever she could. When she left for Canada in 1940 from Spain at the tender age of ten, to escape the ravages of war, her mother had sold all their possessions and purchased them both the finest furs she could buy, purely to keep them warm for the journey.

Mark's time in Scotland, a period of almost eight months, was spent trying to locate the niece of a man who had passed the previous year leaving no Last Will and Testament, a man of considerable wealth. He had travelled through most of Scotland during this time, chasing one false lead after another, but he was enjoying the beauty of the country so much that he was quite happy for the false leads. Hiding his true feelings from his company during his weekly reports was, at times, a little difficult. He would lie at the side of a beautiful loch, gaze up at the trees and mountains around with barely another soul to interrupt his thought process. Mark was generally a loner and thoroughly enjoyed taking a long afternoon stroll, culminating at a local hotel for an evening meal and a dram or two of a fine Highland Malt.

Having never partaken in a drink of whisky before setting foot on Scotland, he was somewhat nervous of the amount on display in the first hotel where he stayed. Fortunately for him, the landlord was overjoyed to have a novice in his midst and the two of them spent several evenings, tasting and discussing many bottles. Mark had narrowed down his preference to either a Highland Malt or one from the Speyside area. He found the Island Malts a little too peaty for his taste and the lighter Lowland Malts were not flavourful enough. Armed with this tiny piece of knowledge, it had stood him in good stead when entering a hotel anywhere in Scotland and he could confidently ask for a malt which he knew would be to his taste. One other major fact he learnt from the landlord during those evenings was to add the tiniest splash of cold water rather than ice. Just one teaspoon of this water would bring out the aroma and slightly soften the whisky, which would then become like velvet to his palate.

Therefore, between the malt whisky, the beautiful scenery and the wholesome stone croft, Mark found his stay in Scotland an idyllic place. The young lady he was trying to locate, was not an easy individual to find. She travelled extensively in the area and he seemed to arrive at one location only to find she had moved on a few days before. The only knowledge he had of her was a name, Emma New, and a twenty-year-old description but he was very good at his job and he did eventually locate her in Wick, showing a group of tourists around the remains of the castle. She was standing outside a battered looking coach, mobile phone in one hand and the last remnants of a cigarette butt in the other. He couldn't believe his eyes. He had travelled hundreds of miles with a scrappy twenty year old photograph and yet, the one day he decided to take off from work, a leisure day to spend sightseeing in this far northern part of the country, there she was.

He had stopped in Wick for a sandwich to sustain him on his journey further north to John o' Groats and Dunnet Head. He knew she had been in the area recently but he was convinced he would have missed her again. His plan was to spend a day in Wick and then travel north. His guidebook had explained that both John o' Groats and Dunnet Head should be part of every visit to the North of Scotland:

"Dunnet Head ten miles to the west of John o' Groats, extends further north, and Duncansby Head, to the east, is probably a mile or two more distant from

Land's End, but John o' Groats is the place you start or finish if you want to cover the length of Britain playing hopscotch or pushing a pea with your nose!"

It was the image of someone wanting to traverse the length of the United Kingdom in such a ridiculous manner that made him inquisitive to visit. He had hoped that he might even get to see the beginning of some such adventure.

The petrol station where he picked up his sandwich had a local visitor guide that mentioned the castle. He thought this might be the perfect place to eat and stretch his legs a little. The map within his guidebook took him straight there and apart from a battered looking coach, there were only one or two other visitors. It was as he was getting out of the car that he saw her.

Walking up to someone and explaining that you have travelled from Canada for the sole purpose of tracking them down and advising them of great inheritance, is not always received well, let alone believed. Thankfully he carried his 'office' in his car so he was able to not only prove he was not some kind of stalker but also that he genuinely was an heir hunter and he did indeed have notice of a sizeable fortune for them. This time had been easier than most. Having the photograph, which she recognised immediately of time spent in Canada with her uncle, had made his introduction believable and yet very sad. She had not heard of her uncle's demise, let alone understood that she was his sole beneficiary.

Mark arranged for them to meet later that evening at a hotel close to her lodgings further south in Helmsdale. It took an hour or so to complete the necessary paperwork and discuss the arrangements but as to how long it would take her to come to terms with the fact that she was the last member of her direct family, was another matter entirely. She had no siblings nor any cousins, her closest family member having been her uncle in Canada who had never married. Emma's mother had passed several years back of bone cancer and she had watched her slow demise over four or more years. Her father was unknown to her, having chosen to not stay with her mother when she found herself unexpectedly pregnant. Emma never wanted him in her life as an adult, just as he had not wanted to be in hers as a child.

Chapter Three

Wednesday mornings were Ava's most relaxing time of the week. She didn't work in the coffee shop on Wednesdays and Sundays and she saw Wednesday as a day for herself. Once she had fed Ricco, sat on the balcony for a while soaking up the warm rays of the early morning sunshine and had at least one cup of steaming dark black coffee, she was set for the day. Ava was a creature of habit and enjoyed spending her day off in the local market, absorbing the sounds, smells and colourful displays that lay before her like vibrant works of art.

This Wednesday, Ava took her usual stroll through the market stalls, picked up some shiny silver fresh sardines, a large aromatic bunch of sweet oregano and a kilo of chocolatey dark coffee beans. She wandered along the stalls admiring the freshly baked bread, the brimming bowls of bright green olives and the fresh cheeses displayed to perfection by the traders. At the top of the market sat two large wooden benches and each week, without fail, Elias would sit, his arms folded over his walking stick, his head relaxed and slightly nodding as he drifted in and out of a silent doze whilst warming himself in the morning sun. Ava approached him and he lifted his head, smiled, and patted the bench next to him for her to sit. She sat and let out a large sigh, a contented sigh. Elias lifted the front of his cap and turned to face her.

"A young man has been around here asking questions," he began, "wanting to know who to talk to about people who live around here…"

His voice trailed off, Ava noticed his eyes were closing and his head had dropped slightly. Elias was known for falling asleep mid-conversation. By all accounts, as a younger man, he had fallen asleep at the wheel of his fishing boat and ended up miles out to sea. He eventually returned home just after nightfall, having left home well before dawn. After that day, he took his eldest boy with him each day. The two of them would be up and out on the boat by four am, returning home with their haul for the day by ten am and then the boy would run up the hill to get to the local school so as not to miss too much of the morning lesson. The school knew of his father's condition and helped the boy keep up with his schoolwork despite the long hours he worked alongside his father. He was a dedicated boy, both to his learning and to his family, caring for his father and younger brother.

His mother had sadly passed away whilst giving birth to her youngest child and Elias had brought them up by himself. One doctor had pronounced that his ability to fall asleep suddenly was due to the shock of losing his wife in childbirth. Another had suggested drinking more coffee and eating less fish. Elias scorned them all, and whilst he continued to fall asleep randomly throughout the day, he slept well at night and had proudly brought up his two boys, both now working happily on his fishing boat and bringing in the daily catch, just as he had in his younger years.

Ava sat quietly with him. It varied between a few minutes to up to an hour or more that Elias would sleep, but she had nowhere special to be so she was happy to sit with him, relaxing and enjoying the day.

There was a kerfuffle by one of the stalls as a local woman argued that last week the tomatoes that she had purchased had not been ripe and tasted bitter. The stall owner hushed her quietly and added beautiful bright red tomatoes to her basket, tapping the side of his nose as if to say, 'It's our secret'. The woman quietened immediately, smiled, and held out her basket to him. Reluctantly, he added a couple more and a small handful of basil. Her smile grew considerably and then strangely, she tapped her nose too, bid him farewell and waved as she walked away. Ava loved to watch people—their hand gestures, their faces, whether full of radiance or saddened, the way they interacted with each other or the tradesmen they had come to see. It all added to the fascinating surroundings of the market.

Gino from the coffee stall opposite where she was sitting gestured to her, offering a cup of coffee. Ava smiled and accepted. A few minutes passed before he came over to the bench with two cups of steaming hot coffee. One for her, short and black, and a milky sweet one for Elias. Gino knew everyone, made it his business to do so and he knew everyone had a preference for a certain style of coffee. The market was bustling but his stall was a little quiet. His daughter, with her raven-coloured mass of curly hair, was managing to keep the customers happy. Gino perched on the arm of the bench, passed over the coffee and leant back to absorb the warmth of the sunshine, his body stretching out like that of a cat. Elias mumbled and came to from his brief slumber. He picked up the cup and took a large slurp, then realised his manners and turned to thank Gino.

A few quiet moments had passed when Gino also mentioned the stranger who had been asking questions. The man had been told of Gino and how he seemed to know everyone. It turned out that he had been asking about a woman who had lived in the area some thirty or so years ago. The photograph he had, showed bright green eyes. Gino had remembered her well. She was a real beauty and a woman with eyes like that was the exception around here. He had told the man that he had not seen her for several years now but was sure that she would be easy to find. Ava cast her mind back to the conversation she had with Joe in Indri's coffee shop recently. Joe had thought the stranger in town was talking about her whereas Gino had said that the woman had lived here many years ago. *That is why it made no sense,* Ava thought to herself.

"To begin with, I assumed he was talking about you, Ava, not too many with your eye colour in these parts, but he said she had lived here thirty or so years ago…" Gino's voice petered out and he looked at Ava a little intently, just as Joe had done. Ava was slightly unsettled, but he continued, "Then I remembered her, but for the life of me, her name escapes me. She must have moved away as I haven't seen her here for a few years now." Elias stopped drinking his coffee.

"Sarah!" he almost shouted. "That's right, Sarah, she was friendly with my wife. She did move away. I think she moved to Gharb, married a toy boy!" With that, he let out a chuckle.

Gino stood up to go back to his coffee stall. He thanked Elias for remembering the woman and said he would pass on the information should the man reappear. Curiosity about the man and his reasons for finding this woman, got the better of them all. Within a few seconds of each other, they all blurted out "I wonder why?" then they laughed. Ava raised her cup to Gino.

"Saħħa" she said, a little odd saying this with a coffee, but whether it was the coffee, the sunshine or their curiosity she was saluting, it made Elias and Gino smile. Ava finished her coffee, said her goodbyes to Elias and took her cup back over to Gino's stall.

"See you next week!" he called from the back of the stall. Ava nodded and turned to walk back through the market.

Gino took the warm handle of the Cimbali coffee machine from his daughter, let her finish serving her last customer and then sent her home for some lunch. The sun was high in the sky now and it would be a while before Gino had too many customers. The next hour or so he knew he would barely see anyone, but that suited him completely. Gino liked his lunches long and lazy. He would take an espresso from the machine, some bread that his wife baked him each day and a hunk of local cheese. There was no better way to describe the way Gino cut his cheese. A hunk, roughly hewn, a salty and yet creamy slab of cheese, which he bit into, alternating between bites of the fresh bread, together with the aroma from the espresso was enough to form a big, yet subtle smile on Gino's face. Gino was approaching fifty now and had been selling at this market, firstly with his father and now with his own daughter for over forty years. He could never see himself living anywhere else. He didn't wish to travel as he could think of no better place to be than right here.

Coffee was in his soul. His father had been one of the first market traders to have a coffee stall mostly selling his home roasted beans and he would tempt his customers with small cups of coffee. Each day, he would return home having sold his supply of beans. Gino was just seven when he started to help his father on the market stall on a Saturday morning. He would get up early with his father and help gather up the beans that they had roasted the day before and fill small hessian bags. The beans were shipped over from Brazil, still green, and Gino's father would carefully roast the beans in a simple heavy pan on top of the stove. He would make them in batches and each batch would take him just ten minutes. The smell from the kitchen each evening was divine and Gino loved being with his father at this time of the day.

The sun was casting a golden glow over the market stalls. They were quiet right now, waiting patiently for the afternoon shoppers to descend. A small cough awoke Gino from his slumber, the warmth of the rays had lulled him into a blissful doze, helped along with a belly full of the bread and cheese. The tall figure was silhouetted in front of him and Gino had to blink several times to work out who he was.

"Just the man!" Gino exclaimed. "Sarah," he added.

Mark moved closer as Gino rose from his chair. He was wearing dark sunglasses and some sort of trilby type hat.

"It was Elias who remembered her name," Gino continued, "she moved away though."

Mark approached the front of the market stall as Gino went back behind to wash his hands.

"According to Elias, she moved to Gharb on Gozo and has since married. I can ask Elias if he recalls her previous name, if you would like? Apparently, Sarah was a friend of his wife but sadly she passed away a long time ago."

Mark gave Gino a broad smile. "That's a great help, it is quite surprising how even the smallest bit of information can help."

Gino shielded his eyes, the sun was now glinting off the sunglasses that Mark was wearing, he couldn't make out the man's eyes, the glasses were very dark and that enhanced the sun's reflections but he could feel the friendliness of the man despite this.

"Coffee?" Gino asked, never shy in trying for a sale.

"Perfect, and any chance of a bite of lunch too?"

Gino took some more of the homemade bread that he too had devoured only a short while earlier, added a large hunk of salty cheese and presented this to Mark.

"So…" Gino trailed the word as though to add the question he was about to ask, before he actually asked it, "this woman…" again he let the words hang in the air as though waiting for an echo to return, but Mark was making him work for his question. "Why are you looking for her?" Gino placed the plate of lunch and the steaming coffee in front of Mark. Then, in the hope of obtaining an answer to his question, for no more reason than idle curiosity and anticipation of an answer, he waved away Mark's offer of money.

Mark took a small sip of the coffee, lowered the sunglasses to the end of his nose and removed his trilby to allow him to wipe his damp brow. He then replaced his hat and took the plate of bread and cheese as proffered, to the first table, and asked Gino to join him. Gino almost leapt out from behind his stall, there were no customers waiting and he wanted to take the opportunity to hear what the man had to say. It wasn't often that they had strangers in town, apart from the plethora of holiday makers, so to have one that seemed to have a distinct purpose of locating a long-lost soul was too curious for Gino to bear.

Mark explained his profession, gave Gino a business card as a form of proof.

"An heir hunter is someone whose business is to search for relatives legally entitled to inherit from the estate or trust of a deceased person, in exchange for a portion of what they inherit." Mark explained that he worked for a Canadian firm in Calgary and would often find himself travelling to far off places in search of long-lost relatives. On these occasions, when the travel was extensive, so would be the inheritance. He would only be sent far-and-wide if the commission he would earn for the company not only covered his costs and expenses but would also make a substantial profit for the firm.

Gino was enraptured at such an exciting job, not that he would change his for anything or wish to travel the globe in such pursuits, but it was an interesting one indeed. The two men sat for a while passing pleasantries and Mark enthused over the bread and cheese that Gino had provided him. It soon became obvious that Mark was not going to say much about his pursuit of Sarah and Gino was unable to add anything more of help other than advising Mark that the journey north to Gharb included a beautiful scenic trip on the ferry.

Chapter Four

Mark awoke early the next day, parted the curtains to give him the morning view of the beautiful bay. He had called Reception a few minutes before to request a tray of coffee and pastries for breakfast. He knew he might have a long day ahead and he wanted a belly full of carbohydrates to set him up for the day. It was the dark-haired young receptionist whom he had first met on the day of his arrival who appeared a short time later with a breakfast tray for him. The tray was circular with a white cloth that draped over the edge. The cloth was square and the corners seemed to drip down from the tray giving it a slight sense of grandeur, far more than it deserved but it was a nice gesture. She had placed the tray on a small wooden table by the window next to the armchair that Mark had become so fond of already. It was slightly tatty and worn but to Mark that just added to the character and its comfort offered so much more than any new smart piece to be found in numerous furniture stores. The coffee smelt glorious and filled the room with its smoky aroma.

Mark opened the window to take in the fresh air from outside and in turn, the air wafted in the gentle hum of daily life. It was still quiet outside at this time of day but the moderate noise of people beginning their day, the occasional toot of a car horn or a shout of morning welcome between two friends was like a warm hug. Mark was beginning to enjoy this little place more than usual for him on his travels. Whether it was the Maltese sunshine, the friendly people or the delightful coffee he was not certain but he was convinced that once this assignment was complete, he would return for a vacation.

Feeling replete and ready for the day ahead, Mark showered and changed into dark denim jeans and a white open neck shirt. He doffed his normal trilby, placed his notebook under his arm, collected his sunglasses from the glass topped desk and made his way to the main reception. This morning there was a rather spotty looking young man behind the smart glass counter. Mark left his room key and made his way out into the morning sunshine. He headed for the nearest bus stop and stood for some time trying to calculate how long it would be for the next bus. He had about twenty minutes or so to wait and whilst he could have ventured further and hired his own vehicle for the day, he rather fancied being driven and hence able to take in the scenery around him. He had grabbed a bottle of water and some fruit for the journey, firstly to Cirkewwa-Mgarr ferry and then onwards by bus again to Gharb.

When he was safely ensconced on board, the bus journey was a delight for Mark. It weaved its way through traffic and along the roads in no particular hurry. It felt as though the bus was on its own adventure and that it too was absorbing the scenery that was in abundance around them.

A small lady with a tightly wrapped scarf alighted at the next stop and Mark watched as she shuffled her bags of shopping between her hands before setting off back the way they had just travelled. A tall man and a young child had got on at the same bus stop and Mark watched as the man guided her towards a seat with a gentle hand on the shoulder. The girl turned towards Mark, she had a tooth missing and she proceeded to push her tongue through the gap in her teeth. Mark smiled back at the girl and in a similar gesture made his eyes go cross-eyed to try to elicit a smile back from her. It was only when she turned away totally nonplussed by the gesture, that he realised he was still wearing his sunglasses, he shook his head as though to admonish his foolishness and turned back to face the window.

It was late morning before he arrived in Gharb and his first stop he decided was a café, somewhere shaded from the heat of the day. He looked about him as he stepped off the bus having first thanked the driver for his journey. The driver looked slightly bemused but smiled and gave a small salute which made Mark smile back. There were a few places around him. He really needed some kind of local guide but the first place that caught his eye looked so welcoming he took his chances. It did not disappoint and inside it hosted a very picturesque space. The main room with its very high headroom, old brick floor, white walls and wooden ceiling, with heavy wooden chairs and tables, was cool. Mark felt a sense of relief from the heat that had become overbearing and had resulted in his shirt sticking to his body. He took a seat at one of the tables and ordered a glass of water and a cold beer. Not his usual tipple but at this point in time, he knew it would hit the right spot.

Feeling relaxed from the beer or maybe just the heavenly surroundings, Mark took his small leather notebook and began to go over the notes he had written inside. His notes began with the very general description he had been given of the lady he needed to find. He had scribbled the name 'Sarah' next to these. *Talk about 'needle in a haystack',* he thought to himself. He had read his notes on his laptop thoroughly before bed last night so he had a little more than a name and a description but it really was nothing much to go on. He was assured by one of his colleagues back in Calgary, that finding a dark-haired, green-eyed woman in Malta would be relatively easy but Mark was not convinced, and assumed his leg was being pulled extensively. As usual, he would start asking in the café, then maybe a church or two, a library, anywhere where a local lady of this description might be known.

The waiter soon came back to see if Mark would like more beer or some food. Mark asked for a ħobża biż-żejt, an open sandwich made from Maltese bread spread with sweet tomato paste, topped with olive oil, tomatoes, and tuna. Just reading the description made him feel so hungry and he realised he had left the fruit that he purchased first thing this morning, on the bus seat next to where he had been sitting. He decided against another beer as he wanted to commit to some more thoughts on his approach to find Sarah but the iced water that he chose was a perfect accompaniment. He was delighted with the sandwich and made a mental note to try to remember the ingredients and attempt to make something similar back home in Canada upon his return.

Wiping his mouth with the napkin provided, he took up the pencil and hovered it over the notebook. His research which had previously led him to Malta, told him of an heir to a considerable fortune, an only sister of a Canadian woman who had passed away late last year in a road traffic collision. The Canadian woman was a widow who had been married to a Hotelier in Banff. Her husband was the owner of many successful and thriving hotels in Canada, the USA and part owner of one in Dubai. His fortune had been amassed through hard work and a heavy dose of good luck. He had purchased a failing chain of hotels in Canada and spent many months improving them, firstly single-handedly and then once the money started coming in, he gradually employed the best tradesmen he could find to bring each one up to a five-star standard.

The one which he part owned in Dubai, he had won in a rare night of card playing when two extremely wealthy gentlemen from the United Arab Emirates and two local businessmen had asked him to join them. He knew his way around the card tables. His father had been a card hustler for many years and had taught him the rudiments of baccarat, poker and blackjack. He too became a formidable player but never a regular gambler. Seeing his father lose all his savings, his house and his car after one bad hand and several large measures of bourbon, left him numb towards the idea of gambling. The night he won the hotel was the craziest thing he could ever have imagined. The two businessmen were showing off their supposed wealth to the two men from the United Arab Emirates, bragging and raising the stakes of each hand to ridiculous levels. The hotelier had successfully bowed out of each hand of cards before the stakes became too high. He had lost a reasonable sum of money and was about to announce he would leave after the next hand.

One of the Arab men had dealt and the cards given to the hotelier were an astonishingly rare treat. Ace of spades and ace of hearts. The businessmen had placed their bets and then the other Arab gentleman smiled and said if anyone could beat his hand, they would inherit his half of the hotel he owned in Dubai. He owned several and the one on offer was the smallest but nevertheless, he must have been confident in his dealt hand. The two local businessmen bowed out quickly, the dealer had shown a hand of two tens. The Arab declared his 'winning' hand of ace of diamonds and king of diamonds. He leant back on his chair his smile sliding from his face as the hotelier turned over his aces. The hotelier was stunned and wasn't sure if this was happening for real.

They had accepted his bet of his last run-down hotel on the outskirts of Toronto, one which frankly he would have gladly turned over to anyone willing to take it on. It needed so much work and the daunting task of completing it was always forefront in the mind of the hotelier. Not only did he not lose it, but he was now part owner of one in Dubai. It took several busy hours between solicitors to tie up the deal but true to his word, the Arab passed over the reins as though it was a tired old horse that had served his master well and was now being retired of his duties. The owner never giving a backward glance.

Mark's information on the hotelier had been easy to come by. He had written to the head of the chain of hotels once owned by the husband of his client and they had passed over a manuscript detailing what could have amounted to a most interesting auto biography had he finished the work, the last chapter being the most revealing to Mark who had read and re-read each line several times. The couple had enjoyed their wealth, the hotel in Dubai being managed by the other co-owner and regular payments being sent to Banff had enabled the couple to travel extensively. They had a young daughter and were to take a long ten-week vacation to Europe. He detailed the excitement of the trip. The stages of planning and the countries due to be visited were listed alongside their reasons for visiting each and every one. Then one word, just one word was written in strange wobbly handwriting. "Gone." Mark had searched for more information but nothing had emerged.

Mark also knew that the hotelier had taken his own life, less than a year after the planned trip to Europe. Bereft from the loss of their only child, he had muddled through his daily existence in the hotel, hiding his emotions behind a shield of professionalism. The shield disintegrated late one November evening and he was found amongst a pile of scattered tablets and empty bottles of bourbon. The details surrounding the loss of the child were sketchy to say the least. Mark's only choice was to locate the sister of his deceased 'client' and see if she could shed any light on the demise of the child, and at the same time, he would enlighten her as to her now considerable fortune.

Mark made some rough comments in the notebook.

Dubai hotel.

Marriage.

Child.

All potentially relevant to "Gone".

To Mark, suicide in men was often linked to either money or love; his beliefs, but nonetheless borne out time and again in the work he carried out. Passing over sums of inherited wealth to either a separated spouse or child was sadly all too often an occurrence. Sometimes a smaller sum would be all that was left after debts were paid off but once more a suicide would have occurred in order to save face to loved ones and not have to take ownership of lost incomes or fortunes.

So, in this case, could he have followed in the footsteps of his late father? Had the hotelier lost the hotel in Dubai on the gaming tables in a casino, which by this time was creating them so much income that the income from the rest of the chain of hotels had paled into comparison. Mark had tried to contact the other co-owner in Dubai but the language barrier and the mistrust of his business in the hotel, had so far drawn him a blank. There were no divorce documents filed either, which meant that at the time of her death, his 'client' was a widow and not an ex-wife of the hotelier.

Chapter Five

The waiter at the café returned to clear away Mark's used plates and glasses. Taking the opportunity to talk to the waiter, Mark enquired of any local women he might be aware of, about fifty to sixty years of age with green eyes. He showed the photograph to the waiter. The waiter studied him and the photograph with caution. Mark recognised the look which emanated from the waiter and reassured him immediately by explaining as best he could, the reason for his enquiry. The waiter shook his head, but Mark could see that the waiter knew something that he was not willing to tell, not yet at least. Mark thanked him, offered him his business card and explained that should he come across anyone matching the description or know of someone who had, then please let him know. He left the café and made his way to one of the local churches.

The first church he came across was a pale cream coloured, very grand building with a dome towards the rear. Mark walked up the steps to the entrance and stepped inside the cool building. His eyes took several moments to adjust to the lack of bright sunshine but he took a seat towards the back of the church and bowed his head. He was not a regular church goer but he knew his place. He heard footsteps behind him and saw that the local priest had entered the building from the side. Mark stood and went to talk to him.

With the same expression as the waiter had portrayed, Mark could see that the priest would need to be convinced of his need for the enquiry. Again, as with the waiter, Mark explained that he needed to find this lady as she had possibly inherited some money and it was his job to locate her and advise her about it. The priest studied him intently. Mark explained that he had been told she had moved to the town some years ago and had since married a man who was supposed to be a bit younger than she was. Mark could immediately see that he had struck gold. The priest's face lit up with what Mark hoped was a realisation that he knew the person he was looking for.

The priest beckoned him to the front of the church and into a side room. The walls were lined with large leather bound books and it soon became apparent that these were the details of the marriages that had taken place in the Bażilika. Each book was dated on the spine and Mark could see that to look at each entry would take a considerable amount of time, when all he knew was that the lady was called Sarah. The priest took down one of the leather bound books, opened it up and started running his index finger down a page. Looking over his shoulder, Mark could see that the priest was reading the list of bride names. He flipped over to the next page and the process continued.

The priest took several more books from the shelf and repeated the process, then he stopped, dabbed his index finger at the page several times and indicated that Mark should read the entry. The bride was Sarah Fisher, age 52, and she had married Benedito Galea, age 28. The priest turned to Mark and offered him a fountain pen, it was a glorious gold pen engraved with Fr. W.H. Noberto surrounded with beautiful swirls. The nib of the pen had a slight slant from years of use and Mark felt privileged to be offered the scribe to make a note in his book. Carefully, he wrote the two names, Sarah Fisher and Benedito Galea, noting their respective ages underneath the names. Passing back the fountain pen, Mark took out his wallet and offered the priest a fifty-euro note.

The priest turned his back and walked further towards the front of the church slightly bowing his head towards the offertory box. Feeling somewhat embarrassed for offering the priest money, Mark took out a second fifty-euro note and put them both into the offertory. Thanking the priest, he descended the steps back to the street which was still smouldering from the overpowering heat of the day.

He looked across the road to the cafe where he had his beer earlier and noticed the place had filled up with customers, the late afternoon drawing them out of their homes and into the beautiful cool surroundings of the cafe. Mark tapped his notebook as though reaffirming the newly acquired information and went across the road where the waiter he saw earlier raised a hand at him. Mark smiled and walked past the cafe further towards the centre of the town. He stopped at the first hotel he came across. Without a guide he had no idea if there was more than one hotel to choose from, but it looked smart and more importantly it looked cool inside. There was a heavy wooden door studded with old iron fixings that stood out like jewels. The hinges were hefty and detailed and the large round door handle was also made of iron, worn down by the hundreds of people who had ventured through its portal, although rather sadly to Mark, it turned out to be merely ornamental these days. Pushing open the door he went inside. The room opened up to reveal a wooden counter which had beautiful floral arrangements each end and between them stood a young man with a bright expression. Heading towards the desk Mark enquired about a room for the night, just the one night should be enough but as was his usual request, he asked for it to be able to be extended should the need arise. The young man nodded, turned and took a small key from a box beneath the desk and passed it to Mark. The key had a small leather fob with the number 124 in gold lettering. The 1 indicated the first floor and room 24 could be found at the end of the corridor on the left side. He asked if there was anything else and Mark requested a tray of fruit and a bottle of red wine be sent up to his room. Nodding in confirmation that he understood, he moved out from behind the desk and opened the door to the stairwell for Mark to ascend.

The room was bright and cheery, not a patch on the one in Mellieħa but more than adequate for a night or two which he might need to track down Sarah. There was a sharp knock on the door which Mark acknowledged and the young man from the reception desk entered carrying a large wooden tray piled up with various fruits plus a carafe of red house wine and a beautiful cut crystal wine glass. Thanking him and offering him a ten Euro note, Mark settled down and the reception clerk left the room. Mark unpacked his few belongings and placed his notebook on the small table which was set under the window. The window had closed wooden shutters that allowed the light into the room by adjusting a central rod.

This room was on the shadier side of the building so Mark opened them up to allow in the remaining sunlight. It was warm in the room but not hot and Mark took his seat on a small green sofa which had bright red buttons and soft yellow cushions which depicted various animals. The first he picked up showed the head of an elephant, the second one had a striking zebra, the stripes of which stood out boldly against the yellow fabric of the cushion and the third was what appeared to be the neck of a giraffe. Mark turned the cushion over expecting to see the head of the giraffe, but the reverse side was plain yellow. He smiled, he liked the quirkiness of the sofa and the cushions. Leaning forward to the tray he poured himself a large glass of the wine.

He slept well. The bed had been firm enough for support and soft enough for comfort. He woke to the smell of fresh coffee coming from outside his window.

He looked out and saw a street vendor pouring small cups of coffee for his customers. Dressing quickly, Mark left his room and went across the road to the coffee stand. He ordered an espresso and indicated a small pastry shaped into a diamond. It was covered in soft icing sugar and smelt of sweet dates and spices. Taking the paper bag wrapped treat and small cup, he sat at a table in the shade of a canopy on the right side of the coffee stand. He hadn't been sat long, was just about to open his paper bag and delve inside for the pastry when the other chair at the small table where he sat was pulled back. Mark looked up to see the waiter from the cafe where he had eaten yesterday. The waiter sat and stared at Mark quite intensely.

"Any joy?"

Mark smiled at the Americanised phrase uttered by the Maltese waiter.

"Yes, actually, the priest at the church over the road from your cafe was able to give me her last name."

"Fisher?"

"Exactly right, so you do know her," this was a statement not a question but the waiter answered accordingly.

"Yes, I do, but when someone comes asking odd questions about a customer, it pays to be cautious. It is not every day that someone comes to the cafe saying they are looking for someone you know and want to give them money. How was I to know you were genuine?"

"So, what changed your mind?"

"I saw you come out of the church, I know Father Noberto quite well, he was my Sunday school teacher. I went to see him and asked what he thought of you."

"And what did he think of me?" Mark was rather enjoying this conversation, this could give him an insight into how people reacted to him. He would read facial expressions each time he met someone with whom he had dealings, usually to advise them of the demise of a relative. Generally, it started with caution, then disbelief, normally followed by shock, although in one case he had tracked down, they were furious.

Mark had explained that a long-lost cousin had at one time been married to a Hollywood star of stage and screen in the 1940s. The cousin and the 'star' had parted ways but had remained married. It was many years ago and no one in the family had been told of the marriage. The Hollywood star had since passed away and his cousin would have inherited the large estate which had been left behind. The cousin had passed away too, and the person sitting in front of Mark, now furious from hearing about the connection to a Hollywood star, would inherit a quarter of a million US dollars. The amount in question was the residue of the estate after debts and taxes had been paid. The anger was not towards the amount, towards Mark or towards only just finding out about the loss of his cousin, but purely that for years he could have bragged about his Hollywood connections and now he felt it was too late!

"Well, he assured me that you were genuine, something to do with you knowing about Benedito being much younger than Sarah."

"I found that out in Mellieħa. Apparently, she had a friend there many years ago who has sadly passed away but her husband seemed to have this snippet of information."

"Hmm," the waiter rubbed his chin, a slight shadow of unshaved skin showed beneath his hand, "yes, that would be about right. She moved here a few years back and met Benedito, he is my cousin."

Mark's job was not normally this easy, he was expecting to have to work hard for his information, to at least visit the local library and look up the census or the local telephone directory. This was too simple but he was exceedingly grateful.

"Sarah is out of the country at the moment, but Benedito will be in the cafe later today. You can come and see him there if it helps, then he can put you in touch with Sarah."

"Do you know where she is?" Mark enquired. "Is it holiday or work?" The waiter assumed that cautious look once more.

"Ask Benedito later, he can explain better than me."

"Let me get you a coffee." Mark stood and reached for his wallet but the waiter declined.

"Can't stand the stuff," he laughed. "I know that is odd coming from a Maltese man, but I only drink cold drinks."

"A coke? Water?" Mark continued to offer a drink to the waiter, sort of in exchange for information, which was undeniably a helping hand, but also, he was hoping for a little background on Benedito.

"Thanks, but I need to get back to the cafe, I was walking to start my morning shift when I saw you here. I only stopped to tell you about Benedito."

"Well, thanks so much," Mark remained standing and the waiter started to put his chair back ready to leave, "Perhaps I will see you later, at the cafe?"

Mark returned the small coffee cup to the street vendor, took his uneaten pastry back to his hotel and went into the bathroom for a shower.

It was almost midday before Mark went down to the hotel reception. There was a short lady with a round face and curly shoulder length hair behind the desk. Mark enquired about staying at least one more night and she confirmed that was fine and would arrange for clean towels to be put in his room.

"Really no need for that," Mark told her, "but if I could just get a plate of cold meat, cheese and bread for this evening, around seven pm, that would be wonderful."

The receptionist agreed to his request, enquired also if he would like a carafe of wine to go with it. Smiling and agreeing to this, Mark left the hotel and made his way back to the cafe. It was not quite as hot as yesterday but being out in the midday sun was never a good idea at this time of year. He kept to the sides of the street where a thin sliver of shadow cast a low black border to the buildings, just enough to give him respite from the heat.

The cafe was busy but Mark found a table tucked into a corner towards the back. The waiter he had seen earlier was serving a couple of tourists and their young family a few tables in front of him. The man was holding a cold bottle of water to his head, cooling him off, and his female companion was wafting the children with a makeshift fan using the food menu. The waiter moved away and quickly returned to the family with a bowl of ice cubes and the children hungrily sucked on the cooling blocks. He placed glasses of lemonade in front of them and a plate of bread and cheese. Looking up, he noticed Mark, nodded his head towards him to acknowledge him and moved back to his serving counter. A minute or two passed and a man approached the table carrying a tray of two bottles of beer and a jug of iced water with thick slices of lemon.

"I'm Benedito," he announced and placed the tray on the table in front of Mark. "I understand you are looking for my wife, Sarah?"

Mark asked him to join him at the table and Benedito sat opposite him.

"Please call me Benny though," he said, "only my mother calls me Benedito and that was when I was misbehaving!"

Mark laughed at the comment, picked up a glass and poured a beer. He started by explaining that until he had spoken to Sarah directly, he could not divulge too much information but he explained about his work, how he tracked down relatives that had received an inheritance. "I understand Sarah is out of the country, may I ask why that is and where she is?"

"Of course, she is visiting a friend in England, a place called Milton Keynes, it is north of London I believe." Benedito seemed to chuckle under his breath at this. "I hear they have fields and fields of concrete cows, not real ones, but ones made of concrete! How crazy are the English, eh?"

"Ah, I know Milton Keynes," Mark confirmed. "I had cause to visit one time to find a man who had become a Buddhist monk. He had inherited money from an aunt in Vancouver, she had no other relatives. I was sent there to find him."

"Did you see the concrete cows?" Benedito seemed fascinated by his one fact.

"Well, it is true that there are some, but just a few, it is an art thing as far as I could tell. There are plenty of real ones too!" Mark noticed Benedito deflate, his face now downcast, he looked quite dejected.

"That is sad, I have a vision in my mind of concrete cows in all the fields. I will need to learn a new fact about Milton Keynes before my wife returns." Mark smiled, the young man was quite endearing.

"They have a lot of roundabouts, if that helps. And the town was modelled on a North American style grid system with roads having an H or a V, indicating whether they run horizontally or vertically."

"Ha!" Benedito exclaimed. "That is better than the cows, thank you!"

"Is there any way I can contact Sarah?" Mark enquired, "I really need to speak to her."

Benedito considered the request and took a swig directly from a bottle of the beer. "I will speak with her later and ask if you can call her."

Mark was really pleased, this trip was going so smoothly, he would be back home to Canada in no time at all.

Chapter Six

Thursday morning followed its usual pattern. The mechanics arrived for their breakfast and Indri served them whilst Ava was tidying the shelves of white crockery, straightening the handles of the tea pots, cups and jugs so that they all faced in one direction, slightly angled to the left. Indri teased her that she was a perfectionist but secretly he too liked the way it looked on the shelves. Ġorġ appeared soon after the mechanics had departed and sat outside soaking up the morning sunshine. It was warm already but Ġorġ had a thick jacket on and had turned the collar up as though to protect his neck from a cold wind. Ava made his pot of tea and placed the pot and his green mug onto the tray along with the jug of milk and saucer of cubed sugar. It was so quiet in the coffee shop this morning that Ava took the tray out and sat down beside Ġorġ for a short while.

"How are you today, Ġorġ?"

"Aye, not too bad, and yerself?" Ġorġ looked at Ava and gave her a smile showing a row of yellowing teeth many of which were missing entirely, no doubt partially due to the several cubes of sugar he added to his morning tea.

"Yes, fine, thank you, but didn't sleep well last night though I'm not sure why." Ava brushed a few crumbs off the table in front of them and a small brown sparrow came and pecked at the ground. "I feel as though I have something on my mind, but I'm not sure what it is, I think I must have taken too much sun yesterday!" Ava chuckled at her own comment and rose from the table. "Can I get you anything else?" she enquired.

"Some toast would be perfect please and a bit of cheese, thanks love."

Ava went back inside the cafe and into the kitchen where Indri was preparing the vegetables and salad for the lunchtime rush. She took some bread and cut two thick slices, popping them under the grill which was glowing red. Buttering them once golden brown, and adding a chunk of ġbejna, she plated up the toast and took it back outside to Ġorġ. He had his head down reading the newspaper. Thanking Ava, he took a large gulp of his hot sweet tea and picked up the buttery toast. Ava looked across the road and saw Ricco up on her balcony, although she could only see the tops of his ears and his tail which was swinging down from the balcony like a pendulum of a clock. The rhythm of his tail reassuring her of his contentment, Ava smiled and returned to the cool of the cafe.

The lunch rush was in full swing when Francisca popped her head around the door. Catching Ava's attention, she busied herself over to the counter and leant over as though to whisper.

"Did you see that young man that was looking for you?" Francisca blushed as though parting with this isolated piece of idle gossip was alien to her and not part of her usual daily routine. "He did seem quite keen to find you."

"In fact, it wasn't me he was looking for." Ava didn't whisper her reply; she smiled at Francisca and poured her a takeaway cup of sweet tea. "There was a lady who lived here before I arrived—I believe her name was Sarah." Francisca paid for her tea and hovered at the counter hoping Ava would impart some more details. A few moments of silence passed between them and Ava realised she was expected to provide more information. "That's as much as I know," she added, "It was Elias who recalled her, she was a friend of his wife's but she has moved away now."

Francisca seemed happy that she had a little more knowledge and Ava realised that it would not be long before everyone in town knew about Sarah and how she was being sought out by a stranger in town. Shuffling out of the cafe, squeezing between the occupied tables and chairs, Francisca left the cafe holding her takeaway cup high above her head making sure that it didn't get knocked by the other customers.

It was almost four in the afternoon before Ava was able to take a few minutes break and Indri joined her out at the front of the cafe, under the sunshade facing the beach. The chairs there were more weather-worn and tired-looking than those to the side of the cafe, the salty spray from the sea whitening the grain of the wood. Ava preferred the way they looked compared to the pristine ones both inside and to the shady side of the cafe, but Indri would complain about how the salt was ravaging his possessions. They sat in companionable silence for a while both sipping on their favourite coffees. Indri yawned and Ava looked across at him, he had looked more tired of late and Ava was concerned for him.

"Are you okay, Indri?" Ava questioned "You look like you need a good rest, a holiday maybe?"

"Hmm, yes possibly." Indri shuffled in his chair, a little awkward from the question. "I am getting older. I love my cafe but working here each day takes a toll on my old bones."

"Take a few days off, a week if you like, I can manage."

"Be careful, I might just take you up on that offer." Indri smiled at Ava. "I cannot recall the last time I took time off, but then again, what would I do all day? I can't just sit around dozing in the sun, I need to keep moving otherwise I stiffen up and that will not do for me."

"Haven't you got a sister in Sicily, perhaps you could pay her a visit?" Ava could not remember his sister's name despite meeting her a few times. She had marvelled at how thick and luscious her hair was, dark like a raven's feathers that glistened in the sunshine, Ava had been envious for certain. "I wish I had more family," she sighed, "a brother or sister perhaps." Ava had always wished for a sibling but her parents would remind her how loved she was and that there was no need to extend their contented family unit.

Indri was quiet for a while. He stretched out his legs in front of him and having finished his coffee, placed the cup on the arm of the wooden chair then lifted his arms up and rested his hands behind his head. His shirt became untucked from his trousers and he quickly lowered his arms and tucked it back in again.

"I just might call her. Do you think you'd be okay for a few days? I really do think a rest would do me good. Ha! Recharge the batteries, eh?"

"Absolutely, go for it! I will be fine and if I need any assistance, I bet May would be only too willing to lend a hand in exchange for a few pots of tea."

Just then the little bell above the door to the cafe tinkled, heralding a new customer. Ava and Indri picked up their drained coffee cups and went back inside the cafe. Indri usually shut the cafe around seven, most people by then would have gone home and he didn't serve evening meals, though there was not an exact closing time. Ava, however, would finish around five and go home to make Ricco his supper, often with scraps of fish from the kitchen that Indri would wrap up in newspaper for her to take home. Today was one such day.

Ava prepared a plate of crisp green salad leaves with some sardines in lemon and herb dressing for herself having given Ricco the heads of the fish. They sat together on the balcony of her flat enjoying their respective evening meals and the remaining heat of the day. Ava still had a feeling that something was troubling her. It was a feeling like knowing you had forgotten something and racking your mind to try to recall what it was. She sipped on her cool glass of white wine and tickled Ricco's stretched out tummy as he lay beside her.

Her mind questioned various things that had occurred during the day and the few days before and yet still, she could not place her concerns. The conversation with Indri about his long overdue trip away could not be anything to do with it. Not only was she more than happy to help him, but she had also been feeling this way all day, waking from her sleep early this morning with a feeling that she couldn't place. The man who she thought was looking for her, turned out to be looking for someone else, so that wasn't a concern... or was it? Ava pondered this thought for a while. Why was that hanging in her mind like a door that was ajar and needed closing? She shut her eyes and let her imagination run. What was it that she knew? Firstly, a man was looking for a local woman that it turned out had lived here for many years. Secondly, she now knew her name to be Sarah and she had moved away a few years ago, married a toy boy, if Elias was right.

The feeling that was unsettling her began to grow and she focussed her thoughts on the various conversations she had taken part in over the last day or so regarding the matter. Joe had thought the man was looking for her and so had Gino originally. Click! The door in her mind shut with a bang! Ah, the eyes, that is it! She was a dark brunette and had green eyes just the same as the woman who was being searched for, and Ava knew that these looks around here were unusual. She wanted to find out more about Sarah and she knew of only one person around the town that might have something more to add.

Chapter Seven

It was Sunday before Ava had time to pay Elias a visit. Friday and Saturday being the busiest days of the week in the café. She put aside her uneasy feelings and worked through the two days, thoroughly enjoying her daily interactions with the customers, most of whom felt like friends these days. Elias was out on his fishing boat when Ava arrived at his home a little before ten in the morning bearing a basket of breakfast pastries for Elias and his boys. They were freshly made on Saturday but Ava knew they would still be welcomed by the family. The youngest lad was in the kitchen when Ava knocked and he opened the door to her with a welcoming smile. *He will be a heartbreaker one day,* Ava thought to herself.

His large brown eyes were rimmed with long black lashes and his dark fringe lay across his forehead in a boyish tousled fashion. Ava knew that, at some point, it would frame the most handsome of faces. He made a pot of coffee and between them they laid the pastries out on old chipped plates and waited for the return of Elias and his eldest boy. Hardly a boy these days though, at the age of eighteen the oldest lad was able to do most of the work for Elias. Under the guidance of his father, he had learnt how to fish and to bring the haul back to shore each day, the reins of bringing in the family income now falling squarely on his shoulders.

Elias and the boy returned home just before ten-thirty and he was thrilled to have a female visitor in his humble home. Though he had known Ava for a couple of years now and had often met her at the weekly market in town, she had not visited him at home. To be truthful, Elias didn't invite anyone back to his house. Whilst not ashamed of the untidiness, he felt he didn't want anyone to feel sorry for him. He had done his very best to take care of his sons since the passing of his wife and not a day went by when he didn't miss her completely, but housework was something he didn't even notice needed doing until the dishes piled high in the sink or the floor held a carpet of dust and dirt upon its tiled existence.

Never having spoken to the boys before—Ava knew of them obviously—but the need had not arisen to make conversation. She was ashamed to realise that she didn't know their names. Elias smoothed out a potential awkwardness by dropping their names into conversation within moments of his return. Christopher, his eldest son was despatched to wash his hands before eating and Jack was thanked for making the coffee. Elias's wife had been English and had insisted on English names for her sons. He explained that his poor wife never knew that her second child was a boy. She had died almost immediately after a difficult labour at home, the midwife and local doctor could do nothing to save her. It broke his heart but he knew she would want him to remain strong for his children.

Had Jack been born a girl, Elias would have named her after his wife. She was Yvonne and he would have baptised the baby in her memory. Between them, Elias and his wife had chosen the name of Olivia for their baby should it be born a girl and Elias would have given the baby the name of Olivia Yvonne. It wasn't to be and Jack was born, slightly blue in colour, late into the night one February, fourteen years ago. Elias gave him the second name of Ivo in honour of his mother. Ivo being the male version of Yvonne. Yvonne derives from Yew, a tree which is renowned for its strength. It seemed an appropriate name given the difficult birth.

Coffee being passed around and both Christopher and Jack heartily tucking into the pastries which Ava had brought along with her, she made her apologies to Elias for her unannounced visit to his home on a Sunday morning. Elias reddened in the face from her apology but reassured her she was most welcome at any time. Asking to speak to him privately, they took their coffees to the rear of the property into a small paved courtyard out of the glare of the sun. The courtyard was edged with various shapes and sizes of pots all seemingly abundant in various herbs, salad leaves and differing types of tomatoes and peppers. Ava was taken aback by its beauty.

"You have the most magnificent courtyard garden," she began, "what a delight to be able to gather your own herbs and salad leaves to go with your freshly caught fish. I manage to grow a few herbs on my balcony but truly this is my idea of heaven."

Once more, Elias blushed from her comments—he was not used to compliments whether personally or otherwise and he was beaming with pleasure at her remarks. He gestured for her to sit on a bench at the back of the garden. It was just a long beam of wood which was supported at each end by two old tree trunks that had long been felled. The wood was cracked and weather-worn with a slight dip towards the middle. Elias noticed Ava run her hand over the dip as though she was feeling the life it once had.

"I sit here every evening, sometimes I fall asleep and wake to the stars above me and the moonlight guides me back to my bed. I told the boys to leave me here if I'm asleep. This was my wife's doing, all this." Elias swept his arm around him in a large circle to encompass the garden and all its pots, flowers and herbs. "I had to amend my first instructions to them though, when they left me out here one night in the rain; I was chilled to the bone when I woke and had to take to my bed for a few days. But being out here each evening brings her back to me, that's why I keep it going, planting the pots up each year with plenty of seeds to give us a little slice of her legacy on our plates." His eyes filled with tears and Ava reached over and gently patted the top of his hand.

"Do you mind if we talk more about your wife?" Ava looked at him, wary of upsetting him further.

"I'd love to; anything to keep her memory alive for me."

"It's about the other day, in the market, when you recalled the name of the lady that was being sought after. Do you remember? You said her name was Sarah and that she was a friend of your late wife."

"I didn't know her well myself, she was a friend of Yvonne. They would spend time at the market together. It was Sarah who taught my wife to speak Maltese and to be able to ask for her produce without pointing at it." Elias smiled, the memory coming back to him with a pleasure that warmed him.

"So, was Sarah born here, do you know?"

"Oh gosh no, I don't believe so. She came here with her first husband as I recall. She used to live in Canada, met him when he was on holiday and they became pen pals on his return. She always wanted a family but never did manage any children. Her husband was a flighty one though and left her for a younger girl. We were all shocked, and after she'd moved all the way from Canada to marry him. Quite the scandal of the time."

"How awful, poor woman."

"Indeed. Yvonne took to her immediately. She felt vulnerable living here and not knowing many people. She hadn't learnt the language at that time; well, not more than a few words which helped her get by. Meeting Sarah when she was also vulnerable, I think they bonded over their mutual feelings. Became quite good friends too."

Ava nodded, she could understand those feelings, to her regret, she also had never managed to have a child. Perhaps now that she had moved on with her life and her relationship had failed, it was a good thing, but who knew?

"Yvonne used to keep diaries though; there may be more information in them if you'd like to see; but what's the interest in Sarah, if you don't mind me asking?"

"Initially, I had none." Ava shuffled on her seat, feeling a little awkward and not knowing whether to own up to her idle curiosity of the woman just because her looks matched those of her own. "But I got to thinking about her description, pale complexion, bright green eyes..." She let the sentence trail off, having noticed Elias's head had slumped against his chest and his breathing now heavy and regular; she knew he was asleep. Minutes passed when Christopher popped his head out of the rear door.

"Oh, he's off again, is he? He might be out for a while, never can tell."

"That's okay, I'm in no rush and if you don't mind me sitting here with him, I'd like to stay. Your garden is a joy to be in."

"Do you mind if I pop out then?"

"Go ahead, should I let him know where you have gone, when he wakes up, I mean?"

"Yes, just to see Sofia, my girlfriend, I'll be back before supper and Jack will be about, he has schoolwork to finish before tomorrow."

"Thank you," Ava smiled at the young man, the boys were most definitely a credit to Elias.

As it was, it was only a few short minutes before Elias woke from his brief slumber. He shook his head a little and rubbed his temples.

"Was I out long?" he looked at Ava and shrugged.

"No, just a few minutes, but Christopher popped to see you—he said he was going to see Sofia and would be back before supper. I hope that's okay, I didn't question whether you would mind?"

"No, she's a fine young woman," he paused and sighed, "reminds me a little of my Yvonne, not in her looks but the way she keeps Christopher on the right side of the tracks, if you get my meaning? Not hanging about on street corners with some of the youngsters around here."

"Yvonne sounds a fine woman." Ava looked at Elias, making sure she wasn't upsetting him.

"Aye, she was that. I was so lucky to have shared a small part of my life with her and she gave her life for my son. I can never repay her for the debt I feel I owe her but looking after the boys and keeping them on the straight and narrow, is all I can do. I hope she would be proud of them."

"I'm sure she would be, they are a great tribute to you." Ava noticed a small tear trickle down Elias's face and he wiped it away with the back of his hand.

Ava allowed a few minutes of silence to pass. A bee flitted between the flowers on a tomato bush beside her and she watched it as it hungrily took the nectar from blossom to blossom. Unaware of the benefit to the plant, it took the sweet offerings ready to be later passed to his companion within the hive before being capped in wax.

"The diaries you mentioned, would you really be happy for me to read them? I give you my assurance that anything I read within them will stay with me, I would not repeat a word. But I have a feeling that I need to get to know Sarah, even if only because we share the same complexion and eye colour. As a child I questioned this so often. My mother assured me that it was just a throwback from my ancestors, but if I'm being totally honest with you, it always made me feel different. My friends would tease me and it would make my mother so cross with them."

"That you do!" Remarked Elias. "I trust you, and I have a good sense where these types of things are concerned, so by all means. I'll get Jack to dig them out of the attic space later today and drop them to you at the cafe on his way to school in the morning. Whether there is anything of interest in there or not I can't tell you. I haven't managed to look at them myself, but just knowing I have them is a connection to her."

"I'll take the best care of them and return them to you as soon as I can. If I can learn anything about her that might put a closure on the strange feeling that I have had since I heard about her, then I'll be happy." Ava laughed nervously and got up to leave. She bid Elias and Jack a farewell and wished them a pleasant afternoon.

Ricco was sprawled out as per usual, on the balcony when Ava returned home. It was a little too warm for her out there in the midday heat and she took a book from her small bookshelf which she had fashioned herself from pieces of driftwood, threaded with rope each end and hanging from an old iron coat hook.

Making a sandwich of cold ham and radicchio lettuce, she poured a large glass of sparkling water and added a few ice cubes to add to the coolness of the drink. Her flat was cool, its walls were made of thick stone and the whitewash on the outside kept the heat from penetrating its inner sanctuary. She had a small old couch that she had come across outside a house the second day she was in her flat.

At that time, her possessions consisted of her clothes and a few essential items, plus towels and a set of white bed linen that her mother had given her when she first left home. The couch was quite forlorn but it had taken her eye. A woman appeared at the door and told her to take it if she'd like it, as she was expecting a brand new one that very day. Ava was delighted but soon found out it was too heavy for her to move. The wooden frame was solid and shone with years of wax polish. The woman called inside for her husband. He was a man who towered above both Ava and his wife. He picked up the couch with ease and asked Ava for directions. Even the small set of stairs up to her flat didn't discourage him and he placed it down in the centre of the room with care.

A few days after she found her couch, there was a gentle knock on her door. The couch-carrying husband stood there, his arms full of lamps, cushions and a set of cooking pots. He offered his arms towards her and although taken aback by the generosity, Ava gladly took the possessions being passed to her. The following day, she purchased flour, sugar and eggs from the local market and together with pine nuts and lemon peel from lemons that she had on her balcony, she prepared prinjolata to her mother's recipe and delivered it to the family. Shaped like a dome, the cake is traditionally prepared for a carnival leading up to Ash Wednesday. It was a small token of her gratitude for the items of furniture that now graced her once bare flat and she delivered it still warm from her oven.

The couch was faded but enveloped her and she loved it. She had whacked the old dust out with a broom and after a fit of choking on airborne particles from years of use, she arranged the selection of cushions on it with a sense of pride. The worn patches were evidence of the love it had received over the years and Ava embraced them as her own. Sundays, being the quietest day in the town, Ava would often be lying on her couch with the latest book she had acquired from the second-hand book stall in the market. She read all types of books, novels of past and present, true crime stories and non-fiction tales of days gone by. She soaked up the words, the imagery and the joyous quiet moments with equal pleasure.

Her mind drifted back to her morning sitting in the garden with Elias. She was excited to see what the diaries that Yvonne had written all those years ago, might tell her about the mystery woman who resembled her. She was more curious about this than she felt she was entitled to be. For some reason, the door in her mind that had shut firmly upon realising her anxious feelings had found direction, had now popped open again and was offering a brief glance of what might lay ahead.

Chapter Eight

Jack arrived promptly just as Indri opened the door to the cafe at nine. He held in his hand a soft woollen bag. It had a look of velvet and was covered in pale yellow embroidered flowers. Jack looked slightly embarrassed as he handed the bag over to Ava.

"The bag was my mother's," he shuffled his feet with his head bowed, "Dad wanted me to give the whole bag to you as there are a few letters from Sarah inside too."

"That is wonderful." Ava took the bag and laid it on the table before her. "I promise I will take the greatest care of it all, you can trust me with her words."

"I didn't know my mum," Jack looked at Ava more directly now, "I want to read them too one day, it might tell me something about her."

"That's a lovely idea, I will get them back to you as soon as I can."

"Erm, can you bring them back in the bag to the house please? I'd rather not carry the bag around again, I don't want my mates seeing me with it."

"Of course," Ava smiled, "I'll pop around with them as soon as I've finished."

Ava made Jack a takeaway cup of milky coffee for his journey and off he set, school bag strapped over his shoulder. Indri came out from the kitchen and Ava asked if she could pop the precious diaries back home before the day began. She really didn't want them lying around the cafe all day.

The mechanics appeared as soon as she returned and Ava was kept busy with their order, her mind a little distracted by the allure of the diaries sitting on her couch. The lunchtime rush passed and Indri then explained that he had spoken to his sister and would indeed take Ava up on her offer of managing the cafe in his absence. He would be gone for two weeks and would pay Ava extra for the increased work she would have to take on. Ava waved him away when he made the offer, saying she would rather see him back rested than a few extra euros in her pocket. However, he then dropped the bombshell that he was leaving that night and Ava was in charge from tomorrow until his return. Indri instructed her to only open for a half day on Wednesday and he would speak with May about helping her out by clearing used plates and cups from the tables and perhaps a little washing up, particularly on Friday and Saturday.

Ava's delight that Indri would get the rest he needed was ever so slightly tainted by the knowledge that she would have less time to read the diaries, but she knew in her heart he needed this break. Ava took his hands in hers. His were soft from years of washing up but showed their age in the wrinkles covering the backs of his hands.

"Promise me you will rest and enjoy your vacation?"

"Oh, I'm going to," Indri assured her. "My sister is going to show me the sights of Sicily but I have made her promise that I will have lots of time for relaxation."

Just before four in the afternoon, it had quietened down a little and Indri insisted that Ava went home early. They had prepared lots of food ahead ready for tomorrow and Indri told her that she was to close each evening no later than seven. She was to shut for two hours after lunch and re-open mid-afternoon that being the only way he could see that she would manage on her own. He fussed around showing her where things were. It felt a little odd to Ava, having worked there for so long now and knowing where everything was kept, but she knew it was reassuring for him to go through the motions. Indri promised to contact her and confirm his safe arrival in Sicily and Ava promised to keep the cafe running smoothly in his absence.

Having slipped out of her shorts and t-shirt from the day and now wearing a loose cotton sundress, Ava sat on her balcony with the little woollen bag to her side. Ricco sniffed the bag, turned his back and took himself to lie under the bench in the cool shadow of the afternoon. The diaries were tied together with a pink satin ribbon and behind them were a few envelopes, all gently opened with a knife, not ripped. She undid the ribbon and looked inside the top one to confirm it was the oldest in the pile.

Like a lot of people, Yvonne had started the year with enthusiasm, writing a short and succinct anecdote of each day. By February, she had missed a few days and come April she was down to odd words. *Doctor 10am* and *Elias Dentist 3pm*. There was still the occasional little line about bumping into someone at the market and trying to understand what they had said to her. The first two diaries held very little information until she reached September of the second one.

Deliriously happy, Elias thrilled, having a baby next year—excited and terrified in equal measure. Ava looked at the year of the diary and calculated that this would be Christopher. She suddenly felt intrusive reading the words written in the diary and could feel the emotion that Yvonne had used in the few words on the page. These were not meant to be read by a stranger. Ava closed the diary and went to the kitchen to get a drink. She leant back against the cool surface of the countertop and let her imagination go. How would she feel if she was writing something now, something private maybe, which would be read in years to come by someone she didn't know? Ava tried hard to imagine. Annoyed? Nonplussed? Intrigued? She really wasn't sure.

Taking her drink back to the balcony, she picked up the diary and smoothed her fingers over the cover. She opened the pages to September and continued to read. In her mind she told herself that like her husband and now her sons, Yvonne too, would want to help her find out about Sarah. This allowed her to continue despite a gnawing feeling in the pit of her stomach that she was intruding.

From September onwards, Yvonne had written more than before. She chronicled how she was feeling, what foods she craved and how her belly had stretched to accommodate the tiny baby inside of her. By late April the following year, she had made notes about how her feet and ankles would swell in the heat of the day and how Elias massaged them for her whilst she would rest. She was happy. Ava flicked forward in the diary to May and sure enough at the end of the month, the 29th, there is an asterisk. Turning the page, to 30th May, Ava read, *It's a boy! Christopher.* A joyous tear escaped Ava's eye as she felt the emotion in the pages of the diary come to life.

It was towards the end of August, the same year that Christopher was born, that Ava read the first mention of Sarah. *Met woman in market today, so kind, helped me buy fresh basil. Meeting next week for coffee.* A few blank pages and then one word *Sarah* against Wednesday 26th August. The following entry on the 27th August read, *Sarah, just lovely. Willing to help me learn more Maltese, what a relief.*

The diaries continued, mostly just doctors, dentists and coffee meetings with Sarah, the occasional birthday noted for someone but most years Yvonne started well in January with notes about the Christmas that had just passed and how this year she would find the time to write more in her diary. But like all the ones before it, it would be a matter of weeks or so before the words would dry up, and it was back to brief notes occasionally. Yvonne certainly seemed to enjoy her friendship with Sarah and the most remarked entries in her diaries would be to do with their meetings and how her Maltese was now improving. *I can ask for almost anything at the market now*, one entry read. *Successfully opened a bank account using only Maltese* was another. These made Ava smile, it was lovely to read how Yvonne was developing in her learning and the friendship that developed alongside.

It soon became apparent that Yvonne believed she might be pregnant again. She wrote that she was reluctant to tell Sarah knowing how much she had longed for a child of her own but had added a note after meeting her later that day, how overjoyed Sarah was for her and Elias. Ava was beginning to like Sarah very much. From late July through to December, Yvonne's sparse notes once more referred to her strange eating desires. *Cold fish sandwiches with chutney—who knew how delicious these are!* and *Coffee tasting foul these days* read another.

The last diary looked so fresh, barely touched. Ava opened it to January. The entries this time were sparse compared to previous years. *Tired and bloated* was frequently written and an asterisk against February 4th. Turning the pages, Ava saw nothing until February 13th. The entry just read: *Hopefully tomorrow—please!* Ava surmised that baby was late and Yvonne was exhausted. The 14th had one small entry, *Not yet*.

Ava's heart was going out to Yvonne. That was the last entry. Ava closed the diary, assuming Jack was born on 15th February, the day Yvonne passed away. A lump formed in Ava's throat. She didn't know Yvonne but she had felt her elation and her sorrow. Her achievements and her friendship with Sarah had been borne out, albeit so briefly in these few diaries. Ava took the ribbon and tied them all back together. It was getting late and she would read the letters another day.

Chapter Nine

Mark woke from his hotel bed and walked over to the small window that looked out over the bay. He had grown quite fond of this little hotel room in Mellieħa and was pleased to be back after his journey. He picked up the telephone and requested a tray of coffee and fresh fruit to be sent up to his room and enquired if there had been any messages left for him. It was too much to expect a call so soon from Benedito but he could hope. Once showered, he decided to take a walk down the hill to the bay before it became too hot. He found a bench beneath a shady tree and the warmth of the sun was enlivening the nearby shrubs and flowers providing the most heavenly scent. Mark was no expert in flora and fauna and had no clue what they were, he was just happy that his senses were being enticed.

An hour of walking and Mark was beginning to feel the heat of the day and returned to his room. The receptionist nodded in welcome and advised that she had a message for him.

"A lady will call you at four this afternoon, she is called Sarah."

"Fantastic!" Mark grinned, this was far too simple for such a profitable case.

He returned to his room and took out his laptop to make notes. He still had lots of questions for Sarah but the search had been so easy it gave him confidence in the rest of his case. His concern was whether Sarah knew of her sister's demise.

It was a little before three thirty when his room telephone rang. He sprang up from the chair by the window and grabbed the receiver in case it stopped ringing before he had time to answer it. He felt strangely nervous as he sat upon the bed to take the call. In fact, it was the hotel receptionist on the line announcing that he had a call from the United Kingdom and was he happy to take it? Hastily agreeing, he held his breath momentarily whilst Sarah was put through.

"Hi, is that Mark?"

"Yes, nice to talk to you, Sarah, thank you so much for calling me. Would you prefer me to call you back so I take on the cost of the phone call?"

"Gosh, that is fine, I'm happy to do this, unless it is going to take a long time, then you can." With that she let out a slight laugh, it was warm and friendly sounding which put Mark at his ease.

"Not too long hopefully," Mark replied. "Firstly, I must establish a few facts, the usual proof that you are who I believe I'm looking for. Your date of birth and can you tell me if you know of Florence Hensley?"

Sarah confirmed her date of birth and that, indeed, Florence was her sister. Mark enquired whether she had spoken to her Canadian family recently.

"Sadly, not for a while," Sarah said. "We last spoke about eighteen months ago, my sister needed hospitalisation, she suffers with her mental health. I never heard if she came out of the facility. I did write a few times, but I have not heard back."

Mark took a deep breath. "Are you there on your own at the moment?" There was a noticeable silent pause from the other end of the telephone line.

"Er, no, I'm here with my ex-sister-in-law, she is right here, but you have me worried now. Is my sister okay?"

"I'm so sorry to tell you this, but no, I'm afraid she has passed away." There was an audible gasp on the phone line followed by a small sob.

"Oh my, oh no!"

It went quiet and Mark was not sure she was still on the line.

"Can I come and see you in Milton Keynes? I understand you are going to be there for a while and there are things that I really need to discuss with you."

It was a different voice that answered him. A lady confirmed that she was with Sarah who was not able to talk now. Mark established that this was the ex-sister-in-law with whom Sarah was staying. He repeated his question and she said she would take care of Sarah and gave him a contact number to use once he had arrived.

Having finished the telephone call, Mark called Reception and asked if they were able to book him a flight, as soon as possible, to the UK? The receptionist agreed to arrange this straight away and get back to him with the details. Mark began to pack his suitcase. He generally travelled quite lightly so the process was a quick one. He left the suitcase on the bed and went down to the reception area. He could hear the young woman on the telephone and surmised she was arranging his flight.

"I have booked a taxi for you, Mr Wheeler, and your flight leaves later tonight. You have plenty of time but I'm afraid the only flight I could arrange will take you into Birmingham. I'd hoped to get you one to Luton but the flights are all full, I'm afraid. You will leave from the airport at nine this evening."

Mark thanked the receptionist and went back to fetch his suitcase. The taxi was due shortly and he wanted to be ready and waiting. One thing that he was not keen on was poor time keeping. He always felt it was rude to arrange to meet someone and then to turn up late without letting them know. He returned to the desk a few minutes later, settled his bill and went outside to wait for his taxi. He didn't need to wait too long as a large estate vehicle pulled up to the kerb beside him. It was cool in the taxi thanks to the air conditioning and the journey to the airport was a comfortable one.

Landing in Birmingham very late that night was so much colder than he had imagined it might be. Mark shivered inside the airport and realised that a warm coat might be necessary. He enquired about a local hotel, preferring to venture further south the next day and was guided to a nearby Travelodge. A basic yet surprisingly comfortable room and a promise of some heating had been enough for him to accept the room on the spot.

Mark decided to take the train from Birmingham to Milton Keynes, a journey of just over an hour and he could enjoy the countryside at the same time. He ventured off to find breakfast and would telephone Sarah once he had eaten. He found a restaurant in the airport that was selling everything from full English breakfasts, American pancakes to light and fluffy omelettes. Not wishing to have too full a stomach for the day ahead, Mark opted for the latter with ham and a large Americano. Deciding he needed a warmer coat too, Mark perused the various outlets within the airport. Finding a reasonably priced lightweight jacket and adding a woollen scarf, which was expensive, he now felt more equipped for the British weather. Mark pulled his suitcase behind him and followed the signpost for the railway station.

There were several trains due to leave and Mark quickly found the one he needed. The train took him directly to Milton Keynes, he would arrive just before one pm. He had enough time to telephone Sarah and she answered quite quickly. He let her know his arrival time and they arranged to meet at the coffee shop at Milton Keynes station. He dozed a little for the first part of the journey. The train was full but he had managed to locate a seat near the rear of the train with enough room to stretch his legs out in front of him. Various stations passed by the window beside him, Coventry, Rugby, Northampton then Wolverton. Next stop was Central Milton Keynes. He gathered up his belongings, put on his new coat and scarf and having departed the train, made his way to the main entrance where he had arranged to meet Sarah in the coffee shop at the front.

Chapter Ten

He noticed her immediately when he pushed open the door into the coffee shop. Her dark hair flecked with grey fell to her shoulders. Her back was to the door and Mark approached the table, turned to face her and announced himself. Sarah looked up at him, smiled and then indicated that he should take the seat opposite her. She already had a large cup of coffee in front of her and Mark asked if she would like any more before moving to the counter to order his own cup.

Returning to the seat by Sarah, Mark noticed that her brightest of green eyes were a little puffy and red. This was a look he had seen hundreds of times and it always made him sad to see how he could have such a devastating effect on people. Many times, in his line of work, those who he would find, had little knowledge of long-lost relatives who had died without leaving a will. Mark's job was to trace the family tree of the deceased and locate the closest living relatives. It was a job he really did enjoy but on days like these when the living relative had been close to the deceased, watching the heartbreak unfold in front of him was gut wrenching.

"I must apologise for my behaviour on the telephone yesterday," Sarah began, "it was such a shock to me."

"No need, that is totally understandable, I wish I didn't have to impart the news to you but sadly that is part of why I need to speak with you."

They both sipped their coffee and Mark took out his laptop from his suitcase and fired it up. It took a minute or two to open and then he tapped away at the keyboard to locate the files he needed. He had completed some of the necessary forms yesterday having spoken to Sarah and confirming her date of birth. He had already added in her maiden name of Fisher, her now married name of Galea but had left a gap to add in her married name for her first marriage. Sarah broke the silence.

"I had always feared something would happen to Florence, she was so sad after losing both her husband and her daughter, spending so much time in mental health facilities. It was lucky that her husband was a wealthy man, it meant she could have the best care available. Looks like it wasn't good enough though, I am still in shock that she has gone."

Mark began to fill her in on the information he had on her sister. She was indeed an inpatient at a female only unit in Toronto. It was known to be one of the best in Canada and had provided a safe place for females with severe mental illness or mood and anxiety disorders. Florence had been at the facility a few times following on from the death of her husband. Each time, upon leaving, it looked as though she would manage to take care of herself, only to return once more, in need of their care. The last such occasion was about eighteen months ago, Sarah knew of this time being the last time she had contact with her sister.

Mark confirmed that she had been a resident, for just a few months when she managed to leave in the night through an open window, unseen by the staff. She had acquired a set of car keys and had stolen the car at approximately two am. Leaving the facility at some speed, sadly she took a bend in the road far too fast and was found the next morning upside down in the vehicle. The emergency service confirmed that they thought she had died on impact.

Sarah's eyes glistened with tears.

"I'm so sad, but at the same time I am not surprised." She looked across the table at Mark, her hands were screwing up a napkin in front of her, she would clench it between her hands then release it, smooth it out and then clench it once more. "How many tragedies can one woman take before it all becomes too much?"

Mark held her gaze and then continued with the information he had.

"I know about her husband's suicide and the death of her daughter, I assume these are the tragedies to which you refer?"

"Yes, though of course, with regards to her daughter, not having found a body always left her with questions. She always clung on to the hope that she was still alive somewhere, albeit everyone telling her that in all likelihood she had drowned."

This was new information to Mark and it pricked his interest, he wanted to learn more. Whether today was that day, he doubted, so he asked if he could meet Sarah again to allow the details surrounding her sister's passing to settle and perhaps, they could discuss her daughter when she was feeling stronger? Sarah readily agreed and it was decided that they would meet again in a few days' time at the same place. In the meantime, Mark would find himself a hotel to stay and would do some research, to what extent he knew not, on the loss of Florence's daughter.

Mark and Sarah left the coffee shop and she took a taxi from the front of the station. He too flagged down a taxi and asked for a local hotel. The driver took him to a place close by, and he was able to take a room for a few days without too much difficulty. He was tired from his travels and opted for room service that evening and was brought a plate of grilled sea bass with a salad that was fresh and appealing. He accessed the hotel Wi-Fi and began his internet search with *Florence Hensley daughter*.

It was a little before midnight when Mark turned off his laptop, sat back and exhaled. The bare bones he had managed to extract were that the family had been visiting Europe and had stopped in Malta to visit Florence's sister. They had travelled to Mellieħa where they had planned on spending a week or so with Sarah. A few days after their arrival, they had gone to the beach late one afternoon and allowed their daughter, Alison, who was almost three, to go down to the edge of the water by herself. In a matter of moments Alison was not visible to her parents and a frantic search began. The child was not found and presumed drowned. Seven years passed and a death certificate was finally issued.

Mid-afternoon the next day, Mark telephoned his office in Calgary and explained what he had learnt so far of the case surrounding Florence Hensley. He asked for all the files which were held in the office to be emailed to him but the only documents they had on Alison Hensley were both a birth and death certificate. Mark really needed a change of scenery to his hotel room, as comfortable as it was. He decided to take his laptop down to the lobby of the hotel and set himself up to do more searching on the internet for whatever facts he could find on the case of the missing child. Naturally the child had been discounted for inheritance as they had the death certificate but now that Mark had discovered that the body of the child was never recovered, he was left feeling a little uneasy. He really needed to have more facts before his next meeting with Sarah so he ordered himself a black Americano with an extra shot and settled down for the remainder of the afternoon.

The pages and pages on the internet describing potential leads, the family anxiety, lost documents and ultimately a decision by the courts in Malta that the child must have drowned, took Mark the rest of the day to read through. He looked in his notebook and turned to one of the last entries he made back when he was in Mellieħa. He had written the word "Gone". Now it made sense, now he knew what Alison's father meant when that final day he could take no more of the grief and loss of his only child. Mark's thoughts turned to Florence. Her child gone and then her husband abandoned her also. He could not begin to imagine how these poor parents were feeling. How does anyone cope with that type of loss, never knowing how their child had lost their life, never knowing for certain?

Footsteps stopped beside him and Mark looked up to see a smart woman in a bright red woollen jacket buttoned up over black pin stripe trousers. She made a small cough to gather his attention or her own thoughts, he was not quite sure.

"Are you Mark Wheeler? I'm Sarah's sister-in-law, well, ex-sister-in-law to be exact."

Mark stood up to welcome her and indicated for her to take a seat beside him. "Can I get you a drink, tea or coffee perhaps?"

"No, no that is fine, I just wanted to come and see you without Sarah. She has taken the news of her sister's death so badly despite saying she is not surprised. I'm concerned for her naturally so I don't want to leave her too long. Only I have these papers for you, they are newspaper cuttings, but I kept them from when Alison went missing. I went out to Malta at the time to help in the search and kept my own record of everything that was printed over there and also back here. My brother was married to Sarah at the time and we all helped, walking the beach, the streets, going into cafes and hotels in the hope that someone had seen her, but all to no avail. It was devastating. Florence and her husband William, stayed for nine months hoping to find something, they never gave up hope."

"I cannot imagine how they were feeling." Mark took the pile of papers and envelopes from his companion. "I will take good care of these and get them back to you."

"It's probably all on the internet these days," she added, "but you might find something here that gives you the full picture. I must go now, I believe you are seeing Sarah the day after tomorrow?"

"Yes, that is correct, and then I need to decide what to do next." Mark stood as Sarah's sister-in-law did the same. "I'm not sure this case is as simple as I thought it would be."

They said their goodbyes and Mark sat down, opened the various envelopes and spread the contents in front of him. She had been right, he had learnt most of this information from the internet already, but it was useful reading the reports at the time. There was a report of a man being seen on a bicycle with a child holding on to him. They had been disregarded quickly when the child turned out to be his daughter who had run out of the house late at night having had a bad dream. Another report described a car in the area, a silver Fiat Panda that had a large dent in the front wing. It had been stopped by the police at the roadblocks that had hastily been set up, but it later emerged that the police officer had failed to search the vehicle in its entirety. However, the vehicle was later found and discounted. There were sightings of people with small crying children, all of which resulted in conversations with the parents, all of which were a dead end in the search for Alison.

Chapter Eleven

Mark knew from being in the heir hunter business that it was possible to accept the official documentation which he had and make arrangements for the considerable inheritance to be passed over to Sarah. His company would gain their twenty percent and he would get a substantial bonus as a result. But he was hesitant. There was something about this that he didn't like, something that was niggling at him and he wanted to delve more into the information that was available before proceeding with the inheritance paperwork between Sarah and his firm. He had spent the previous day trawling websites in Malta and some in Canada too, all of which brought him to the same conclusion as the coroner, that to all intents and purposes it must be accepted that the child had sadly drowned.

But there was a fact that made Mark uneasy; the policeman who had stopped the car, the silver Fiat Panda, had left the police service at the age of thirty-four. Mark had looked for information on the policeman and had found that he became a school teacher and left the police before the verdict into Alison being missing had been officially given. Coupled with the fact that he had failed to search the vehicle correctly when it was first stopped, made Mark very curious. He decided he needed to get back to Malta and investigate this further.

Mark checked out of his room, it had been a very brief visit during most of which he had been holed up in the hotel, but he was aware how valuable the trip had been. He decided to spend some time before meeting with Sarah later that day, to look around the local area. He recalled his last trip to find the Buddhist monk and took a taxi to the beautiful Willen Lake on the south side of the city where he took the white steps up to the Peace Pagoda which sat near to the Buddhist temple. He had seen images of the pagoda before but being there now, he marvelled at the tranquillity that it exuded. Four white stone lions stood guard to the entrances and a beautiful gold statue looked out across the lake.

Mark stood back and took a few photographs on his phone to show Benedito later, hoping that his disillusioned image of Milton Keynes concrete cows could be altered when he saw the beauty of the pagoda. It was a much warmer day today and Mark would have enjoyed a walk around the lake amongst the ducks, swans and geese that resided on its watery edge but he was trundling his suitcase behind him ready for his return journey which was making the walk a little difficult. He chose instead to sit on a slatted wooden bench and observe the local wildfowl from there.

A short while later, Mark walked over to a nearby cafe and ordered a sandwich and coffee, sadly the cheese and pickle affair was not a patch on the ħobża biż-żejt which he had had only a few days earlier but it sated his hunger and that was sufficient. He ordered a taxi and went outside to wait for it.

His next stop before his meeting was to locate the concrete cows. He wanted to take a photograph back to Benedito for him to see. The taxi driver knew of some replicas that stood on one of the 'V' roads in the city but told him that the original structures were now housed in the local museum following various types of vandalism and graffiti over the years. Mark was able to grab a quick shot of the replica cows as they drove past on his way to meet Sarah before his return journey. It was a small gesture for Benedito, though one which he imagined, would be gratefully appreciated. How these kinds of random rumours get spun out of proportion was fascinating and part of him didn't want to disillusion Benedito, but having already disappointed him with his previous explanation, he felt it was necessary to give him something more concrete in affirmation. Mark smiled at his own unintentional pun.

Sarah turned up a little before three in the afternoon. Mark was already sitting at a table in the same coffee shop where they had met previously. She joined him and Mark was relieved to see her eyes looked greatly improved from a few days ago. He ordered her a coffee and asked after her well-being.

"I'm feeling a little better," she began, "I think it has begun to sink in. I just wish I had known and I would have travelled to Canada for her funeral."

Mark just nodded and allowed Sarah to speak more.

"Though I've always felt that funerals just serve to make money for the funeral directors and the church or chapel concerned. Why this process must happen is beyond me. The family has already gone through the loss, and then a day of ritual and compounded grief is added on top. I'd like to cut out the middleman, the profiteer, when it is my time. I'd like my body taken away and my ashes returned to my loved ones for them to dispose of how they wish." Sarah looked sadly into the middle distance. "I don't suppose my sister's ashes are available now?"

"I can make enquiries, but I fear it is unlikely. As there was no family present, they may have been interred at the crematorium. I will let you know as soon as I am able."

"I'd appreciate that, if that is all I have left of my family then I would like a special place for her to rest, somewhere I can visit, plant a rose tree perhaps."

"That's a lovely idea." Mark smiled warmly at her. He was relieved to see she had been able to talk freely of Florence without being overly upset.

Mark opened his laptop and the relevant files held within, pertaining to the inheritance.

"I need to discuss with you the possibility that you may inherit some or all of the money that is left in her estate after taxes have been settled. But I would like to carry out some further investigations back in Malta surrounding the disappearance of Alison, before we complete the paperwork. Are you happy with that arrangement?"

"Of course, I'd love to hear anything that you discover with regards to Alison but is there really anything left for me to inherit, surely all the time Florence spent in mental health facilities must have taken a considerable chunk of her wealth."

"I'm sure you are correct and there would have been a lot more if she hadn't needed to do this but I am still talking of a large inheritance here, I believe it will finalise at somewhere around twenty-six million Canadian dollars, after our fees."

Sarah looked positively pale. Already of a pale complexion, it was as though her face went from pale pink to blanched white in a matter of seconds. She slumped back into her chair and her mouth dropped open, aghast at the information.

"Never, surely not!" She shook her head as though to dislodge the thought from her mind. "How can that be? That is a vast sum, this is too much, too much!"

Mark turned his laptop to face her and it clearly showed Can$ 33,268,177 being the value of Florence's estate and then minus the twenty percent which would be taken by Mark's company, the inheritance value amounted to Can$ 26,614,541.

"This is why I firstly need to ensure that there are no other living relatives that could lay claim to all or part of this money and also why I am able to travel across the globe to find you. I hope you understand."

"Yes, yes, that I understand, I am totally flummoxed though. How did I not know how much money Florence had? Where did it all come from?"

"The sale of hotels mostly," Mark advised. "Her husband had amassed many five-star hotels across Canada and USA plus part ownership of one in Dubai, which alone was worth many millions of dollars."

Ordering a second coffee each, Mark wanted the meeting to last a little longer, he really hoped to learn a little more about Florence. Sarah had seemed to recover from her shock and the colour was returning to her cheeks. He closed his laptop, there was nothing now that he needed to make notes on and it made the situation feel less business like.

"If you are happy to talk, I'd love to know more about your sister."

Sarah lifted her head to meet his gaze, she stared for a moment and then nodded slowly.

"Growing up was idyllic, I suppose. We were very close and being just the two of us, we would share so much, clothes, books, you know, that kind of thing. Our parents were not poor but nor were they able to give us much, honestly though, we never felt deprived and what little we did have, we cherished." Sarah began to smile with the memories, it was lovely to go back to those times in her head, relive the pleasantness of childhood.

Over the next hour or so, Sarah continued to tell Mark about Florence, how she'd met her husband and how Sarah had moved to Malta to be with her first husband. The way she seemed to glow each time she spoke of her sister was not something that could be faked and it reassured Mark that the bond between the sisters had been strong and genuine. She explained how Florence had met her husband whilst working at a hotel, she was waiting tables when he began working in the kitchens. Their friendship blossomed and before long they were a couple. Sarah, being a year and a bit younger than Florence, had missed spending so much time with her sister now that she was with William, and initially became a little jealous. Florence realised quite quickly what was happening and would include Sarah in their days out. This was how Sarah met her ex-husband. He had been on holiday, travelling across Canada from Toronto to Vancouver and they had met one evening in a bar.

Sarah's reminiscences were warming to be a part of, and Mark settled back in his chair. She spoke of how happy she was to hear of Florence's pregnancy and safe delivery of a baby girl. Sarah by this time was living in Malta with her husband and sadly had not managed to conceive. The joy of hearing about her niece was a special moment, one which Sarah still cherished. The telephone had rung late one evening and she had answered it with a little trepidation as one does when the phone rings late at night. Her sister was on the other end, the joy in her voice so wonderful to hear. She had needed a caesarean section to deliver the baby as she was breach but she was recovering well and the little baby, to be called Alison, was "pink and soft and smelt of fresh cotton", being how Florence described her.

Sarah knew that William was now working hard in setting up his own chain of hotels. He had amassed a few in one large purchase of run-down properties and had spent a lot of time on the renovations. Time was at a premium but Florence had promised to visit Sarah with baby Alison as soon as they could get away. It was three years, almost to the week that she had heard of Alison's birth that the family arrived at Sarah's house in Mellieħa. It was to be the first of many visits that Florence made, over the next twenty years or so. Sarah recounted her version of that fateful evening and Mark listened intently not wishing to miss a single fact.

It was about four in the afternoon, the intense heat of the day had subsided a little and Alison was keen to play in the sand on the beach. Florence, William and Sarah had taken the short walk to the beach with her. Sarah's husband not wishing to go, had remained in the house with a promise of preparing food for them all to have upon their return. Alison had run ahead and had pulled off her little sandals the moment her feet hit the sand. She had asked if she could go for a paddle and the three adults had agreed, with Sarah telling Alison not to go any deeper than her knees. The beach sloped so gently that there was no concern for her safety, just that she should not go deeper without an adult present. The three of them turned their backs for what seemed like a few seconds, purely to also remove their footwear. They had all been wearing trainers and socks so the process took a few minutes, no more.

William had turned first; Florence was sitting on the sand and Sarah was beginning to sit down when he remarked that he couldn't see Alison. Florence had leapt to her feet immediately and she and Sarah had sprinted the few metres down to the water's edge. They had looked all around but she was not visible.

William clambered over some small rocks on the beach to see if she was hiding but he saw nothing. Then he ran back up the beach, back to the road to see if he could see her. Sarah and Florence ran up and down calling out Alison's name, the panic setting in like a raging fire in their bodies that they were unable to quell. There were only a few other people on the beach, everyone started to help search; no one had seen anything.

William called the police and within a very short time, several roadblocks were put in place. A massive search of the whole area began, including a helicopter search both locally and over all the beaches. Sarah continued her story explaining about the people who had been questioned, most of which Mark had read about either on the internet or in the newspaper clippings that Sarah's ex-sister-in-law had given him. That reminded him that he still had them and he leant down to his bag to fetch them out.

"These are for you," Mark passed over the papers, "it was interesting to read all the different things that were written about the case."

"Thank you, yes I know, as hard as it is, still to this day, this is all we have left of Alison and it may not be much but I cherish these pieces of paper."

Sarah went on to explain that Florence and William had stayed with her for nine months following the disappearance of their young daughter. Leads were followed and hopes were raised and dashed again as each one turned out to be false. Sarah mentioned the Fiat Panda and how despite initially it hadn't been searched, that it had been found very soon thereafter and checked thoroughly, then subsequently discounted. This was the part that concerned Mark the most, this was what he wanted to try to get more information on.

Four months after their return to Canada, William committed suicide, not able to live any more with the responsibility he felt for the loss of his child. His death threw Florence into an even deeper depression, but despite this, Sarah was able to encourage her to return to Mellieħa many times over the next twenty years. Each evening she spent there, she would wander along the shoreline, sometimes calling out Alison's name. It was heartbreaking.

Lastly, Sarah told Mark how eight years ago (her marriage having failed ten years prior to that), she finally decided to leave Mellieħa and had moved to Gharb. There she met Benedito, a man much younger than herself but they had fallen in love and married within six months of meeting. She was happy and felt slightly relieved to have moved away from Mellieħa. No longer reminded each day she saw the beach, but honestly, she would still look at every young person she encountered and look for any resemblance, even though she knew in her heart that Alison had been lost to them all, that afternoon on the beach.

Chapter Twelve

Ava had set her alarm clock, not something she usually did as she would regularly wake around eight, take a quick shower before heading over to the cafe where Indri would have a hot espresso waiting for her. However, she was opening the cafe up herself today and wanted to make sure everything was perfect. It was a little after seven am when Ava silenced the small silver alarm clock that sat on the cabinet beside her bed. It was given to her by her mother when her father had passed away. It had been his clock and Ava treasured it knowing how her father had wound the small key at the back each evening to make sure the clock would trill the morning hour for him.

She had such fond memories of time spent with her father, so tall, so broad shouldered that up to her early teenage years he would still lift her and sit her on his shoulders. His hair was thick and dark and would smell of engine oil from working beneath his battered old car. He loved his car and would spend hours tinkering with the engine and touching up the paintwork. It was dark emerald green and, to keep it pristine, he would often be outside with a spray can making sure it was as glossy and as perfect as it could possibly be.

Ricco was curled up on the bed when Ava returned from her shower. She took a small blue saucer from the cupboard and opened the fridge where she had some sardine heads wrapped in newspaper. Ricco was not a fussy eater, years of living on the streets had made him most adaptable to eating whatever came his way, but sardine heads were a favourite. He sniffed the air, stretched and tumbled off the bed, curled himself around Ava's legs before lowering his head and delicately nibbling at his breakfast.

By a quarter to eight, Ava had begun to move the cafe furniture outside to the pavement. The array of tables and chairs sat in the morning sunshine waiting for their first visitors of the day. The cafe was eerily quiet to Ava and she turned on the little radio that sat behind the counter to break the silence. Nothing too intrusive, just some gentle classical piano music was enough to make her feel more comfortable.

The clock had barely ticked past nine when Mikiel and the rest of the local mechanics arrived. Ava had already begun to prepare their drinks, one kafè iswed, two kafè latte and Joe's green tea. Joe came inside for the order whilst the others sat at the small tables outside. He stood by the counter ready to take the tray from her and gave her a big smile as she placed the last of the drinks on the tray.

"I saw that man again," Joe remarked, "you know, the one that was asking about the lady. He is staying at the Solaqua hotel overlooking the bay, I was there last night with my family for dinner and he came in pulling a small suitcase."

Ava had started to prepare their breakfast, the order of bread, ġbejna cheese and ham never wavered so she was confident that the food would be welcomed.

"He has been looking for a lady called Sarah," Ava told him. "She was a friend of Elias's wife, but she has moved away now." Ava placed the last of the food onto a second tray and lifted it to take it outside whilst Joe carried the coffees. "Perhaps he has not yet found her?" Ava was not one for gossip and wanted to end the conversation quickly. She swiftly moved to the open door and gave her 'good morning' welcome to the rest of the group. Each man raised himself briefly from their chairs as they returned the 'good morning!'

Indri had left Ava a small list of food that needed ordering along with the respective telephone numbers for the suppliers. Ava began to make the necessary calls between serving the other early morning customers. There was a note at the bottom of the page to say that the 'craft ladies' would be having afternoon tea today, a day earlier than usual as it was a special birthday for one of the group and could Ava arrange for a cake from the bakery.

It wasn't too busy so Ava decided to prepare a cake herself. She had all the ingredients to hand and cherished moments like these when she was able to use the skills passed on to her by her mother. Undecided to begin with between a prinjolata or torta tal-lewż. She eventually chose the former being more of a celebration cake than the almond tart, and she began to pare the skin from several lemons in preparation. She would bake it just after lunch so that it would be still slightly warm when they arrived, whip up some cream and serve it with a dusting of extra cinnamon. She was sure it would be a delight.

Like clockwork the ladies arrived just after the lunchtime rush had subsided. The cafe smelt wonderful from the baking and Ava had arranged their tea things on a tray, draped with a pretty embroidered cloth and added small plates and cake forks in preparation for the birthday treat. May looked quizzically at Ava and she explained that Indri had let her know about the celebration so she had prepared a prinjolata for them to enjoy between their knitting and sewing. May opened her bag and lifted out the most beautiful white cardigan knitted to perfection. Its lace like quality and scalloped bottom hem together with its delicate pearl buttons was a beauty to behold. The rest of the ladies began to file into the cafe and Ava left them to it, all marvelling at the latest design that May had created for the boutique. One of the other ladies proudly showed off her patchwork cot quilt, perfect neat little squares of colour co-ordinated fabric all bound together by a ribbon edge. It was stunning, and Ava could see the joy that making these items gave to each of them.

May came up to the counter an hour or so later, to thank Ava for making the beautiful cake.

It was voted as the most delicious cake they'd all eaten for many years.

"My mother-in-law was a fabulous cake maker," May had told her. "I can knock up something more basic, but my skills lie in my sewing and knitting rather than in the kitchen."

"Honestly May, it is so easy, anyone can make it." Ava thanked May for her kind comments and promised to add it to the menu whilst she was running the cafe. She knew Indri would be more than happy with the addition. "Are you still able to help me out on Friday?"

"Most certainly, what time would you like me? I can be here all day if you wish. I might need the occasional sit down though." May chuckled. "My legs are not as young as they used to be and standing all day will be tricky."

"Gosh, no, just from about eleven until three or four, if that is okay with you. That will cover most of the busiest time when I need a little help to clear the tables and get the dishes washed, otherwise I will manage fine."

Just then May turned her head quickly to the window facing the street. "Look, it's that young man, the one with the notebook, the one asking all those questions." May hurried back to her friends, desperate to let them know that the stranger in town had reappeared.

The man stopped outside at one of the tables and sat down removing his hat and placing it on the chair beside him. Ava took her notepad and went out to greet him. He was the only person sitting outside the cafe, the 'craft ladies' always preferring to either sit inside or out at the front facing the sea. Ava offered him the menu but he held up his hand to stop her and asked her for an espresso together with some bread and cheese if she had some. He was staring at her and it made Ava feel a little uncomfortable. She acknowledged his order and went back inside to begin making the coffee. Glancing out of the window, Ava could see him take out his small brown notebook and make a note on a clean page.

Just then, the 'craft ladies' appeared in front of her, and all speaking at the same time, they thanked her for the extra trouble in making the cake for their little celebration. May stood towards one side and was making gestures with her head, nodding it over to the left. Ava could see she was indicating to the rest of the group the whereabouts of the man with the notebook. Ava thanked them for their custom, said she looked forward to their visit next week and smiled at them whilst they chatted in hushed voices leaving the café.

Taking out his order, Ava placed the espresso and a small saucer containing cubes of white sugar, a small jug of milk in case he preferred his coffee that way, and a white plate of crusty bread cut into thick slices, some creamy yellow butter and two large pieces of local cheese.

The man thanked her, and again, he seemed to stare too much and for too long at her, once more making her feel slightly on edge. She had barely returned to the kitchen when Jack, Elias's youngest boy came running inside.

"Ava, come quick, it's Dad; he has fallen asleep just outside and is in a heap on the floor!"

Ava dashed out from behind the counter and followed Jack to what appeared to be a large puddle of black clothing that lay slumped into a pile on the edge of the road. Between them, they were able to gently lift him and place him in a chair outside the café. Jack held onto him from behind preventing him from falling forward whilst Ava checked him over briefly for any damage. The only good thing about Elias's condition was that he would fall so gently that he rarely hurt himself but would crumple downwards like a floating feather. Lying asleep in the road was another matter however and although the locals were well aware of Elias's episodes and were accustomed to seeing him fall asleep randomly, no one wanted to see him on the floor, let alone in the road. The good thing was that Mellieħa was not a place that hosted many tourists apart from in the height of summer and like the man sitting at the table outside the café, anyone not local was unusual so Elias didn't have to worry about strangers reacting badly to his affliction.

With Jack holding onto his father, Ava was able to fetch him some water. She returned with a large jug of iced water and glasses for both Jack and Elias once he woke. Jack was still sitting with his arms around him so Ava helped him to reposition his father and lift his feet up onto another chair so he looked like he was more comfortable. Jack gladly took a drink of the iced water, the coolness was a welcome relief. Elias was snoring softly and hearing his snuffly exhales encouraged both Jack and Ava that it was nothing more than another episode for him. Ava left Jack with the water, returned to the kitchen and brought Jack out some left-over prinjolata, it was only then that she remembered she had another customer who had sat outside and had witnessed the spectacle. Ava turned to him, smiled and said, "This poor gentleman has narcolepsy and we try and do all we can for him."

Mark smiled. "You seemed to have it all under control, and I felt it best to just keep out of the way. But I must settle my bill with you and let you take care of him."

Ava nodded, went inside and came back with a small slip of paper with the total for his coffee and bread.

"Was everything okay for you?" she enquired.

"Most definitely," he replied. "That bread is one of the best I have tasted in Malta, but I have to admit that I am eyeing up the cake which you gave to the young man, if there is any more, I would like to take a piece away with me, if that is possible?"

"I made it for a special birthday for one of our regulars, but yes, I do have one piece remaining. I will package it up for you."

"How much more will that be, on top of this?" Mark gestured towards the slip of paper.

"No charge for the cake, it was the last piece and you have saved me from eating it and feeling guilty!" Ava laughed a little before returning to the kitchen to wrap up the piece of prinjolata.

The man had stood up and was chatting to Jack when Ava returned with his cake. He held out the required money to her which she took, placed in her apron and retrieved his change. Mark held up his hand, refusing the cash. He looked at Ava once more, again very intently and then enquired, "So, have you lived here all your life, it's such a beautiful place, I can't imagine anyone wanting to leave?"

"No, I moved here a while back, I'd heard so much about it and wanted to relocate after a difficult time I'd had. But you are quite right, it is the kind of place where people tend to stay. The beach is quite beautiful and the people here are so friendly, I feel like I've known the village for years."

Chapter Thirteen

Taking a taxi to Valletta to the National Library, Mark listened to music on his phone. He was trying to compute all the facts he had learnt on his journey so far. For him, music was the way he felt able to think about things without putting pressure on himself. He would use the same method to recall forgotten facts or just purely to get himself to sleep when he was troubled by something in the far corner of his brain that wouldn't let him switch off.

Mark arrived in Valletta and set off to find the nearest bar or café to have some lunch and a much needed coffee. He wandered for a while before settling on a place on a street corner. He glanced quickly at the online reviews and settled into a seat outside. A waiter greeted him shortly and he ordered an espresso with an apple pastizzi. There was a large canopy overhead for which he appreciated the break from the heat of the day. The pavement beside him was made up of small squares and the seats for the café were situated within the narrow road that ran along one side.

The espresso arrived with his warm pastizzi and a small glass of iced water. The waiter placed the coffee and cake in front of him and asked if he required anything further. Mark asked for the Wi-Fi code and began to remove his laptop from its bag. He had so very little to go on to start his search for the one-time policeman, that he was not hopeful, but as always, he would not give up easily.

Opening his laptop, he located the files on the disappearance of Alison, he had added notes from the cuttings he had seen in England and together with his own summations, he looked through the documents he had acquired thus far. One of the newspaper cuttings had named the policeman as Ġakobb Farrugia, at the time, a young policeman who had done all that was asked of him in searching all vehicles in the road blockades that had been hastily erected. Within a few months, Ġakobb left the police and took up a position as a teacher in a primary school—the lowest level of teaching apart from nursery level and to Mark this seemed an odd career change from being a policeman.

The pastizzi turned out to be as delicious as it had smelt. Mark took his time eating it, savouring each mouthful. Connected to the Wi-Fi, he began with an initial search on the internet for anyone with the name Ġakobb Farrugia on Malta. He had carried out this search previously and had found four likely candidates for his match to the man for whom he was searching. There had been many more suggested people from his search, some easily discounted for age or location, others he had put a query against but he would start with the four that he had first found.

Assessing his list, Mark initially chose to message an older-looking man who had very little on his Facebook page. Knowing that the policeman would now be in his sixties, Mark chose who he thought looked about the right age. He started by looking through the photos and details which he had shared on his profile. There were the usual family photos of birthdays, holidays and weddings plus one of this Ġakobb holding a granddaughter. All very normal looking. Mark sent his message.

I am looking for Ġakobb Farrugia who may have lived or worked in Mellieħa. He went on to explain that he was visiting from Canada and needed to ask some questions. He didn't want to mention that he was looking for an ex-policeman, there were some facts best kept silent for now. Not wanting to wait to hear back from everyone, he sent the same message to all four possible people, each time having looked through whatever Facebook profile they held. Obviously, this method was very sketchy at best but it was a decent starting point these days.

Having finished his pastry and espresso and having downed the very welcome glass of water, Mark closed his laptop and proceeded to the library to make further enquiries. He was not certain whether Ġakobb would still be teaching and if so, whether there were any registers or records available. Mark had plumped for the National Library in Valletta, being the first one to come up on his Google search. He had barely entered the building when his phone signalled that he had a message and he went back outside the confines of the building to access it. In fact, he had two messages, having not heard the first one and chose to look at them in chronological order.

The first message, from one Ġakobb Farrugia, explained that he had never been to that part of Malta and assumed that Mark had the wrong person. The second message was a little intriguing as it just said, *Why?*

Looking around him, Mark spotted a small wooden bench under some trees and moved over there out of the direct sunshine so he could sit and see his phone screen more clearly.

He pondered for a while on his best response, he didn't want to mislead this Ġakobb Farrugia, but he also didn't want to reveal too much either.

Deciding on honesty being the best policy, he explained that he was looking for an heir to a Canadian estate and that he understood that there was a Ġakobb Farrugia that used to live or work in the location of Mellieħa who might be able to help with his enquiries. He concluded with, *all information you may be able to give me, is treated in the strictest confidence.*

Mark sat back and waited. The hairs on the back of his neck now pricked. His phone pinged again, this time from one of the other people whom he had messaged, explaining that he had indeed visited Mellieħa in the past, but had never resided there. Mark thanked him for his response and said he had probably messaged the wrong person.

He got up from the bench and made his way back to the library. The building was much cooler than the outside temperature and that alone was a welcome relief. Mark sat down inside the grand entrance, chose a small sofa with a low coffee table in front of him and plugged his laptop in to recharge. He was approached by an official looking man enquiring about his business. Mark took out a business card and explained as best as he could, how he was trying to find the proverbial needle in a haystack. Tracing the location of an ex-policeman from thirty-three years ago or so, whom he now believed was a teacher. The man sat beside him on the sofa and studied the business card held between his rather pudgy fingers.

"He'd be retired now," he began, "won't still be teaching, so you won't find him on any current list of employees at any school, I shouldn't think."

Mark went quiet. He felt a little foolish for not realising this and quickly did some mental arithmetic in his head. The man was right. There was little doubt that he would be retired. If his Facebook contact was not the right man, he could have a far bigger problem than he first thought. The newspapers at the time had recorded the policeman as thirty-four, add on another thirty-three years and he would be somewhere around sixty-seven by now. The library employee left him to his work and Mark made some more notes on his laptop. He was about to leave when an older man sat in front of him and announced that he too was an ex-policeman. He had spoken to the library official who had explained that Mark was looking for an ex-policeman turned teacher.

"Is this about the young girl that went missing?" the man in front of Mark wasted no time with small talk, that was certain.

Mark gave him a business card but hesitant to give away too much information, he briefly explained that he was looking at all avenues into Alison's likely drowning and that any policeman serving at the time might be able to help him. He assured him that he was not investigating her death, merely dotting the i's and crossing the t's for his office.

"My name is Reginald Micallef and I was also a policeman on that case, at the same time as Ġakobb Farrugia. He was a good policeman who made one serious mistake. But we later traced the vehicle when it was scrapped. It belonged to a man on Gozo from Munxar. He scrapped it about two weeks after the disappearance of the little girl. His paperwork was good, he was a mechanic and would often scrap cars that he had taken in." Reginald seemed to ponder a moment. "I wonder if that paperwork still exists?" he added.

"I don't suppose you recall the name of the mechanic?" Mark knew it was a long shot but in light of the high profile of the case, he thought it worth an ask.

"No, I'm afraid not, but I know where the scrapyard is. I could enquire for you?" Reginald seemed to be filling out his chest like a preening bird. "It would be good to put my investigative skills to work again, I'm bored being retired."

"I don't want to put you to any trouble," Mark countered, but silently hoping that Reginald would look into this for him. "If you can point me in the direction of the scrapyard…" he trailed off his sentence.

Reginald looked directly into his eyes, adjusted his sitting position and then leant back on the seat.

"Honestly, I doubt there is anything to find, but it'll be easier coming from me. Where can I contact you?" Mark gave him his hotel details and pointed out the email address and mobile number on his business card. Before Reginald left, he stood, shook Mark's hand and told him he would be in touch soon.

His laptop was charging nicely and Mark spent the next hour or so reading through his notes thus far and adding in some further detail. He emailed his office in Calgary to let them know about his encounter with Reginald and his potential contact with Ġakobb Farrugia. He relaxed back into his chair for a few moments, massaged his temples and sat forward again just as his phone pinged. The message was brief:

I am Ġakobb Farrugia, I am a retired school teacher from Mellieħa but I have no connections to Canada.

Mark looked at the message, it had to be him, surely?

I'd like to buy you a coffee, Mark began his reply. *Could we meet up later today, perhaps? I think you may be able to help me with my research.* He then added some details about his firm in Canada and suggested that Ġakobb check his identity should he have any concerns.

The clock in the library ticked by, seeming to Mark to suddenly be loud and intrusive into his thoughts. His gut feeling told him that this was his missing link, this was the man who could tell him more about the day Alison went missing. Almost twenty minutes passed and he gasped when his phone pinged again.

4.30 at St Julian's Bay, I have about thirty minutes I can spare.

Thank you, Mark was beginning to pack up his belongings whilst replying to the text. *I'll see you there, I should recognise you from your Facebook profile.* Mark hit send, closed his laptop and went over to the librarian's desk.

The library official he had first met was talking to a customer. Mark hesitated for him to finish his conversation and was going to just say thanks for the use of the Wi-Fi.

"Hopefully, Reginald was of some use?" the librarian began once his customer had moved away. "He's my brother and I thought he might be able to help."

"Thank you, yes," Mark said, "he is making some enquiries for me. Thanks for the use of the Wi-Fi and I've been able to recharge my laptop."

"Pleasure is mine, good luck in your investigations. As soon as you mentioned Ġakobb, I thought it'd be about the little one that went missing. I'm Eric, by the way."

Mark shook Eric by the hand, left the library and went back outside into the searing heat of the day. He looked around for a nearby taxi, hoping he could find one quickly to get him across to St Julian's Bay. He had checked that it was approximately eight kilometres away, so it wouldn't take too long, but he wanted to be there when Ġakobb arrived.

Chapter Fourteen

Ava's first few days of running the cafe by herself had gone quite smoothly. Not that she had been concerned that it wouldn't but she was genuinely pleased with herself. May had been a great asset. She had not only cleaned tables, done lots of washing up but had also encouraged Ava to do some more baking to add to the existing array of pastries that the cafe offered. Her birthday cake for May had been a great success and Ava had already received two orders to make a prinjolata, one for Gino from the coffee stall in the market, and the second for Christopher, Elias's eldest boy, who had heard all about the delicious-looking pastry from Jack. He was sad to hear that he had missed out on the last piece that Ava had baked the day his father had collapsed in the street outside the cafe.

Christopher wanted to treat his young brother and father. He had recently taken on much more of his father's fishing work and his income had been relatively good of late. He felt it was about time that they enjoyed something fine to eat and had produced the delicious smelling cake one evening after they had finished their simple meal of fish and salad. The three of them had finished off half of it in one sitting, and they had all agreed that it was one of the best things they had eaten in a long while.

It was Saturday evening when Ava remembered that she still had the letters that Yvonne had kept with her diaries and pouring herself a large glass of iced water infused with lemon, she collected them and put her legs up on her couch and began to read. The first couple she opened were obviously love letters that Elias had written her when they were first together. Ava skipped over them, not wanting to pry into the contents, but it was the third letter that spiked her interest. She read it quickly, turned the page over to read the last sentence or so, then turned back to read the letter again, this time much more slowly and carefully.

My dearest Yvonne,

I'm just dropping you a quick line to explain that I need to cancel our arranged rendezvous this week. My sister is visiting from Canada for ten days and I need to be with her. Each time she visits, whilst I love seeing her, my heart breaks to see her wander Mellieha beach each evening, crying out for her long-lost child.

I know coming back is such a traumatic time for her, but the way she gazes into my eyes, staring without blinking for what seems like minutes at a time, is so hard for me to take. I feel guilty that I have the same bright green eyes as Alison, Florence's own being more hazel in colour and I know that she sees the eyes of her baby within mine.

She is obviously still struggling with her mental health but lately she tells me, she has been more stable, hence she feels well enough to visit. I do hope that it doesn't set her back but I understand her need to be here again.

Look after yourself, make sure you have plenty of rest. This pregnancy seems so much harder for you, maybe it is just the heat? I'll pop by on Monday, the week after next.

Until then, Sarah x

Ava read the letter twice more. Her mind went back to the first time that Joe mentioned that there was someone looking for her, and the way he stared into her eyes. Then she thought of her parents. Are these things genetic? She wasn't certain about that but she also knew that both her parents had dark brown eyes. Ava stopped her irrational mind from working. Just because she had bright green eyes and Sarah also had bright green eyes, it meant nothing, surely? There were no other letters that held Ava's interest. There were a few more from friends overseas, two from her mother and one from a cousin announcing a visit. She put the letters back with the diaries and placed them all in the woollen bag to give to Elias.

Later that evening, Ava took a stroll over to Elias's house and knocked on the door. Almost immediately, Christopher pulled open the door and gave Ava a great big smile. She apologised for the intrusion and gave him the bag, explaining briefly that his father had let her read the diaries. Christopher looked into the bag.

"I've always said that I would read them too," Christopher's smile began to fade, "but I'm concerned that the mother I remember will be altered by anything I read."

Ava wanted to reassure him that there was certainly nothing awkward or sinister within them, but she respected that his memories of his mother were his

81

alone and she didn't want to suggest replacing them no matter what little he might or might not glean from the pages.

"Please let Elias know that I am truly grateful to have been able to read them." Ava went to turn away but Christopher stopped her, asking her to stop for a coffee with him and Elias in the courtyard garden. "That's an offer I cannot refuse." Ava stepped inside and followed Christopher out the back into the sunshine that was now laying speckled shade through the trees whilst still leaving enough light to provide the evening with a warm embrace.

Elias was laid back in a chair, a newspaper spread over his mid-section and his feet up on an upturned pot. He almost jumped up from the chair when he saw her and he began to apologise for not hearing her arrive.

"Don't worry, Dad," Christopher said. "You were out for the count for the last ten minutes or so. I thought about making coffee and have asked Ava to join us. She has brought Mum's diaries back."

"Anything interesting or helpful?" Elias asked of her.

"Well, I must admit I felt a little intrusive, especially as I didn't know Yvonne, but it was lovely to see how her friendship with Sarah developed. There was also one letter from Sarah that mentioned her sister visiting, which was interesting." Ava didn't elaborate.

"Ah, yes, that must be Frances, wasn't it?" Elias looked at Ava and motioned for her to sit next to him. Christopher had retreated inside to make coffee.

"Florence," Ava corrected.

"That's it!" Elias looked at Ava, shook his head gently from side to side and continued, "As much as it has pained me for years, losing my Yvonne, I cannot begin to imagine what that poor woman went through. Losing her child like that, I don't think that is something you ever learn to accept."

"How did the child die?" Ava sat forward on her chair as Christopher came back with a tray of cups and a pot of coffee. He poured three cups and offered one to Ava.

"Well, that's the thing, you see," Elias took his coffee and leant back in his chair placing the hot cup beside him, "they assume she drowned, she was never found. Awful it was. I went out to help search for her many times. We scoured the beaches, the buildings with outhouses, knocked on every door possible. It was as though she had vanished into thin air. That's why they think she must have drowned but a body was never recovered." Elias's head drooped, both

Christopher and Ava thought he'd fallen asleep, but just as quickly he lifted it up again. "I guess she'd have been about thirty-five or thirty-six by now."

Ava was sipping her coffee and looked at Elias, who was studying her. Just like Joe had done before, it was a little too intense for her liking. He got up from the chair and went inside.

She could hear what she assumed were drawers being opened and closed and then an "Aha!" from within.

Elias returned with a few pieces of paper. They were a little scuffed up around the edges but he passed one to Ava.

"These were what we handed out to anyone and everyone we saw. There is a photo of the girl and a good description of what she was wearing that day. Tragic, just tragic."

Ava took the sheet of paper; it was obviously a little faded from age but the photograph hit her first. She had seen a photograph, not dissimilar from this one, in her parents' photograph album. She would have been about three or four years old. The face shape and the eye colour the same although the hairstyle was different, but this was weird. Ava was looking at a photograph of herself as a young child.

Chapter Fifteen

Mark arrived at St Julian's Bay shortly after four pm. He found a bench that looked out across the water and placed his laptop bag between his feet. It wasn't the best vantage point to watch for anyone approaching but he had a little time to sit and enjoy the warmth of the afternoon sunshine. Hotels surrounded the bay and Mark had been sitting with those behind him, his view being of the varied boats that bobbed on the water. There were many people milling about, some obviously on holiday holding the customary ice creams in hand, sunglasses on and shorts in a rainbow of colours. Mark checked his watch, picked up his laptop bag and turned towards the central area of the bay. He spotted Ġakobb Farrugia as he descended the steps of one of the hotels along the front. Mark raised his arm to signal his presence and Ġakobb nodded his head, making his way across the pavement to meet him.

The two men shook hands and Mark gestured around with one arm whilst asking if Ġakobb had a preference for a café. Ġakobb started to walk back to the hotel from where he had come and they went inside. The coolness of the air-conditioned lobby was a stark contrast from the heat of the day, despite the midday temperature now waning. Ġakobb indicated to Mark a small table with two glasses of iced water which he had already requested and then asked Mark for his coffee preference.

"These are on me," Mark started to say, but Ġakobb wafted his suggestion away with one hand. The coffees arrived a few minutes later by which time Mark was part way through his introduction. He had explained his business to Ġakobb previously and the man had indeed contacted his office in Calgary to verify his story.

"My interest in Alison Hensley is purely to make sure that I have explored every avenue before I finalise this case." Mark had explained that he was tracing relatives of a Canadian woman which had brought him to Malta. "The woman in question was related to Alison." Ġakobb knew that he had information to help

Mark. He knew that the burden that had laid on his shoulders, and his shoulders alone, for over thirty years needed to be told. With a look of downtrodden melancholy, Ġakobb began to speak.

"You probably know by now that I was once a police officer. I had a good career ahead of me and in one split second, with one bad decision, that was gone."

Ġakobb told Mark of the day when Alison went missing, how the police set up roadblocks and how he, amongst other police officers, were sent out to stop every vehicle that they encountered for the rest of that day and for the next two days. One vehicle in particular was a silver Fiat Panda, driven by a car mechanic that Ġakobb recognised. This man lived on Gozo but had been to mainland Malta that day for spare parts. He had a brief chat with the man but, distracted by the fact that he knew him, he let him go without a proper search of the vehicle. It was several weeks later when the case into the missing girl was beginning to wind down slightly, that Ġakobb was going through some paperwork. He recalled the vehicle and it came flooding back, that he had not made a thorough search.

Immediately, he reported to his superiors and was subsequently sent to Gozo to track down the driver. The task was not too difficult and he arrived in Munxar to the home address of Lisa and Stephen Muscat. Stephen Muscat ran his own car mechanic business, repairing and selling second-hand vehicles. Lisa was a troubled woman, nervous in nature, fragile in appearance. They had one daughter, Ava.

"They quickly provided Ava's birth certificate when asked and I saw the child playing happily in the garden with a little dog. Nothing concerned me at the time, and when I asked to check the vehicle, Stephen explained that he had sold the vehicle to a local scrap dealer who wanted it for parts. He showed me the car he now used, a dark green Fiat Panda and assured me that the dealer would be able to show him the silver Fiat Panda he had traded with him."

Ġakobb had then gone to see the dealer who had shown him the vehicle in question and he had conducted a thorough search of the car. He had asked for a forensic team to check it over and they were unable to find anything untoward.

"But," and this is where Ġakobb's voice wobbled, "I was asked to leave the police service. I had potentially put the life of that little girl in danger and quickly and quietly I was advised that I should leave and never speak of this error again." He looked up at Mark, his eyes now glistening with tears. "I had a gut feeling that all was not right at that house. The mother looked terrified, but Stephen reassured me that she was a nervous soul and he took great care of her and their daughter. The child appeared happy and content, but it was an instinct, something I couldn't place. I contacted my colleagues from the police department to look further into the family, but everything checked out. However, I wasn't convinced and I didn't know why."

Mark waited, partly to make sure that Ġakobb had finished speaking but also to fully digest what he had said.

"You were happy that the child's documents were genuine?" Mark asked Ġakobb.

"Without a doubt; you get to know what to look for."

"And the vehicle checked out?"

"I know, I know, it sounds ludicrous that I still had concerns, but I did."

"Do they still live there, on Gozo I mean?"

"I think Stephen passed some time ago but as far as I know, Lisa still lives there. My wife saw her not that long ago. She told me that she seemed far less nervy these days."

Mark had been making notes on his laptop the whole time that Ġakobb was talking. Some of this he already knew, but there were a few details of interest—names of the family concerned with the stopped vehicle and the information of the scrap dealer which Reginald had also mentioned. He let out a long sigh, he wasn't sure if there was anything to find. The police had conducted forensic tests, the child of the family checked out, it sounded to Mark like a dead end. Mark looked at his watch, thanked Ġakobb for the time he had given him and got up to leave.

"If you find anything out about the child, would you let me know?" Ġakobb looked pleadingly at Mark. "This has been on my mind ever since that day and one day, I'd like to lay that ghost to rest. It's like having a black cloud on my back the whole time and whilst I know in my head that the child most probably drowned, in my heart, I believe differently."

The two men shook hands and Mark agreed that any information he was able to learn that might reassure Ġakobb he had covered all bases (albeit not immediately after the child had disappeared), then he would do so. Ġakobb looked like a broken man and Mark had so much sympathy for him.

Later that day, back in his hotel in Mellieħa, Mark wrote up his notes from his meeting with Ġakobb. He contacted his office in Calgary and let them know that he would follow up on the Muscat family and was waiting for news back from Reginald. He too would visit Gozo as soon as possible and hopefully have a chat with Lisa Muscat. Mark was beginning to feel that all the loose ends were forming a nice solid knot and his work on Malta and the Hensley fortune would soon be passed to Sarah. Paperwork had checked out with the Muscat family and surely that, along with the confirmation of the forensics carried out on the vehicle that was not checked properly, meant that the little niggles that Mark had surrounding the day Alison went missing, could now be silenced.

Mark took an evening stroll down to the beach. It was a beautiful evening—the lights from the buildings surrounding the bay cast a golden glow across the sea and the sky appeared as layers of orange and purple that reflected into the sea like molten glass. He chose a small bar overlooking the boats that gently lolled from side to side, the last warmth of the day just enough to keep the breeze off the sea at a comfortable temperature. Wherever he travelled, he liked to enjoy the local foods and had been lucky to sample some great cuisine and unlucky to have some rather dubious dishes too in various parts of the world. Tonight, he would order the most requested dish from the menu and see what that would bring.

The waiter appeared and Mark ordered a beer alongside his meal of stuffat tal-fenek. There were a few other diners, mostly couples although a couple of families with young children sat nearby. Mark had three nephews and two nieces and loved spending time with them in lieu of a family of his own. He had never really hankered for his own family, which considering his chosen career, was obviously a good thing.

The waiter appeared with a brimming glass of beer and a large white bowl which smelled delicious. Placing them both in front of Mark, the waiter offered black pepper which Mark refused, then he left him to his repast. His bowl of rabbit, cooked with vegetables, red wine and lots of garlic was the perfect blend of aromatics. He knew his grandfather, after whom he had been named, had kept cages upon cages of rabbits during World War Two. At the time, his grandfather was living near London, and this meant a readily available source of meat to feed his family. The breeding nature of the animal inevitably saw that he was never short of a supply, and his wife Edith was happy to skin and gut the animals for the table.

Mark would listen to tales from his grandfather of how one rabbit had been allowed out of its cage and nibbled its way through his shoelaces. During the war, shoelaces amongst many other items were in short supply and this had been a tale recounted many times over the years. Whether that particular rabbit was soon destined for the pot, Mark never knew, but as a young child he recalled giggling at the tale and would ask for his grandfather to tell him more stories about the rabbits.

The waiter returned to remove his tableware and Mark ordered a whisky to finish off his meal. Opting for a small jug of water to accompany his drink, he settled back into his chair, stared out over the bay and absorbed the last remnants of the sunset before it faded into night. Tomorrow he would head to Gozo, tick off the last remaining boxes on his checklist and begin to make plans to return home. He let out a contented sigh. Malta was a truly beautiful island. He had enjoyed this trip, met some lovely people and had a wonderful dose of Mediterranean sunshine. What more could he ask for?

Chapter Sixteen

Ava held the piece of paper in her hand, her mind whirring frantically. She realised she was crushing the corner, let go of it and let it fall into her lap. She looked at Elias, he was staring at her.

"I … um … I …" was all Ava could muster.

Elias looked concerned. He motioned for Christopher to leave the garden by nodding his head sideways towards the back door. He took Ava's hands in his and once more gazed into her eyes.

"Oh lass," he seemed to take a small gasp for breath, "is this you?"

Ava couldn't speak. She stood up, letting the paper fall to the floor, made her way through the house and left without saying another word. This wasn't real. Somehow, she made her way back home, her ears were ringing and she felt faint. At the foot of the stairs to her flat, Ava sat down and laid her head to one side on the cold stone wall. She was confused, numb, shocked and full of disbelief. If she hadn't seen the photograph for herself, she would never have believed it. But seriously, how could this be?

How long she sat there, she didn't know but she found herself back in her flat with Ricco purring around her ankles as usual. The evening had now turned into night and Ava poured herself a glass of iced water and sat on her couch. Her head was still reeling and she had so many thoughts whizzing through her mind that she felt sick. The water began to steady her stomach and she sat stroking Ricco who had curled himself up beside her. It was morning when she awoke— thankfully a Sunday and she wasn't needed to open the cafe.

Her back hurt and her head thumped with a mighty headache. Moving, and groaning as she did so, she went to the cabinet in the bathroom and found herself some painkillers. Taking these, and a glass of water, she moved out onto her balcony and sat with Ricco trying to wake herself up. Weirdly she felt hung-over but knew she hadn't had a drink last night. Ricco rolled onto his back and she gently stroked his belly, letting the warm sunshine cradle her soul. Gradually the events of the evening before began to appear. The painkillers were reducing the headache and the pains in her back, so she decided to brave a coffee—not something she would normally do with a headache like this, but she felt the need to sharpen up her mind.

Taking a cafetiere from the cupboard, she added two heaped spoons of coffee and put the kettle on to boil. Like stills from an old black and white movie, she visualised intermittent flashes of images. Firstly, the photograph of the child, then Elias staring at her, then her mother and lastly an image of the letter from Sarah to Yvonne. She shook her head rapidly from side to side as if to clear the thoughts from her mind. The kettle boiled. She poured the steaming water into the cafetiere and took it, together with a white porcelain cup, out on to the balcony. She was still dressed in her clothes from the previous evening, so left the coffee to brew whilst taking a brief cool shower and then re-dressed in some denim shorts and a floaty white blouse. She put flip-flops on her feet and went back outside. Ricco hadn't moved. Ava poured the coffee and let its steamy aroma drift into her senses. The coffee was strong and bitter. Ava hungrily drank from the cup and poured a second, leant back on the bench, closed her eyes and let the coffee do its work.

Ava heard her mobile ring. She glanced down at her watch and knew this would be her weekly catch up call from her mother. She just stared at her watch, the second-hand pulsing clockwise around the dial. The trill from her phone faded into the background and Ava just continued to stare until the phone stopped ringing. A minute or so passed and there was a beep indicating a voicemail had been left. Pouring the remaining dregs from the cafetiere into her cup, Ava drank the virtually cold coffee before taking the cup back into her kitchen. In almost robotic fashion, she fed Ricco some cold chicken from her fridge, added some cat treats to a bowl before finding her sunglasses and sun hat and heading out of the flat.

She walked back to where Elias lived and knocked purposefully on the door. Elias opened it up almost before she'd finished knocking. He too was wearing a sun hat and was obviously on his way out. He jumped back in surprise. Ava hastily began her apology for leaving the way she did the evening before. Elias removed his hat and insisted she went inside. It was cool, and Ava was relieved, her headache already beginning to build again. Jack appeared from upstairs, rubbing his eyes as though just having woken. He offered them both tea and went into the kitchen to boil the kettle.

Taking Ava by the hand, Elias led her outside. She appeared to still be in shock so he quickly sat her down on a stone bench in the shade and waited for her to speak again. He was very concerned, his heart was racing and he was certain that he would fall asleep any minute. Jack appeared with the tea and Elias relaxed. When he came to a while later, the tea was already poured and Jack and Ava were deep in conversation.

"Alright, Dad?" Jack looked over at his father and handed him a cup of tea. "Trust you to nod off when we have company!"

Elias knew his son was making a gentle joke at his expense but he was relieved that he had been there and Ava was still with them.

Ava started to apologise once more for her departure the previous evening but Elias wouldn't hear of it. She went to stand up to leave but he asked her to sit and stay a while. He wanted to make sure she was okay.

"Look," he began, "there might be a perfectly simple explanation to all this."

Ava just stared into the distance. She seemed unable to make a sentence let alone one that made sense.

"I don't know what to think." Ava looked at Elias, her eyes brimming with tears. "It's obvious that it can't be me in that photograph and yet, I know it is. I feel numb."

"Have you spoken to your mum?" Jack was clearing the tea away, Ava looked up at him as he spoke. "She will know that it's not true, won't she?" He finished filling up the tray of tea things and took them into the kitchen. Elias and Ava could hear him begin to wash the cups.

"I can't," was all Ava could say.

Elias took hold of her hand once more, patted it gently and gave her a most tender smile.

"I don't know your mum, but if she is anything like her kind and sweet daughter, there is nothing for you to worry about."

"But, what if I'm *not* her daughter, what does it mean?"

Jack had finished the washing up and they could hear him chatting to Christopher inside.

Christopher appeared at the doorway and came over to sit with Ava and Elias.

"Jack has just told me." Christopher sat next to Ava, took her spare hand into his and, like his father had done, began to gently pat the back of her hand.

"Perhaps you have a doppelganger, it will just be a coincidence, I'm sure." Christopher, ever the level-headed one, tried to reassure Ava. He had the flyer in his hand, the one Elias had shown Ava the previous evening. "This photograph is from a long time ago, it could be any young girl on the island."

"Do you think so?" Ava looked at Christopher. "Do such things actually exist?"

"Oh definitely, you've only got to look on the internet to find people that live on opposite sides of the world, only to have a chance meeting and find out they're the spitting image of each other." Christopher released her hand, he had noticed that she had relaxed a little. Ava suddenly began to feel claustrophobic and wanted to leave. She stood up and made hasty goodbyes before heading back to her flat. This time, neither Elias nor the boys had tried to encourage her to stay. They all had concerned looks on their faces but Ava felt she needed to digest everything and make sense of it all, one way or another.

As she was making her way back, her mobile beeped again, reminding her of the voicemail. She waited until she was back in her flat and dialled the code to retrieve the message.

"Hi darling," Ava immediately recognised her mother's voice, "I was wondering if you'd like to pop over here for lunch today? It's been a few weeks since we got together. I have fresh red mullet from that little shop in Victoria. I thought we could grill it with some salad. Anyway, call me back and let me know. Love you!"

Looking at her watch, Ava realised that it was now after ten-thirty and her mother would probably be worrying by now why she had not heard back from her daughter. Ava picked up her mobile and called her mother.

"Hi darling, thanks for calling back," her mother answered before the third ring.

"Hi," Ava tried to keep her voice level and cheerful, "lunch would be lovely, I should be able to catch the 11.45 ferry. Can I bring anything?"

"Just yourself, darling," Ava's mother replied. "See you in a while, I'll start preparing the salad." With that, Ava's mother hung up.

Ava had just enough time to brew up another cafetiere of coffee, pop a couple more pain killers and change into a cool sundress. She put some biscuits down for Ricco, poured him some fresh water and tickled his head before heading down and across the street to the cafe. Indri had a small car that he used to go to the wholesalers, and Ava was on the insurance. She had never really wanted to drive, found the whole experience a little daunting at times. Drivers on the road were always too aggressive and impatient for her liking. But her father had not only insisted that she learnt to drive, he taught her himself and she passed her test on the first attempt. Despite her father's car sitting in the garage at her mother's, and her mother not being able to drive, Ava saw no reason to have the vehicle on Malta. For the odd occasion when she needed a car, she was happy to use Indri's.

Before leaving for the ferry, Ava popped inside the cafe and picked up a couple of left-over pastries from the day before. She wouldn't be able to sell them the next day, although she was prone to turn them into a custard baked dessert for her customers, there were enough to take a couple to her mother and still have plenty to use the next day.

The ferry got her to Gozo just after twelve thirty and by this time Ava was already convincing herself that Christopher had been right, and the photograph she had seen was a child with a striking likeness to Ava, but obviously not Ava herself. This was the only possible answer that made sense. Ava decided to put all thoughts of it out of her mind and enjoy the day with her wonderful mum.

The heat of the day was beginning to peak and the roads had begun to shimmer like an out of focus film footage. She recalled being taught at school how the air closest to the road would become hotter than the air just above and the difference in temperature would produce the blurred shimmering effect that was a daily occurrence during the hotter months on the islands. The car was quite old and certainly didn't have any modern conveniences like air conditioning, or power steering for that matter. But Ava didn't mind. She had learnt to drive in her father's old green Fiat Panda, which also had neither, so with the windows down she accepted the warm breeze on her face and made her way from the ferry terminal to her mother's house in Munxar.

Lisa, Ava's mother, was these days more stout in stature than she would like to be. She was standing outside the rear of the house, in the cool shade of the olive trees which lined the rear of her property. She had collected several olives and was turning them over in her hands when Ava appeared in the garden. Lisa would rinse the olives, place them in a bowl of boiling water before allowing them to dry in the sunshine. Ava adored the fresh olives but knew that straight from the tree, they were bitter and to her taste, inedible. However, the short process followed by her mother, who would then rub them in olive oil and rosemary, made them totally delicious.

Looking up from her task, Lisa put the olives back into a bowl and crossed the garden to give her daughter a hug. Ava tried not to tense up, but the knot in her stomach made the hug a little awkward. Lisa pulled back, looked Ava in the eyes and asked her what was wrong? She had sensed the tension and it was not normal.

"Just ignore me, I fell asleep on the couch last night, woke with a headache and such pain in my back." Ava was never able to lie convincingly but nothing she had said was untrue. She just left out the reasons behind her unusual sleeping arrangement.

Lisa prepared the lunch of red mullet, fresh salad leaves with the olives from the garden and Ava added the pastries from the café onto a separate plate. They took the plates out into the garden but stayed close to the house, under the shade of a canvas covered gazebo that backed onto the kitchen. Lisa had made the canopy herself and it was a great addition to the garden. She would sit under the canopy in the middle of the day and yet keep cool from the rays of the sun or take her evening glass of local red wine outside and enjoy the chirp of the crickets late into the evening. She loved this little space and despite living here on her own since her husband died, she took pleasure in the place that they had created.

Ava wasn't sure if she should bring the conversation around to the leaflet that Elias had shown her. On the one hand, she had no desire to upset her mother by even asking such ludicrous questions but at the same time, she had an insatiable need to scratch the itch that was burning within her. She decided on a gentle approach.

"Where are all the photograph albums from when I was little?" Ava looked over to her mother who was currently pushing the remnants of her fish salad around her plate. Lisa stopped, looked up and seemed to hesitate before answering.

"Which in particular?"

"I'm not certain, I just fancied a trip down memory lane. See some photos of Dad too." Ava smiled reassuringly at her mother, hoping she was not showing the signs of nervous anxiety that were building up inside her once more. "I honestly cannot remember the last time we looked through them. I was probably a young child."

"I'm sure they are around somewhere," Lisa began to tidy the plates away and took them into the kitchen. "They will be in your father's old study I suspect." She called from the kitchen, "It's not somewhere I like to go—too many memories."

"Can I fetch them?" Ava asked when her mother returned to the garden. "I'll happily take them home with me if you would find it too upsetting."

"Let's eat these delicious treats," Lisa put a small plate in front of Ava together with a dessert fork. "We can look for them in a while. Isn't the garden looking dry?" Lisa had changed the topic and Ava wasn't inclined to push the conversation back to the albums.

Their chat turned to plants in the garden, which ones were suffering from pests and just how much watering the rest took. It truly was a beautiful space, curving brick pathways interspersed with delicate blooms which always looked so fragile in the heat. Tall grasses and cobbles of smooth pebbles filled another space that enveloped little enclaves of herbs and a small rose garden in one back corner that always seemed to produce the most stunning blooms, in turn giving off the headiest of aromas in the sunshine—all encapsulated by the tall olive trees adding their own fragrance into the mix.

The heat of the day was beginning to diminish when Ava decided to head back to the ferry and onwards to her little flat. She knew Ricco would be wanting some more food soon and she was able to use that as a good excuse to leave. She didn't need an excuse really but she always felt a twinge of sadness leaving her mother alone.

Picking up her bag and a small container of fresh olives which her mother had parcelled up for her, Ava was about to leave when she remembered the photograph albums.

"Could I take them with me?" Ava looked directly at her mother, looking for hints of concern but she didn't see anything to worry her. "I'll bring them back next visit."

Ava crossed the hallway and entered her father's study before Lisa had chance to reply. She went straight to the bookshelves, running her fingers along them whilst she searched for the albums that she could vaguely recall from her childhood. There were a multitude of books, mostly engineering textbooks dating back decades, sitting alongside various manuals for vehicles old and new. Right at the far end of the shelf, she saw two leatherbound albums and reached for them. Clasping the two books close to her, she made her way back out of her father's study before making eye contact with her mother.

"Is this all of them?"

"Well, yes…" Lisa was looking down at her feet. "Of course, we didn't have a camera until you were about three, so there are no baby pictures sadly." Lisa continued to look at her feet.

"Oh?" Ava was surprised by this, having seen a small black and white photograph of a baby on her father's desk. "Who took that one?" Ava pointed at the desk and the back of the little silver frame that seemed to have pride of place. "I can only be a few months old in that one?"

"I think we were given it." Lisa began to walk away and Ava could hear her voice shaking, it was very unsettling to hear her mother like this and she began to feel uncertain about leaving. She heard her mother clear her throat from the kitchen before she returned to the hallway. Ava noticed a small corner of a tissue peeking out from her mother's hand.

"Are you okay?" Ava was genuinely concerned that her request for the photographs had upset her mother, or was it going into the study, she wasn't sure.

"Yes indeed, darling." Lisa seemed to pull out a more stable voice from inside her and hushed her daughter to the front door. "Let's not make it so long next time, I do miss seeing you."

Ava agreed. She adored her mother and hated herself for even doubting that this whole silly notion that loomed in her head could possibly have any truth to it. Clutching the photograph albums, she opened the little car, waved her goodbyes and set off for the ferry. The albums seemed to burn a hole in the seat beside her and Ava couldn't wait to get back and have a look through them.

Chapter Seventeen

Early the next morning, Mark spoke to the young girl who was sitting at Reception to enquire about the times of ferry crossings to Gozo. She handed him a leaflet for the ferry company and explained that there were many ferries each day and he shouldn't have any difficulties getting over to Gozo.

Mark took his time over the breakfast in the hotel restaurant. There was a great supply of cereals, pastries, meats and cheeses plus some eggs and bacon too. Spoilt for choice, Mark decided on a selection of cold meats and croissants with some scrambled egg on the side. He wanted to make sure that he could get over to Gozo, follow up on his queries and get back to Malta without needing to stop off for lunch. Now that the end of his travels was in sight, he felt a bit more of an urgency to get the job done. The quicker he was finished, the more time he would have to himself before needing to fly back home.

Fuelled with breakfast and coffee, and with laptop case in hand, Mark took a taxi to the ferry terminal. He only had to wait twenty minutes for the next crossing which he took on foot. The crossing was about forty-five minutes and Mark sat back, relaxed, and enjoyed the view. He arrived at Mġarr shortly before 11.30am, it was a Monday morning and was pretty busy. He got off the ferry and looked around for a taxi to take him to Munxar. He had managed to obtain an address for Lisa Muscat from the electoral register but he had not managed to find a telephone number so hadn't been able to contact Mrs Muscat to ensure she would be available.

The morning was a little on the cloudy side but Mark was grateful for the cooler weather today. He walked up and down the side of the road looking for a taxi but there didn't seem to be any available currently. He found himself a bench, ready to sit and wait for one to appear when his mobile rang.

"Mark, it's Reg," the caller began. "I'm at the scrap dealer, I've got information of interest."

Mark sat up sharpish, dropping his takeout cup of coffee in the process which spilled its hot contents all over the pavement in front of him.

"Ah shoot!" Mark exclaimed. "I've just dropped my coffee everywhere." There was a chuckle on the end of the phone line.

"And that's before I tell you what I've found," Reginald added.

"I've just arrived myself, I'm trying to get a taxi to take me to Munxar," Mark told Reginald. "But why don't I get a taxi to you instead?"

"Wait there," Reginald instructed, "I'll come and get you, it won't take long and I can tell you what I've found on the way to Munxar."

Reginald didn't give Mark time to agree or disagree, he'd already hung up before Mark could draw breath. Mark sighed, picked up the paper cup and lid from the ground and found the nearest recycling bin. The closest one was next to a coffee vendor and Mark decided to get himself another coffee whilst he waited for Reginald. He ordered himself a cappuccino and went back to sit on the bench overlooking the sea. He had just about finished his coffee when a vehicle tooted from behind. Mark spun around and saw his driver, one foot out of the car, waving at him. Throwing away his second paper cup, Mark headed over to the car. He had barely sat down in the vehicle, never mind put his seatbelt on when Reginald began to tell him of his findings.

"Unbelievable! Just totally unbelievable!" was how he began. He then continued to explain to Mark what had happened.

He had arrived at the scrap yard and was introduced to the owner. This owner had bought the scrap yard almost three years ago and only last year had begun to deal with the paperwork that was held in storage. Nothing had been discarded and the new owner had decided to look through everything to see what was necessary to be kept and what could be thrown away. One of the files he came across contained notes from the previous owner regarding a silver Fiat Panda that had been forensically checked by the police some thirty or so years ago. The previous owner had made his own notes in the file for the car stating how there was nothing untoward found and he could continue to break up the car and sell the parts.

So far, so good. Only when the new owner went to look at the documents in detail did he notice a large red question mark against the registration plate. This had made him curious and he had made some general enquiries with regards to the vehicle. It turned out that the registration plate that the silver Fiat Panda had when it was scrapped did not match the identification number of the vehicle under the bonnet. The new owner had researched the registration plate and whilst it had certainly come from a silver Fiat Panda, it had not come from the one that had been brought in for scrap.

Mark blinked several times, trying to take in what he had just heard.

"So, the Fiat Panda that was checked by the police, was not necessarily the one that had been stopped in the roadblock?" Mark looked across at Reginald, who was slowly nodding his head.

"That's my feelings," Reginald said. "I'm not saying it wasn't the same vehicle, but it's a discrepancy that appears to have been missed."

Mark asked Reginald to pull the vehicle over into a lay-by so he could process what he had just heard. He wanted a clear head before he arrived at Munxar and at that moment, he was feeling a little confused. They pulled off the road and Reginald stopped the engine.

"So…" Mark paused and then continued, "a silver Fiat Panda was scrapped by Stephen Muscat, the same registration plate as that stopped in the roadblock. This was then, a week or two later, checked forensically for evidence of the missing child, but the registration plates did not match the vehicle identification number, so therefore, it could be a totally different vehicle." Mark looked at Reginald who was smiling with what appeared to be a sense of pride. "Have I understood you correctly?"

"Exactly."

"And there was no evidence found of the missing child. However, there may have been another Fiat Panda, that would have contained evidence, but the number plates had been swapped onto this vehicle, and this vehicle was scrapped."

"Exactly."

"So, is there a way of tracing the vehicle identification number of the car that would have matched the registration plates?" Reginald smiled once more.

"Already checked," he began. "No vehicle matching the correct identification number has been scrapped on Malta or Gozo in the last thirty years. I could check overseas, but that is as much as I have been able to do so far." Reginald looked straight ahead, out of the front windscreen. "So potentially," he added, "that car is still around but has false registration plates."

"Wow," was all Mark could come up with.

"So, we could carry out a search for any silver Fiat Pandas that are on Gozo and Malta. All vehicles over four years old must pass an annual compulsory

Vehicle Roadworthy Test, so that is our starting point. That should give us information of any existing vehicles to check."

"Okay, and is that something that we can look at?" Mark was feeling excited, could this be a new lead?

"Well, I'm not sure that I can, being retired, but we should be able to get the local police to request information from Transport Malta. I've still got a few contacts in the police and with a handshake or two, maybe they will be able to do the search for us."

The heat of the midday sun was beginning to burn through the windows of the car and with the wispy clouds now having evaporated, Mark was feeling the need for refreshment. The two men decided to find a local bar or restaurant and then Reginald would take Mark to Munxar later that afternoon. Despite these new findings, Mark still wanted to visit Mrs Muscat to satisfy himself that she was nothing to do with this case. It was getting more curious again.

They headed to Victoria and found a restaurant called The Grapes where they both chose a glass of iced lemonade and sat outside at a small table with a green checked cloth. Mark was still full from his morning breakfast but Reginald happily ordered himself a bolognaise ragu as well as a basket of bread. Whilst waiting for their order, Reginald put in a phone call to an ex-colleague who still worked in the Malta police to ask him about obtaining information from Transport Malta, having explained as briefly as he could, why he wanted the information. He finished the conversation with the phrase 'I owe you one!' before putting his phone down just as his meal arrived.

The waiter brought the drinks and Reginald's meal to the table. Mark gratefully sipped on his lemonade and took out his laptop having established that Reginald was happy for him to make notes on their findings from the morning. "Reginald?" Mark enquired.

"Stop there," Reginald began, "just Reg please."

"Sorry, Reg it is. Why do you think this was missed before? Surely a full police check would have found this anomaly?"

"I suppose," Reg was between mouthfuls, "once they'd found the vehicle, they were just trying to cover their backs and get the forensics checked ASAP."

The men were about to leave when Reg's phone rang. It was his colleague who had already come up with a list of vehicles for him. Reg nodded, said the odd 'Aha' and then finished the call before Mark had been able to pay the bill.

"I have a list of vehicles being emailed across to you, my contact said it didn't take long as there are not many Fiat Pandas still on the island, let alone silver ones. So, he has sent the list of them all, a total of six."

Reg ordered another couple of drinks, sat back down and Mark followed suit. Sure enough, the list was in Mark's inbox. There were six Fiat Panda's between Malta and Gozo, two metallic grey, three ivory and one described as Dark Racing Green. All of these had their corresponding registration plate. One stood out like a sore thumb!

Chapter Eighteen

By the time Ava got back home, fed Ricco and settled herself onto her couch, she really couldn't face looking at the photograph albums. Whether that was fear of what she might or might not see, or simply that her previous night spent sleeping on that same couch meant that she felt tired beyond belief, she wasn't certain, but she put them both upon her coffee table and had herself an early night.

The next morning, being Monday, Ava opened the café and tried hard to put all thoughts of the perplexing matter out of her mind. The morning took its usual form. The mechanics appeared followed by Ġorġ. She smiled, greeted and served whilst happily chatting to all, but her mind would not rest. It was only when May arrived to help out, did she feel she could relax a little.

"You seem troubled today, everything okay?"

Ava really did not want to bring May into her confidence yet; the matter had to stay between her, her mother and Elias. Too many people having an opinion on her situation would only add confusion.

"Yes, thank you, May, just a little distracted that's all. What with Indri being away, I'm feeling the responsibilities of this place." Ava rotated her arm in a circle to indicate her meaning of 'place' was the café.

May gave a lopsided quizzical look, she wasn't convinced. She had known Ava for a few years now and she was also a good reader of people. She felt there was something troubling the girl.

"Well, if you need me for more hours, or just an ear to listen, I'm at your service."

"May, you are a real trouper, I know I can rely on you always, but it's only another week and Indri will be back. Thank you for the offer, I'll bear it in mind." With that, Ava went into the kitchen to sort out the clean plates for the lunchtime rush leaving May to finish clearing some tables.

After the lunches had been served, Ava left May to the washing up and went across the road to her flat. She welcomed the couple of hours during the early afternoon when she would close the café to customers. Usually, she would use the time to prepare cakes and desserts for the late afternoon trade, but today, she had other thoughts on her mind. Climbing the stairs to her flat, she felt a sense of frisson come over her. Ricco welcomed her with his usual greeting, twisting around her ankles, mewing and purring at her return. She took a large glass from the cupboard and filled it with cold water from the fridge. Taking the water to the couch, she sat down and stared at the albums.

A few seconds passed before she took a large breath and opened the first album. Her mother was right, there were no tiny baby photographs, these all started around the age of three. Helpfully, her mother had written beneath each photograph, the date and location so it was relatively easy to age herself in them. Ava saw a sadness in herself at that early age, there were no smiles, no silly faces which you would expect of a toddler, just a solemn little girl. The first page held her attention for a long time. Staring back at her, was the child from the leaflet that Elias had shown her. In these photographs she had a wonky fringe and her hair was cut much shorter around the back. That too was not cut straight, it appeared to be much longer on one side than the other. Despite not having the leaflet to compare the photographs, Ava had burned the image into her mind and she now felt certain that she was the child whose face was on those leaflets. She was the child that had been lost. Ava felt sick, ran to the bathroom and promptly emptied her stomach of the little she had eaten for breakfast!

She washed her face with icy cold water, having let the tap run for some time to get it as cold as possible. She lifted her face up from the basin and studied it in the mirror above. The bright green eyes returned her gaze.

Back in her kitchen, she telephoned May and let her know that she was unwell and asked her to put a sign on the door of the café saying they had to close for the day. May wouldn't hear of it, not only did she insist on running the café for the afternoon, but she would also arrange for one of the craft ladies to pop in and help her. She assured Ava that it would run like clockwork and that Ava should rest. She would check on her later. Ava didn't have the strength or words to form a negative response, she numbly accepted the offer and finished the call.

She went back to her couch, sipped some of the water and turned over the next few pages in the album. By her calculations, she was around the age of four before she saw a smiling child, one that looked like they were happily playing, swimming or just generally being four. Then around the age of five, came the obligatory first day at school photographs. By now, Ava would grin at the camera, her eyes twinkling—those bright green eyes. She hesitated over the photographs containing her father. Sadly, these were few and far between, seeing as it was usually him that was behind the lens of the camera. The few in which he featured would be a little off centre or heads slightly cut off at the top and Ava could tell that these were taken by her mother. She stroked the photographs gently with her fingertips, she missed him greatly.

Closing the last page of the first album, she noticed that the inside cover of the back of the album was a different colour to the front. It appeared to have a piece of paper carefully glued over the original. Running her fingers over the piece of paper she felt something beneath, not much but a couple of small rectangles about the size of a photograph. Ava fetched her small penknife. It had been her father's and he always carried it in his pocket. It was the one thing that she knew she wanted to keep when her father passed away. She prised open the blade from its shell-like cover and gently lifted the paper away from the back of the album. It had been stuck fast and it resisted her attempts to begin with, but with gentle persuasion, she was able to loosen two sides and let the hidden objects reveal themselves to her.

There were three in total, three photographs of a young child, a girl with dark hair and dark eyes who had the same shape face as Ava's father and the small button nose of Ava's mother. Holding them in her hands, she flicked from one to the next then back again, staring intently at each one. She knew they were not photographs of hers. The nausea came over her again and she ran back to the bathroom.

Having washed her face once more in icy cold water, Ava left her flat and headed for Elias's house. She knocked firmly on the door and waited. Moments later, Elias opened the door and stepped back as Ava walked inside without saying a word. She headed straight for the courtyard garden and sat on a small, curved stone bench that was supported by two stone squirrels at each end. It was cold beneath her but that was a good thing, steadying her temperature. Elias waited a few minutes for Ava to speak but when that didn't happen, he went back inside and put the kettle on to boil. He soon appeared with two mugs of steaming hot tea and placed one gently in Ava's hands.

"Do I assume the meeting with your mum didn't go well?" Elias sat himself down next to Ava and put his tea beside him on the ground. He never knew when he would fall asleep and having a very hot cup of tea in his lap when that happened was best avoided.

Ava didn't respond immediately, but when she did, the tears flooded her eyes. "It is me… it is me… I'm the lost child."

The tears ran down her cheeks and Elias let them fall. She needed to let this out and whilst he felt he would be able to console most crying, having brought up two young children single-handedly, he didn't feel it was right to stop the flow. He just waited.

At least ten minutes must have passed before Ava spoke again. She also placed her tea on the ground beside her, not that she wasn't grateful for the drink, but her hands were shaking and she was already spilling its contents into her lap. She then explained to Elias how she had taken comfort in what Christopher had said, and not wanting to upset her mother, she had just asked for the photograph albums. She described the first few photographs to Elias and then she told him of the three hidden ones glued behind a piece of paper inside the back cover. Elias let her talk. He sat himself as upright as possible, not wanting the narcolepsy to kick in. When she finished talking, he took her hand in his and leant back in his chair. He had noticed that Christopher had appeared at the back door—how much he had heard, he wasn't sure but knowing he was there, was a relief.

Elias came to with Christopher kneeling in front of Ava and they were looking at the leaflet of the missing child. Beside them were Yvonne's diaries and the letters from Sarah which explained about the mother of the missing child, her sister, who walked the beaches at night calling out for her lost baby.

Ava had drunk her tea and had by now a little more colour in her cheeks than when she arrived. Elias sat up and made a small cough to announce his woken state. Christopher smiled at him and gave him a reassuring pat on the knee.

"Your tea will be cold now, Dad. Shall I make some more?"

Elias shook his head, he hadn't really wanted the first one but it seemed an automatic response, to make one for Ava when she arrived.

"Ava has explained it all to me too now, and honestly, we do believe that she is this missing child. But still, there must be a reasonable explanation, I'm sure of it." Christopher smiled up at Ava from his seated position on the floor and Ava gave him a small smile in return. "I've offered to visit Ava's mother with her— well, drive her there at least. I'm sure any conversations between them don't need to involve me, but I don't think she should be driving after such a shock.

105

I've already called May and asked her to run the café again tomorrow, saying Ava is unwell. I think she felt pleased to be needed if I'm honest." With that last remark, Christopher let out a small chuckle. "I'm going to walk her back home and then pick her up first thing tomorrow."

Ava didn't speak during this exchange between father and son. She sat still, cradling her empty mug, her tear-stained face and swollen eyes testament to the shock that had hit her like a thunderbolt.

Chapter Nineteen

Reg and Mark arrived at the address for Mrs Lisa Muscat a little after two-thirty. The sun was still high in the sky and the temperature remained at its maximum for the day. There was very little shade to be found near the property but Reg managed to manoeuvre the vehicle beneath some dappled shade from a row of olive trees. They had the windows down already to keep them cool and they sat for a while to discuss what to do next.

"We can hardly approach her and ask if she has a connection to the missing child?" Mark said.

"Err, no, that is something I don't think we should mention," Reg added.

A few minutes silence passed between them when they noticed the door to the garage was ajar and they could quite easily see a dark green Fiat Panda sitting in the garage. Mark opened his laptop and went to the email which he had received earlier that day. On the list of vehicles, there was an addendum, the one listed as Dark Racing Green had an asterisk beside it and a note stating that the vehicle had undergone a colour change a little over thirty-three years ago. Reg was first to speak.

"Stephen Muscat gets stopped by the police during the roadblock in a silver Fiat Panda. The vehicle fails to be thoroughly checked at the time but within two weeks, he has traded that vehicle in, or so it was believed, and that vehicle was forensically checked. We have now determined that the registration plate of the checked vehicle did not match the identification number under the bonnet. We have in our possession a list of all existing Fiat Pandas, one of which has had the colour changed to Racing Green and here we are staring at a dark green Fiat Panda sitting in the garage of the deceased Stephen Muscat!"

Mark didn't know what to say, Reg had said it all. They were looking at the vehicle that potentially had taken young Alison from her parents all those years ago and it had been hiding here for all that time.

"Time to leave," Reg said. "This is for the professionals now." And with that he started the engine, turned the vehicle around and drove away. Neither man had noticed the lady hovering behind the curtain, looking out of the front window.

Lisa Muscat sank into the armchair which had been supporting her weight whilst she observed the two men sitting on her property for the last ten minutes or so. She'd been on her way back to the garage, to put in a second bag of fresh strawberries that she was now freezing, when she first spotted their arrival. Ever cautious, she had hidden herself behind the curtain to see if she knew who they were before she would open the door. They had been in deep conversation but it was when one of them pointed towards the garage that her heart leapt into her throat. Moments later, they turned the car around and drove away.

This, together with Ava asking for photographs only yesterday, made her extremely anxious. Lisa began to feel faint and put her head down towards her knees inhaling and exhaling slowly for a few minutes. Gathering her thoughts, she made her way through to Stephen's study and began to look for his small dark blue book with all the important information in—passwords, notable dates and of course, details of what to do.

Stephen Muscat had been a car mechanic for years, not a profession he really chose but one perhaps that chose him. He fell into it really, started work helping his father with his mechanic business. They worked well together and experienced many years of ups and downs which came with running your own company. They never earned a huge profit, and many a time they went without wages in order to keep going. They were both immensely proud of the business which they grew together and Stephen continued it on, long after his father passed, right up until the day before, he too, lost his life. A sudden heart attack took him as he was making his way upstairs in the middle of the night. He had gone to the kitchen for some water and to find some indigestion tablets. He often got indigestion, especially if he ate too late in the evening, and this was the case the night before.

Lisa had been distracted in the garden and she had not made his meal until after seven in the evening. Stephen being an old-fashioned patriarch had not even thought to prepare the food for the two of them, despite his wife being particularly busy, but had waited for her to provide. He grumbled all the way down the stairs; each step seeming to increase the pain within his chest— rummaged around for the packet of indigestion tablets, grabbed a glass of water and was halfway back up the stairs when the final pain made his heart surrender. It was over in seconds and the doctors that spoke to Lisa had confirmed that he would not have suffered.

She knew of the little blue book in which he kept all the important information that she might need and he had told her many years ago, that should the time arise, this was where she should turn with regards to the car. She found her mobile phone, called the local scrap yard and made the appointment to take the vehicle there that afternoon.

Reg and Mark made their way back to Malta. They took the first ferry they could get and despite having to wait a while as the first two ferries were already fully booked, they arrived back in Malta by late afternoon. Reg dropped Mark back at his hotel and joined him in the bar so they could further discuss what to do. To Mark, this was out of his comfort zone. He was used to the strange and quirky trails he often needed to follow in order to track down his heirs but this was definitely one of a kind and he felt very uneasy.

Reg went to the bar and ordered them both a cold beer. The table held a small bowl of peanuts and when he returned, Mark was absentmindedly eating them one after another.

"Hungry?" Reg teased.

"Um, yes I suppose so," Mark replied then realised he hadn't eaten since breakfast so it wasn't surprising. "I'll order something at the bar, can I get you something too?"

Reg took the menu from the small table in front of them and never one to pass up on some free food, asked for a toasted cheese and tomato sandwich.

"What now?" Mark said, having returned from the bar. "Surely we need to let the police know?"

Reg took a long drink, wiped his hand across his mouth, put down his beer and sighed. "Yes, we must speak to one of my old contacts in the morning, it can wait until then. But don't breathe a word of this to anyone. We could have it all wrong and there could be a perfectly innocent explanation." Reg didn't believe this for a moment but it was, nevertheless, the right approach.

Mark opened his laptop and began to add a few more notes. He had written down the number plate of the car in Lisa Muscat's garage in his notebook. It was not really necessary seeing as it was listed on the email he had received earlier, but old habits die hard and Mark was used to making notes in his book. He had included the details of the scrap yard owner together with brief notes about the documents which the new owner had come across.

Later, he would construct an email for his employer.

The two men ate their food in friendly silence, commenting only on the quality of the beer and food. Both had a second glass of beer and Reg took the opportunity to follow his sandwich with a slice of warm apple pie. He left Mark shortly after finishing his dessert and said he would call him tomorrow after he had spoken to the police. If necessary, he would collect Mark and take him to the police station tomorrow, just to confirm his interest in the matter.

Mark headed back to his room. His mind was fully wired and he couldn't sleep despite the two large beers he had drunk earlier. Realising he was still hungry he ordered room service of bread with olive oil and balsamic vinegar. He would really have liked some cheese too but resisted the temptation, however, he did ask for a glass of red wine to accompany his bread. Less than ten minutes later, a soft knock on the door indicated the arrival of his supper. He tipped the young man who had brought him his tray and sat down on his favourite chair by the window and sated his appetite. From what had earlier felt like finding the proverbial needle in a haystack, he now thought he had not only found the needle but he had found the thread too and pulling on that thread could possibly create an almighty crash. He did sleep eventually, but it was very fitful and he did not feel at all rested by the next morning when Reg woke him early, just before seven with a telephone call.

"Sorry to call so early but I stopped by the home of my old colleague on the way back from the Solaqua last night. We sat up talking into the small hours about the old days which was not good as he was due to start an early shift this morning. Anyway, he rang me as soon as he arrived at work and wants me to bring you along this morning, there has been a development."

"Right… um… I'm not yet showered," Mark hesitated.

"Ah, sorry there, Mark, I'm an early riser, always have been, it came with the job I suppose. Look, I'll pick you up just after nine, if that is okay?"

Mark confirmed and threw back the bed covers before heading to the shower. He stood under the steaming water for quite a while hoping it would refresh him but after a few minutes he decided it was not going to work and would opt for strong coffee instead. After dressing he made his way down to the restaurant and piled his plate high with a various selection of breakfast on offer. He wasn't going to go hungry today, he would make sure of that. A double espresso later together with copious amounts of bacon, eggs and pastries of all descriptions, he stood outside the front steps of his hotel and waited for Reg. He didn't have to wait long as Reg came to a halt beside him two minutes before the hour.

Mark was just sorting out his laptop at his feet, having pulled on his seatbelt and adjusted the back of the seat to a more upright position when Reg launched into a monologue.

"She's only contacted the scrap dealer asking for the car to be scrapped. Fully smashed up, mind you, no breaking up for parts. Claimed that her husband had an agreement with them that it should be compacted immediately, she even quoted him a conversation that her husband had with the previous owner 'who had given his word' she reckoned, that this could be done immediately. She claims he had made the provision for this to happen when she could no longer face seeing the vehicle in his garage after his demise!" Reg seemed to gasp for breath before continuing, "The scrap owner thought that following on from his and my discussions yesterday morning, this all seemed a little odd, but he agreed to take the vehicle in for scrap."

"Surely it has not been compacted already?" Mark felt horrified.

"No, he was too smart for that, told her that there was a fault but it was due to be fixed today, and promised to compact it as soon as the machinery was repaired. Apparently, she looked a little concerned but left it there with him. She was with him under an hour after we left her house. I think she may have seen us clocking the vehicle in the garage."

They arrived at the police station and Reg bounded up the steps to the building ahead of Mark. Mark had neither the energy nor inclination to climb them hastily, but he made his way up to the top, by which time Reg was already inside chatting away to the officer on the reception desk.

"We are here to see Guzeppi," Reg began. "He is expecting us."

The desk sergeant picked up a small telephone beside him on the desk and tapped out a short three-digit code. He spoke a few words of Maltese into the receiver and hung up. "He will be here shortly."

Reg continued to chat to him in Maltese, Mark had no clue what they were saying. It had been a relief when he arrived on Malta to find that everyone he encountered could speak fluent English but he had heard the Maltese language being spoken between people and was fascinated by the sounds it made. Mark made himself comfortable on a chair near the open doorway and Reg soon followed and sat beside him.

"He prefers to speak Maltese," Reg informed him, "it gave me an opportunity to use it. 'Use it or lose it', they say, don't they?"

Mark realised that he didn't know much about Reg and was about to question him further when a half-glazed brown door opened up ahead of them.

"Come through!"

This was obviously Guzeppi and Mark followed Reg through the door into the depths of the police station. They twisted their way down dark narrow corridors. Some of the overhead strip lights were blinking on and off and it was obvious that the building needed a little bit of attention. They came across a small office which housed a large metal desk, a wall of varying styles of filing cabinets, boxes of paperwork everywhere and two, not that comfortable looking, chairs on which Guzeppi indicated that they should sit.

"Well, this is quite something. I honestly believed that there was nothing more to find with regard to Alison Hensley. Who'd have thought, after all this time, that we may have discovered the actual vehicle she was abducted in?" Guzeppi sat down opposite Mark and Reg, rested his elbows on the table and stared intently at the two of them. "But you must leave this to us now, I can't have you getting involved, is that clear?"

"Of course," Reg replied for them both. Mark nodded in approval and felt greatly relieved that the matter was being investigated, but also a little surprised that he and Reg had managed to discover the car, and its dubious history, quite so easily.

Chapter Twenty

Christopher had left Ava lying on her couch. He had kindly made her a cup of coffee and prepared her a sandwich from whatever contents he could find in the fridge and insisted that she should eat. She really had no appetite but she didn't want to offend him after he had gone to so much trouble. So, whilst the young man sat on the floor and tickled Ricco's outstretched tummy, she ate most of the sandwich which he had prepared.

"You have very little food in your fridge," he stated. "I'll pop back to Dad's and bring you some of the catch from today. We have some beautiful gilthead bream and some squid too, plus I'll collect some fresh tomatoes from the garden. At least you will have something simple you can prepare if you are not feeling so good. It is important to eat."

Ava just nodded, she seemed to not be able to make conversation. Stunned was an understatement and it was all she could do to not vomit again.

"I'll be back shortly," Christopher added. "In fact, I'll cook up the fish so you can just take it from the fridge when you want some."

True to his word, Christopher appeared after a while with a bag in hand containing the fish and the tomatoes along with some extra herbs and some courgettes that Elias had insisted, he bring. He set to in Ava's kitchen, first gutting and descaling the bream, then he removed the rod like gladius from the centre of the squid and discarded the remaining innards that were not eaten. Putting all the intestines of both the bream and squid on a saucer, he fished through them for bits he felt were inedible and then laid the saucer on the floor for Ricco.

Ava had fallen asleep and Christopher continued silently in the kitchen, gently pan frying the bream and squid, adding some olive oil, garlic and herbs to the pan before putting the fish into a terracotta oven dish and covering it with a cloth whilst it cooled and he prepared the courgettes. These too, were pan fried in garlic, herbs and olive oil. He had become quite a cook over the years, preparing very simple yet delicious food for his father and brother. By the time the courgettes were cooked, he had sliced up the tomatoes, not cooking those but tossing them in the oil with the courgettes and found another oven dish to place these into. The fish was now cold and he put the dish in the fridge. At least it was safe from Ricco in there.

He was about to leave when Ava woke; her mobile had rung and it had disturbed her. It was May, checking how she was feeling and filling her in on the various activities of the day. Ava thanked her profusely, assured her she would be okay and another day of rest would be all she needed. Whilst May seemed to accept this, Ava couldn't convince herself that this was the case. Christopher made his farewells, told Ava of the food in the fridge and left her to her evening.

He arrived the next morning as promised. It was just before eleven and he had already been out on the boat and brought in today's haul of fresh fish. He had showered well, not wanting to smell of fish on the car journey to Gozo. Christopher had suggested Ava call ahead to make sure her mother would be there but Ava refused. Not only would she not know what to say, but she also knew that her mother would be concerned, as she should really be working, and visiting her mother on a workday was definitely something that didn't happen. No, she would work out what to say when she arrived.

The ferry to Gozo was reasonably quiet, it was the early and later ferries that tended to be busier so they didn't have long to wait to board. Ava looked very peaky and Christopher was concerned that she might not be up to her day ahead.

"Do you want me to come inside with you when we get to your mother's house?"

Ava looked at him, she didn't know how to respond. On the one hand, she didn't want to be alone but on the other, what would she say to her mother about this young man who had escorted her. She just shrugged.

Christopher had put the location of the house into the satnav on his phone and they were now heading to her mother's when Ava asked him to stop the car.

"I can't go through with this, I just can't. What the heck will I say?"

Christopher pulled the car to one side of the road and switched off the engine.

"Start with the photographs," he suggested. "Explain how you found them and see how she responds. I'll come inside and we can say that Indri's car wasn't working and I offered to help you return the photograph albums."

Ava blindly nodded but looked terrified. He reached into the inside pocket of his jacket and pulled out a silver hip flask.

"Dutch courage?" he said, offering her the contents of the vessel.

"Um… I don't know… maybe?" She took the flask but just held it in her hands whilst Christopher started up the car and continued towards the house.

When they arrived, he parked the car then jogged around to the other door and helped Ava out. She was very unsteady on her feet so he held onto her arm whilst picking up the two photograph albums with his other hand. They walked towards the door but Lisa had seen the car approach and despite hesitating behind the curtain, once she saw Ava get out of the vehicle, she went to the door.

"Hi, I'm Christopher, a friend of Ava's."

"Hi." Lisa looked frail and, like Ava, lacking in sleep. "Come in." She didn't ask questions, she already knew what this was about.

Lisa led the way through to the garden patio under the gazebo. She held out a chair for her daughter to sit and beckoned for Christopher to sit too. Then she sat herself down, lowered her head but didn't speak further. Ava too, was silent, and some time passed before Christopher felt the need to start the conversation.

"We have brought back your photograph albums," he started. "Ava wanted to return them to you as quickly as possible."

Ava was now staring at her mother but her mother's head was facing down to the ground. A tear fell from Ava's cheek and then another and another.

"Who is the child in the hidden photographs?" Ava blurted out. "Why would you hide them behind glued down paper?"

Lisa knew the game was up. "That is Ava, my darling, that is the real Ava."

"So… who… am… I?" Ava managed to stutter out the question.

"You, my sweet child, are the angel sent from heaven."

Ava glared at her mother, stood up so abruptly that her chair fell to the floor behind her and marched off down the garden.

Christopher had no idea what to do or say. He stood up and went back inside the house. He knew this conversation should happen between Lisa and Ava, without him as an interloper but he stood just inside the door in case he was needed. The house looked well-kept and homely. He imagined Ava growing up here and what a lovely place it was to have been raised in. It was not furnished with fancy decoration but it gave off an aura of warmth in the same way he felt about his own home. This might have been a home of love but somehow it was also a home based upon a lie.

Christopher could hear a lot of sobbing going on. He looked out, Ava was sitting on the grass further down the garden and Lisa was still seated at the table. It didn't appear that more words had been spoken between them. Lisa stood and started to walk towards Ava. Ava's shoulders were visibly shaking from the crying and Lisa went to offer comfort. To Christopher's surprise, Ava allowed Lisa to take her into her arms and Ava laid her head on Lisa's shoulder. They continued to cry but no words were exchanged. Then there was a pause in the crying as Ava pulled away and stood up, walking towards the house.

"I'd like to leave now." Ava looked at Christopher, he nodded his head and opened the front door for her to make her exit.

"I'll check on Lisa to make certain she is okay." Christopher had opened the car door too and Ava had climbed inside. "I won't be long."

Ava pulled the door closed and put her hands over her face. Christopher quickly went back inside and found Lisa still sitting halfway down the garden, sobbing.

"I need to take her home," he started to say. "I can easily bring her back again, whenever she would like."

Lisa turned to face him, her eyes already beginning to swell and the tears pouring down her face. She just nodded.

"Will you be okay?" He was genuinely concerned and felt awful leaving this woman in such a desperate state. "Can I call someone to be with you, a friend maybe?"

Lisa shook her head, stood up from the ground and tried to force a smile.

"This day had to come, although I hoped and prayed that it never did. Please understand, I love Ava, this Ava," she pointed towards the car, "from the bottom of my heart."

"I can see that, and Ava knows that too."

With that, he turned and left, making his way back to the car where Ava was still covering her face with her hands. They hadn't gone far when a dark-coloured Hyundai went by them, neither driver knowing who was in the opposite vehicle and maybe, at this point in time, that was a good thing.

Christopher took Ava back to her flat, settled her on her couch and made her a coffee. She just stared straight ahead. He had wanted to call her doctor but Ava had refused. She couldn't talk to anyone right now. She needed time to process this. Christopher noticed a slip of paper pinned to the side of the fridge which simply said, 'Indri's sister' and a phone number written beneath. Rightly or wrongly, he wrote down the number and would later call Indri once he was back home. He knew that Ava wouldn't make it in to work tomorrow or the next day for that matter and he felt Indri should know at least some of what was going on.

Chapter Twenty-One

Lisa shut the front door as Christopher drove Ava away. She turned her back against the coolness of the door and then slid to the floor. The tears had stopped flowing but her heart was racing. She stared straight ahead in a trance. Her thoughts turned to Stephen, he would have known what to do. He had taken charge of everything in their marriage and she felt so lost without him. Her breathing became rapid and moments later she fainted onto the cold stone floor. She didn't hear the car stop outside, nor the doors opening and closing, it was only the knocking on the door that she became slightly aware of, but she lay still, semiconscious.

The knocking became harder and roused Lisa from her faint. She tried to sit but the room was spinning and she let out a groan. A man was peering through the letterbox and noticed Lisa slumped on the floor. He let the letterbox close shut and ran around to the back of the house to see if he could gain access. A second man followed. Going into the house via the back door through the kitchen, they found Lisa and immediately checked for a pulse. Lisa groaned again and the men let out a sigh of relief.

"I think she has fainted," the first man explained, "can you fetch some water from the kitchen?"

Moments later, the second man reappeared with a glass of cold water to find that Lisa was now sitting up against the front door, her eyes were open but glassy. He presented the water to her but it was the first man who took the glass and offered it up to her lips.

"Sip it slowly," he instructed, "there you go." The man removed the glass. She had taken a little into her mouth, but some ran down her chin and dripped onto her dress. Once more he offered the glass, again she sipped, almost mechanically and without conscious thought. The second man had returned from the kitchen with a damp tea towel which he used to dab at her forehead, she was beginning to come round.

A good ten minutes or more had passed before Lisa had been guided to an armchair. She rested her head back and suddenly noticed the two men in front of her. Gasping audibly, she tried to sit up, a look of horror across her face.

"Mrs Muscat, my name is Guzeppi Verra. I'm an inspector with the Malta police and this is my colleague, Police Sergeant Zeppa Gatt. I'd like to ask you some questions, if you feel able?"

Lisa's face relaxed but only slightly, she was gripping the arms of the chair with both hands. Guzeppi lowered himself onto his haunches so he was less domineering over her and smiled gently.

"We just need to ask some questions about the car which you took to the scrapyard yesterday afternoon."

"It was my husband's car, I don't drive. I wanted to get rid of it, seeing it in the garage reminded me too much of my husband." Lisa spoke clearly yet her voice gave away her emotional state, her words sounded rehearsed.

"I understand." Guzeppi had now pulled a small chair towards him and sat upon it. Holding himself on his haunches was pulling on his thigh muscles and he rubbed them gently as he sat facing Lisa. "But I understand your husband passed some time ago, did you not wish to scrap it sooner?"

"I couldn't face doing it before now."

"Yes… yes… there is a lot to deal with when someone passes. The grief is just part of it. It must have been so very difficult for you."

Lisa didn't comment, she just stared at Guzeppi, her body was so tense and she wasn't sure what to say.

"Look, can we call someone to sit with you, or your doctor maybe? You are very pale and I'm not happy just leaving you here alone."

"There is no one, and I don't care for my doctor. Perhaps I am coming down with something, I'll take myself off to bed."

Guzeppi was still uncertain about leaving her, but it had just been a faint, and further questions could wait for now. He asked Zeppa to make her some hot tea with sugar and helped her up the stairs to her room. By the time Guzeppi had fetched the tea, Lisa was dressed in a nightshirt, the curtains were drawn and she was lying in bed with the covers up to her chin. He placed the cup beside her and let her know that they would lock the back door and let themselves out of the front. Lisa said nothing in reply.

Back in their car, Guzeppi in the passenger seat and Zeppa taking the wheel, the two men headed back to the ferry terminal.

"Odd, don't you think?" Guzeppi began.

"What's that?"

"It's not an offence to scrap a vehicle, but not once did she ask why we wanted to know."

Zeppa flicked his head quickly sideways to see Guzeppi nodding his head, his lips pursed, obviously deep in thought.

"Let's stop at the scrapyard, I'd like to speak to the owner, I need to make sure that no one touches that car."

Zeppa nodded, pulled to the side of the road, and looked up the address on his mobile. Setting the address into the satnav, they changed direction and made their way to the scrapyard.

The scrapyard was fronted with two, three metre high, rusty corrugated iron doors. There was a large sign with a picture of two German shepherd dogs and a warning in both Maltese and English stating 'Guard dogs loose—BEWARE!' Guzeppi telephoned the owner and asked if they could enter, to be told that the dogs were on chains so they would be safe to go inside. He got out of the vehicle, opened the gates which screeched across the floor beneath them. The dogs sprang into action, their barking loud and aggressive but Guzeppi was not fazed by such, and beckoned Zeppa to drive the car through whilst he shut the gates behind them. As Zeppa drew level, he told him to park up near the office and he would walk. The gates screeched once more and the dogs joined in with the cacophony of sound.

The office, such as it was, appeared to be an old shipping container tucked away in a corner of the yard, barely visible due to the mountains of scrap vehicles and parts thereof which surrounded it. Zeppa noticed the dogs were pulling at their chains, their mouths snarling and their front paws leaping off the ground. He hoped those chains were strong. Guzeppi strolled towards them, stood a metre in front, and stared at them. The dogs relaxed, their barking stopped and he then stepped forward and offered the back of his hand for them to sniff. Zeppa stayed in the car.

"Come on in!" called the owner from the makeshift door to his office. The container had two large doors at one end and these were propped open with old tyres and exhaust pipes. It appeared that they never closed. Guzeppi noticed the dark green Fiat parked up to one side with a bright orange cone sitting on its bonnet.

"Stops anyone touching it!" the owner had noticed Guzeppi looking.

"Couldn't it get knocked off, or blown by the wind?"

"Doubtful."

Guzeppi gave a slight shoulder shrug to one side, it didn't seem very secure to him.

"I need to get a team of forensic officers to come and search this vehicle so I need to be certain that it is not moved or touched in anyway. Have you or anyone else been inside?"

"Well, I have," the owner replied. "The lady didn't drive so one of the lads dropped me off and I drove it back here. Here's all the paperwork she gave me. Not much as you can see.

"The registration and licence, also the VEH006 which I obtained a copy of, from Transport Malta. This is the official document submitted when a vehicle goes through a change of colour. Mr Muscat had recorded the colour change using the correct documents and it appears that he sprayed the car himself."

Guzeppi took the papers and said he would need to keep them for now. The owner just nodded in agreement.

"What's the interest in it?"

"I can't go into that just yet. It's part of an investigation. My officers will be along in the next few days and they may decide to bring the vehicle to Malta. We will let you know what is happening as and when we know."

Guzeppi bade his farewell and joined Zeppa back in the car, then put in a phone call to the station asking for a forensic team to be sent to Gozo as soon as they could. How much they would find after all this time was uncertain. It was unlikely that there was blood to be found and he was certain that Stephen Muscat had vacuumed the vehicle to within an inch of its life but it had to be done. One way or another they needed to know if this was the car that had been stopped in the original roadblock, although he was certain it was. But whether they could prove that the child was ever in the vehicle, remained to be seen.

Heading back to Malta, Guzeppi took the time for forty winks. He was getting older and spending some of the night talking to Reg rather than sleeping was catching up with him. He stayed asleep until they made the ferry, then slept once more when they had landed on Malta although it was only a short drive back to the station.

Zeppa parked up and in doing so, Guzeppi grunted out of his sleep, rubbed his eyes and exited the car. The two men made their way through the building to Guzeppi's office where there was a bright yellow post-it note sitting on top of a file on his desk. It was the old case notes from over thirty years ago. He had requested they be found from the archive earlier that day. The post-it note said that forensics were going to Gozo tomorrow for nine am. The team were currently looking at a property in Valletta where there had been a suspicious death over the weekend which took priority. The next few hours were spent with the two men reading through the old files, making various notes, and drinking copious amounts of coffee.

Chapter Twenty-Two

It was just after eight am on Wednesday morning when Ava woke with a start, hearing knocking on her front door. Throwing back the covers which didn't best please Ricco who had been curled up at her feet, she grabbed a dressing gown and padded over to the front door. Opening it wide, she was amazed to see Indri looking back at her, his face a picture of grave concern.

"You're back early!"

Indri stepped inside the flat and held out his arms to Ava. She stepped towards him and crumpled like an old tissue. He held her close in a paternal way and Ava took the embrace and welcomed it. He patted her back and then held her at arm's reach, peered into her eyes which were still swollen from all the tears and shook his head.

"I only left you alone for a week and look at you!" Indri was smiling and hoping that his teasing would cover up the way he was feeling. He'd taken a call from Elias's eldest the evening before and managed to get himself on a late flight out of Sicily, arriving in time for Christopher to meet him at the airport and fill him in on what had been going on. He was genuinely concerned for her.

"You are to take at least the rest of this week off." Ava tried to argue but Indri wouldn't hear of it. "I couldn't wait to get back from my sister's place. It was too busy and too noisy for me. I was pleased to see her but a week was more than enough. So, Indri is ordering you to rest. If you need me, come across the street but I won't let you work."

"How did you know?"

"Young Christopher called me, told me the basics. It's not my business to interfere but I'm here if you need me."

"Thank you, Indri, you are a good friend. I feel shocked, I had no idea." Ava sat down on her couch, she felt exhausted despite waking from many hours of sleep. "I'd like to go and see Elias, see if he can contact the friend of his late wife. I'd like to talk to her, not that I have the faintest idea what to say!"

"You just take it easy, there is no rush. Make sure you are feeling steady before you do too much. It's been one hell of a jolt!" With that, Indri left and made his way back to the café where May was in full swing in the kitchen preparing the morning breakfast for the mechanics who would be their first customers, no doubt.

Ava took a long shower, dressed in white shorts and a dark pink t-shirt that really could have done with an iron, but she didn't notice. Putting on her usual flip-flops, she made her way across to the café for an espresso and pastizzi. She couldn't face making anything for herself but she was feeling a little light-headed and was certain a lack of food was the cause. Ava sat on one of the seats facing the sea. It would be quieter out there and she was hoping that she didn't need to make polite conversation with anyone. Indri had spotted her move swiftly through the café, disappeared quickly behind the counter and prepared her espresso and an apple pastizzi. He didn't mention to May that Ava was out there, she was tucked away in the kitchen and for now, he wanted Ava to have the peace and quiet which she needed.

"Here you go!" Indri put the plate and cup beside her, smiled and left.

Ava held the coffee to her face and breathed in the smoky aroma which always delighted her senses. The sun was warm on her face, she stretched out her legs and kicked off her flip-flops. Closing her eyes, she let the sound of the gentle lapping of the waves flow into her mind. Many years ago, she had learnt a little meditation and she tried her hardest to let the soothing sounds calm her. Generally, she was quite good at the process, and would often use it to lull herself to sleep or just add to her relaxation when taking a bath, but today it wasn't having the greatest of effects.

The pastizzi, however, was very welcome. She hadn't realised quite how hungry she was and tucked into its flaky goodness with relish. Indri had spotted her from inside the café, devouring the pastry, grabbed another and took it outside to her. He didn't say a word, just left the plate beside her and went back in. Ava heard the voices of the mechanics approaching the café and no doubt Indri had too. He needed to prepare their order.

Ava stayed put, long after finishing her two pastizzis and coffee, she wanted the coast to be clear before she ventured through the café once more. She also knew that Elias wouldn't be back from the fishing boat until after ten. Checking her watch, she rose from her seat, popped her head inside the café to see Indri outside on the pavement chatting to Ġorġ, she was able to quickly walk behind him so that he didn't notice her passing by. Making her way to Elias's, she began to think about the lady she now knew to be called Sarah and realised that this lady was her aunt.

Christopher opened the door, still smelling heavily of fish. He apologised for the aroma, invited her inside and suggested she went straight through to the courtyard. Elias was already outside, a bucket at his feet, slitting open the bellies of some of the morning catch. Jack was sitting beside him and the two of them quickly and deftly descaled, gutted and cleaned up the fish. They were masters of their craft. Elias looked up and welcomed Ava warmly. She sat slightly away from the men, the aroma of the fish was a little too strong for her at this time of day.

"Excuse the pong!" Jack quipped. "We do this first before we shower."

"Don't let me stop you, I just wanted a quick word. Do you have any contact details for Sarah, the lady who was friends with your late wife?" Ava directed the question at Elias but it was Christopher who answered.

"I don't believe we do, she moved after Mum died and there was no reason for her to keep in touch with us."

"Yes, that was my fear," Ava began, "just that I'd like to try and find her."

Elias looked up, still holding a fish in one hand.

"You could ask Gino, he saw that man that was looking for her, he might know how to get in touch." As he spoke, the fish wobbled in his hand. Had its belly not been split open and half its insides spilling out, Ava would have thought that it was alive.

"Ah, yes, I could certainly try him and he will be in the market today. Thanks Elias, I didn't think of that, I'm sorry to have disturbed you all."

"You're always welcome here, anytime." Elias gave Ava a big smile and it was only then that she noticed that he had many teeth missing from his mouth. Ava left and headed up through the town towards the market.

Gino was in his usual spot at the top of the market. He had a small line of customers forming a queue for their chosen beverage so she sat on the bench that overlooked the street-filled stalls and waited for a lull. The sun was at its height now and Ava was wishing she had brought a hat with her. She shuffled sideways so that she was partially under the shade of the trees which surrounded the market square. The queue soon dispersed and Ava approached Gino's stall.

"Espresso please, Gino?"

"Hey, I don't suppose you have one of those prinjolata for me? I could sell ten of those cakes a day!"

"Sorry, no. But I'll happily make you more if you would like. I enjoy doing it."

"Sit yourself back down, I'll bring this over to you. Mind if I join you for a few minutes?"

Ava went back to sit down in the shade and waited for Gino to join her. He took a while as two more customers arrived and he made their coffee first before bringing hers and one for himself. His daughter had arrived to give him a break so Ava's timing was perfect.

"So, how many could you make me and how often?" Gino was looking very hopefully at Ava.

"Can we discuss this at another time, Gino? I have a pressing matter that I need to deal with, but I could probably have time to make you a few each week if you'd like."

Gino then noticed that Ava was looking a lot less than her usual cheerful self. "Everything okay with you?" he asked.

"Yes, I'm okay, just tired. But I wonder if you can help me. Do you have a contact number for Sarah, the lady that knew Elias's wife? I'd like to talk to her."

"Sorry, no, I don't but you could try asking that man that is over from Canada. I have his business card and he was trying to track her down. If he has, you may be in luck." Gino got up, went over to his stall and reached inside bringing out the business card that Mark had given him. Ava held the card between her fingers; *This is where it all began,* she thought and a big part of her wished she had never heard of Mark Wheeler.

Leaving Gino in the market, Ava took the business card, promising to return it to Gino as soon as she could. She made her way to a quieter part of the market to make the call.

"Hello, is that Mr Wheeler?"

"Yes, that is me, how can I help you?"

Ava hesitated. "Well, my name is Ava Muscat, well, I think it is, have you got a few minutes to talk?"

Mark almost dropped the phone in shock. He was sitting with Reg in the Solaqua bar waiting to hear back from Guzeppi how the forensics team were getting on with the car.

"Ava?" Mark repeated back to her. "Ava Muscat from Gozo?"

"Um… yes… that is me. You sound like you know who I am."

"Well, not exactly but I would definitely like to talk to you. Would you like to meet up, we could get some lunch perhaps?"

Ava didn't feel at all hungry having eaten two apple pastizzis earlier, but she agreed to meet him.

"Can I come to you?" Ava asked. "I could do with a change of scenery." Not strictly true, she just wanted to talk to him away from anyone she might know.

"Certainly, I'm staying at the Solaqua Hotel in Mellieħa Bay, do you know it?"

"I do indeed, I live down the hill near the beach. Any chance we could meet somewhere else?"

Once more, Mark was shocked by the lady on the end of the telephone. If this was the child of Lisa Muscat, there was a possibility that this was the child that had been abducted all those years ago. Reg had been researching the Muscat family and had found a birth certificate for Ava Muscat, who would have been approximately the same age as Alison. There was also a record of a period of time where Lisa Muscat was being medicated for depression following the daughter's prolonged illness from meningitis. There were no more birth records as far as he could find. Mark and Ava agreed to meet at St Julian's Bay at twelve. He knew of the hotel where he had met Ġakobb Farrugia, he explained where it was and ended the phone call.

Turning to Reg, who was sitting beside him this whole time, he explained that possibly, just possibly, he had just been speaking and had now arranged to meet with Alison Hensley. Reg looked aghast.

"*The* Alison Hensley? The child that was taken all those years ago?"

"I think so. But I don't know if she knows who she is."

"Blimey mate, that's incredible. Can I come along for the ride?"

"Well, yes, but let me talk to her on her own for now, I don't want to frighten her off even if you are no longer a serving policeman." Mark chuckled a little at this, but Reg was already nodding his agreement.

"Good idea; if we get there early, I can ensconce myself nearby and listen in."

The two men tidied up their papers and Mark closed his laptop. It was very unusual for a prospective heir to find him but this was a most unusual case and he didn't believe this lady had one iota of an inkling that she was who he believed she was.

They parked up easily, near to the hotel but to be safe, Reg had got out of the car a little way away and had walked the last bit. If Ava was to see Mark arrive, he didn't want her to see Reg getting out of the car at the same time. Mark made his way to the bar, Reg was already sitting near to a group of seats tucked into a quiet corner. Ordering a large white coffee, Mark took the drink to the corner seating and waited. He realised that he hadn't given Ava any idea what he looked like so he watched the door hoping he would notice a young woman entering the lobby on her own. He didn't need to wait long, he knew it was her right away and he had a funny feeling that he had seen her before.

As she approached the bar, Mark stood up, leaving his coffee on the table. After all, he was hoping that Ava would agree to sit in the corner with him, and went to speak to her at the bar.

"Ava?" he asked.

"Yes, are you Mark?" Ava hesitated and then said, "I served you the other day at the café by the beach, you had the last piece of prinjolata!"

"That was you? Of course! It was delicious by the way. How is the man who collapsed?"

"Elias? He's fine. I saw him this morning."

Mark bought Ava her drink. She asked for fresh orange juice saying she had drunk far too much coffee already today. He indicated where he had been sitting and, to Mark's relief, she followed him over to the corner. She didn't notice Reg sitting nearby or she didn't concern herself with it. Either way he was pleased.

Ava began the conversation, asking if he had found the lady for whom he had been searching. She went on to say that she had discovered that Elias's late wife had known Sarah and Ava would like to get in touch. She was obviously skirting around the real reason, Mark believed, but he let her continue her story.

"Well, it is difficult for me to just pass over someone's contact details without their prior knowledge."

"Yes, I suppose it is…" Ava trailed off and her face looked sad, her eyes were filling with tears and she didn't seem to be able to control them. Tears began to fall down her cheeks and Mark reached inside his jacket for a clean handkerchief which Ava gladly accepted. He waited for her to mop her tears. She laid her head back on the wall behind her and sighed. "I'm so sorry, I have had a tough few days. Can I tell you something in confidence?"

Mark was concerned, he knew Reg was listening and he knew that whatever she told him, wouldn't be kept in confidence.

"You believe you are not the real Ava Muscat."

Ava bolted upright in the seat and stared at him in disbelief. "How on earth do you know that?" Ava wasn't sure if she was angry or relieved. If he knew who she was, then perhaps he could tell her!

"Please don't be frightened or concerned, I think I may know more about you, but I am not certain at this stage. I have been looking for Sarah and I have found her, but she told me some things that I need to clarify. I think that you may be part of a much bigger picture. How much do you know?"

Ava relaxed once more. She had a good feeling about this man and had already contacted his company in Canada before meeting him, just to establish that he was a genuine person and not some fraudster. She hadn't given them any details as to who she was and thankfully, they hadn't asked her.

Over the next hour, Ava told him everything that had happened over the last few weeks. Including the bits about how people thought that Mark was looking for her initially, but soon she had heard that he was searching for an older lady. She then told him of her strange curiosity, how she had spoken to Elias and how eventually Elias had shown her the flyer from the original search for the missing child. She left out the bits about visiting her mother, she wasn't sure she wanted him to know about her, she wanted to protect her from all of this. Mark let her finish then he took a gamble.

"I've not been working alone," he started to say, "I've had a man helping me these last few days and he knows more about you, or at least who you might be, than I do."

Ava blinked at him repeatedly, she was feeling a little unsteady and she took a large gulp of orange juice. "Okay… should I be worried?"

"Heavens no. He just happens to believe you might be this child that you saw on the flyer and he was part of the original team who had investigated her disappearance. His name is Reginald Micallef."

"Blimey!" Ava was trying to absorb all this information and was not sure if she could take much more but she pressed on anyway. "Could I talk to him?"

"I'm so pleased that you said that." A voice came from behind her as Reg stood up and moved around to where Mark and Ava were sitting. "Sorry for the subterfuge but we didn't want to frighten you."

"Oh, believe me, I'm not frightened. I'm terrified, but not of you."

Reg sat down next to Mark and introduced himself properly. He explained how the case into the disappearance of the child had possibly been flawed and

128

how, by sheer coincidence, Mark had spoken to Reg's brother in the library and he had contacted Reg. Since then, Reg had happily been helping Mark investigate the case.

"Case?" Ava queried.

This time Mark took the reins, not wanting to include Lisa into the conversation at this point.

"Well, as you know from the business card, I am an heir hunter, do you understand what that means?"

"I think so. Do you trace people who don't know they have inherited from a relative?"

"Yes, that is right."

"So, that is why you are looking for Sarah, she has an inheritance that she does not know about?"

"That was my case originally, but there has been a twist."

"Oh?"

"Well, Sarah would have inherited from her sister…" He let the sentence hang in the air, wondering if Ava would pick up on it. Silence ensued so he continued, "It was when I contacted Sarah that I learnt about the child who had gone missing, this child being her sister's only daughter…" Again, he let the sentence hang. This time he could see the cogs whirring in Ava's mind.

"And you think that I might be that child?" Ava slumped forward onto the table, her shoulders sank into her body and she laid her head on the cold surface. She hadn't passed out, but she sat there for a while, just to be certain that she wasn't going to do so. "I don't believe this is happening to me!" Ava still had her head on the table but both Mark and Reg could just about make out what she was saying.

"Are you okay? Would you like a brandy?" Reg had already got up to go and get one when he realised the table was wobbling, Ava was nodding her head whilst it rested on the table, making it jiggle back and forth.

Reg returned quickly with a large balloon of golden liquid with an ice cube floating on the top. He passed her the glass seeing that she was now sitting upright again, but there was no colour in her cheeks. She looked transparent.

"Look, there is no rush here, let's take this one step at a time. Would you like me to contact Sarah and see if she would like to meet you? But I do think we may need to do a DNA test."

Mark was carefully observing her; the last thing he wanted was for the poor girl to collapse.

"Let's talk about the other business, another time. We would have to have a DNA anyway. How does that sound?"

"Yes." The simple reply came.

The two men sat with Ava whilst the colour began to return to her cheeks, aided by the large brandy that she had consumed.

"How did you get here?" Reg asked Ava once she looked a little brighter. "You can't possibly drive after all that brandy."

"No, it's okay, I came by bus."

"Well, I'd rather we dropped you back home, if that is alright with you? I don't like the idea of you being on a bus right now."

"Thanks." Once more just a simple reply. Ava had a mind like a spinning top and all she wanted to do was make it stop.

Mark settled the bar bill and between them they helped Ava to Reg's car. She was silent all the way back to Mellieħa. They dropped her in the market at her insistence. She didn't want anyone to ask why she was seen getting out of a strange car. The men agreed, on the understanding that Reg would follow her at a distance so that they could be certain she made her way home safely. Ava gratefully accepted.

Chapter Twenty-Three

Ava had taken the rest of the week off work and at Indri's insistence she was only going to work part time for the next week too. She was still feeling exhausted. She was sleeping but her dreams were disturbing and she would wake without feeling the slightest bit refreshed. Between them, they had convinced May that she was recovering from a bug and was just a bit off colour. May was continuing to help Indri during the busiest times and this was working out well for all concerned. A few days had passed. Ava hadn't heard from Mark about Sarah, and she was feeling uneasy that perhaps Sarah didn't want to meet up. She received the call on Sunday morning.

Ava was out on her balcony with Ricco. The sun was warming up nicely for the day and she had her coffee in one hand and was stroking Ricco's head with the other when she heard her phone ring. She hadn't heard from her mother since she left with Christopher, but thus far, Ava didn't know what to say or how she was feeling so she hadn't called her either. The phone ringing was quite possibly her mother, so Ava got up slowly to find her phone, hoping that it would stop ringing before she got to it. It wasn't her mother.

"Is that Ava?"

"Yes, who is this?"

"My name is Sarah, Mark Wheeler gave me your number, I hope that is, okay?"

"Oh gosh, oh my, oh lordy!" was all Ava could say.

"Sorry, perhaps I should have let him call you first, I'm so sorry."

"No, no, it's fine, I'm just surprised that is all. Hang on, let me sit down." Ava made her way to the couch and collapsed onto it in a heap. "Sorry about that, I was half expecting that to be my mother and I wasn't sure if I wanted to speak to her."

There was a definite pause before Sarah spoke again, "Mark believes you may be my niece, do you think that is possible?"

131

Ava shook her head, trying to make a sentence form that didn't sound like nonsense. "Well, I don't believe I am who I thought I was, and I don't believe my mother is my real mother, if any of that helps?" Ava wasn't sure she had achieved a sentence that wasn't nonsense after all, but she carried on. "So, I may be your niece, but I had no idea!"

Sarah paused again before she spoke. She wanted to suggest they meet but was it too early? Mark had said that Ava would need a DNA test before they were sure but she really wanted to meet her.

"Would you be happy to meet me?" Sarah began. "If you are not my niece then so be it, but I'd like to meet you. I have a strong feeling, from what I have heard, that you are." Sarah was trying to hold her voice stable, she couldn't really believe that she might be speaking to Alison. She didn't want to get her hopes up like the old days when Alison first went missing, but this was the first positive news for so many years. She had to try and follow it through.

Ava was shaking, she dropped the phone on the floor and scrabbled around for it.

"Hello?"

Ava heard Sarah speak before she was able to pick up the phone and talk.

"Sorry, I dropped my phone," Ava reassured Sarah. "Yes, I'd like that. I feel that I have got to know you a little already. I know Elias, he had some letters from you to Yvonne which he let me read. I hope you don't mind."

Sarah and Ava continued to chat for quite some time. Ava filled Sarah in on Elias and the boys and Sarah explained a little more about the time when her niece went missing. In the end they agreed to have dinner that evening. Sarah suggested Gozo but Ava wasn't feeling up to crossing over to the island again just yet. She made the excuse of not having a car so Sarah agreed to pick her up and they would find a restaurant at which to have dinner, away from Mellieħa, later that day.

Ava opened her fridge, took out the cooked fish and vegetables and put them into a small container. She decided to take herself for a walk. The day was beginning to get much warmer so she picked up her sun hat, made some coffee in a thermos and grabbed two bottles of water as well. She changed into her walking boots, picked up her sunglasses, and laid a kiss upon Ricco's head before heading out the door. The sunglasses were obviously for eye protection, but also to prevent anyone asking awkward questions should she bump into them, seeing that her eyes were extremely red and swollen still.

She set off and headed towards Popeye Village on Anchor Bay and then along the cliffs. The sun was glorious and she loved being so close to the sound of the waves. It was cleansing her soul if not her mind. She recalled visiting the tourist attraction with her school and staring in wonder at the quaint wooden buildings that formed the film set. To this day she had not seen the Popeye film. She didn't own a television or computer, nor did she like the idea of watching it on her phone, therefore, she was not likely to see it. The wind coming off the sea was certainly bracing and she needed to hold onto her hat. After about thirty minutes, she found a small, raised rock that was flat enough to sit on and not too close to the cliff edge. By now she had removed her hat. There was little point in trying to hold onto it and she had stuffed it into the small shoulder bag along with her lunch. She sat with her elbows perched on her knees having poured out a cup of coffee and gazed out across the glorious azure blue sea. Up here she was detached from what was happening to her and she began to relax a little.

Looking at her watch, she realised that it was approaching midday and she was hungry. The phone call from Sarah had meant that she had completely forgotten to eat breakfast and her tummy rumbled in complaint. She drank thirstily from one of the bottles of water and took out the container of fish and vegetables which Christopher had put together and began to tuck in. She had only taken a mouthful when she stopped mid-chew, chewed a little more and stopped again. *This is amazing!* she thought to herself. 'However did he manage to make this taste so good!' She devoured the whole container, marvelling at each bite. 'This boy knows how to cook!' Making a mental note to tell Indri of his capabilities, she finished up the whole lot and with a quick check around to make sure no one was about, she picked up the dish and licked the surface clean.

The walk was really doing her some good and she realised that she was looking forward to meeting Sarah later that day. She had seemed easy to talk to on the telephone so she could certainly see why Yvonne had taken such a liking to her. Her full belly and the heat of the sun was beginning to be too much, and despite the wind off the sea keeping her cool, she knew that it was time to head back. She could do with a siesta before meeting Sarah, and her flat with its thick stone walls would be nice and cool, despite the heat of the day.

Once back down on the beach, she saw Jack by the water's edge with some young children, they were peering into a small plastic bucket and he had quite a crowd of little ones around him. Ava wandered over to see what was happening. Jack stood up and waved as soon as he saw her. He covered his eyes from the glare of the sun with the hand holding the bucket which was sloshing water all over him and making the children squeal with delight. As she approached, she realised that they were gathering up little hermit crabs and watching them in the bucket, just like she did as a child. It took her back to those happy memories where she spent such glorious days with her parents. It felt like a stone dropped into her stomach at the thought. One moment she was reliving the wonderful days on the beach and the next she was left cold, realising she had no idea who she was.

Jack beckoned her over and she knelt down beside him. The children huddled around the bucket were giggling as the little crabs wriggled around in the water. Jack had placed a small pebble in the water to give the crabs something to climb on or under, there were at least three in there as far as she could see. A little dark-haired boy whose back was covered in sand, jumped up and down each time one of the crabs peeked out from inside its shell. Ava looked around, wondering where the parents of the children were. Jack noticed her looking. "I volunteer at the local kids club, so I'm in charge of this mob for a couple of hours today."

Jack gave one of the children a high-five. "It's fun and I get to be a kid again!"

"For a moment, I thought you were the Child Catcher," Ava chuckled, and then the same stone from before plummeted into her belly.

"Ha! I haven't quite perfected the walk." Jack laughed. "Here, let me try." He told the children to copy him and started to tiptoe about, stop, as if hiding behind a post, and then look around him. The children followed, loving the new game.

"Children… where are you? I know you're here somewhere." Jack made his voice a little higher, and in a sing-song tone, it was uncannily similar to that of the Child Catcher. Ava left them to it, waved her goodbyes as Jack continued to pretend that he couldn't see the children following in his wake. Ava hadn't seen much television growing up, but she knew that film well, and right now the Child Catcher was the last thing she wanted to think about.

Yet it had sprung into her mind from nowhere.

Back at her flat, Ricco was curled up like a soft downy cushion on the balcony bench. Ava grabbed a glass of iced water from the fridge and joined him out there. The street below was pretty quiet since it was a Sunday. Most people would be gathered around tables full of food, chattering with their family and friends. Ava had never felt lonely being by herself, Ricco was good company and she liked being on her own. No one else to please or provide for in her downtime. She went back inside, changed into a linen nightdress, and climbed into bed. She set the alarm on her watch for five pm, put on an eye-mask and lay down having already chosen some gentle piano music to hopefully lull her to sleep. Whether it was the fresh air or the delicious fish that she had eaten, it didn't take long. Ricco joined her and curled himself up between her ankles. She didn't notice him there. She was sound asleep.

Her alarm trilled and Ava woke with a groan, lifted up her eye-mask and silenced it as quickly as possible. She flopped back on the pillow and realised that she had slept solidly for over three hours, possibly the best sleep she'd had in a week. Throwing back the covers, she gently lifted the sleeping Ricco out of the way and tidied the bed again. She didn't like to get into an unmade bed, it made her feel slovenly. Each morning she would make certain her bed looked tidy, straighten up the covers by pulling them taut and arrange throw pillows at the head of the bed. It always looked inviting. She headed off to the bathroom and stood under the shower letting the water complete her awakening. After drying off, she dressed in a cotton sundress and piled her dark hair up into a messy bun. Putting on a slick of lip gloss and touching her eyelids with a hint of olive green eye shadow, she was ready. She didn't need mascara, her lashes were so dark and she really didn't like to wear a lot of makeup.

Then, nervously, she sat out on the balcony waiting for Sarah. She didn't have to wait long, Sarah was ten minutes early but Ava was more than pleased. She hoped the butterflies in her stomach would come to a rest soon. Ava called to Sarah from the balcony, asked her to wait and told her she would be down in a moment. She left Ricco dozing on the balcony, popped some sardines on a saucer, topped up his water and went down the stairs. Sarah stood at the bottom of the stairs, her mouth wide open. Suddenly realising what she was doing, she closed it quickly but continued to stare.

"Hi... wow! I feel like I'm staring at my younger self." Sarah knew instantly that this was, without doubt, her long-lost niece. The tears fell instantly and she pulled Ava in for a hug. She didn't wait to see if Ava was okay with this; she had waited thirty-three years for this moment.

Ava let Sarah hug her. She wasn't sure how she felt, but the warm embrace, and the emotion that she sensed from being held by her, was something that seemed familiar and she didn't resist. Sarah released her from her tight grip.

"Oh gosh, I'm so sorry, you must think I'm mad," Sarah was shaking, "but I recognised you immediately, honestly, you couldn't look any more like me or my sister if you tried."

Ava suggested they get in the car and head to the restaurant quickly—she really didn't want to be seen, or have to explain to anyone, what was happening here. No doubt word would spread soon enough but for now, she couldn't cope with that. Sarah agreed, apologised profusely and got into the driver's seat. They left Mellieħa, headed up the hill and out towards Mosta.

It was around twenty minutes' drive and for the first few minutes Sarah kept glancing sideways at Ava. One time, Ava grasped the wheel, more to show Sarah she needed to concentrate than anything else. Sarah took the hint and once more apologised. "I've brought some photos with me, would you like to see them? Family ones."

"I'd like that."

"How are you feeling? This must be such an awful shock for you. Believe me, I'm reeling in disbelief, but in my heart, I always hoped that you'd be found."

"There is no easy answer to how I'm feeling," Ava looked down into her lap. She pressed her tongue behind her teeth, hoping it would stop her from crying. "It's a lot to take in and, for the most part, it feels totally unbelievable."

They arrived in Mosta and found a little carpark near Mosta Dome church and made their way to a Lebanese restaurant across the road. Sarah had booked a table and had asked for one overlooking Mosta Dome if possible. The view was breathtaking and the cooking aromas were delightful. Sarah took charge and ordered a meze platter between them and it came piled high with all kinds of interesting and tasty delicacies. They both opted for tea with mint which was served in little glass cups.

"Are you ready to see some photos?"

Ava took a deep breath and nodded, whilst Sarah took out a small package of printed photographs from her bag. The first one, she explained, was herself at the age of twenty-four. Ava took the photo and stared, it was a close up shot and the first thing she noticed were Sarah's eyes. She touched the photo lightly and then looked at Sarah who was gently nodding in agreement. Her long dark hair swept over her shoulders and was held back with a simple pin. Ava held on to it for some time. The next one that Sarah showed Ava was of a very similar lady, slightly older but not by much. Sarah said that this one was her sister and, in this photograph, she was about twenty-six. The same long dark hair but her face was a little more rounded.

"You look so alike," Ava said. "I can see myself in you both."

"This one is the time when she was pregnant. She was so happy."

Ava passed back the photo, the stone plummeted in her stomach once more. She understood what this meant but it was surreal.

"I didn't mean to upset you, I'm so sorry."

"No, I'm fine, it's just so much to take onboard. You are telling me, that in all likelihood, this is my mother, my real mother."

Sarah paused and let Ava take that thought and process it. Mark had said that he had told Ava that her sister had passed away, but she wasn't sure how much of this information was penetrating. She could see how tough this was. Sarah had put the photo of Florence on the table, and Ava slid it back towards herself to get a closer look. This felt so weird.

Sarah didn't want to push things any further. She didn't want to frighten Ava anymore and she could see how difficult this all was for her. In her own heart she was doing joyous summersaults, intertwined with bouts of sadness that it had taken the death of her sister for this to happen. There was still all that to process, for herself as well as Ava. She wondered about mentioning her actual birth name but held back for now.

Ava sipped her tea and ate a little of the food. It was exceedingly good but she was feeling so peculiar it meant she had lost her appetite. She leant back into the chair, and asked Sarah to tell her about the day that she was lost. Sarah began by explaining how she had moved to Malta with her first husband and how she longed for her sister to visit. She was so excited to meet her niece and when they arrived, it was the best feeling ever to see her sister after such a long time. She told her about the trip to the beach and how the child had disappeared within seconds of them arriving.

"Which beach?"

"Mellieħa."

"You're kidding me! The very beach that I look at each day. Good Lord!" Ava covered her face with her hands and shook her head from side to side.

Sarah went on to explain how she couldn't leave for a long time. How her sister would visit, go to the beach, calling out her name. But when she got re-married to a man from Gozo, she felt that it was then the right time to move on.

"As far as I knew, I have lived on Gozo all my life. I only moved to Mellieħa a few years ago when I split with a boyfriend. I only chose it because it was somewhere that had a flat available for rent which I could afford. I started working at the café across the road almost immediately and I haven't looked back." It was Sarah's turn to look stunned.

"So, all this time, all these years, you never left Malta? Well, only as far as Gozo!" Sarah looked incredulous. "How on earth did the police not find you sooner?"

Ava shrugged. She went on to tell Sarah what a lovely childhood she'd had. How she was much wanted and loved, but, and she knew this for a certainty, she had always felt a little different. Her mother had always reassured her, but deep down, she felt something, but didn't know what.

"And are your parents who brought you up, are they still living?"

"My mother is. My father passed suddenly a while back. I loved him dearly."

"Does your mother know about all this?"

"Yes. But she only told me a little on Tuesday, I don't know what happened. The last thing she told me was that I was sent from heaven! I saw red, got up and left in case I said something I later regretted. We haven't spoken again since. I feel bad about that but I really don't know what to say. She's my mother, the only one I know, and I love her very much."

Sarah fell silent. To hear that Ava loved the mother that had taken her was a bitter pill, but in another way, she was very happy to hear that she had received a happy and loving home from these people. The fact that they had destroyed her family in the process, was another matter—one she wasn't ready to talk to Ava about just yet. The poor girl looked so fragile, she didn't want to break her further.

"It all feels like a dream that I will wake up from. How has this happened to me?" Ava sat staring at Sarah, into those same bright green eyes, just like her own. "I don't know what to think, or say, or do."

"Look, let's just enjoy the evening, not talk about family stuff. I'll tell you about Benny, my husband, and my recent trip to the UK."

"That sounds good to me."

Chapter Twenty-Four

Mark had tried to call Sarah the evening before but she hadn't picked up her phone. He waited until after nine on the Monday morning before trying her again. He wanted to know how her meeting had gone with Ava and whether they had talked about getting a DNA test. The previous evening, he had sent a lengthy email to his office and ten minutes after it had sent, he got a phone call from his line manager.

"Are you telling me, that you have cracked a thirty-year-old case into a missing child!" His boss said. "That's above and beyond, gee—you'll be after a raise!"

Mark chuckled down the phone. He stated how things were certainly up in the air still and how he needed Ava to get a DNA test to make sure, but yes, it looked as though he had. He also explained that he hadn't yet told her of the inheritance. He knew that his firm would pay for the test. After all it was in their interest to get the case settled and for him to return to Canada swiftly. But this case was different and he knew he couldn't rush it.

"Well, okay, but I'd like you back by the end of the month. That gives you two weeks, make sure you have it all tied up by then." With that, his boss finished the phone call.

Mark then spent the rest of the evening looking into the files he had on the Hensley family, both Florence and William. He had a lot to explain to Ava and he wanted to get his facts right. This girl was going to need therapy for certain. He decided to do a Google search on William Hensley. There was page after page of information on his hotels. How he had gone from working in the kitchens in one hotel to owning a multi-million dollar chain of hotels in Canada and around the world. A real 'rags to riches' story. One article caught his eye. This one was headed 'The Hensley Legacy'. Mark opened it and began reading:

The Hensley Legacy

In the early 1800s, along the east coast of Canada, Samuel Hensley was living as a young man. Part French and part Cayuga, an American Indian tribe that originally lived in the area around Cayuga Lake in what is now central New York state. They belonged to the Northeast Indian culture area and spoke an Iroquoian language. He couldn't read or write but he was good with his hands and would tinker with engines from a boy. He went on to help his father who turned his hand to any type of building work in the houses of the wealthier people in the area.

Samuel learnt to build walls and dig drains. He could craft wood with precise skill and yet he was able to make a steamboat engine come to life that would otherwise have sat idle. He could apply wallpaper with a deftness of hand which you would not associate with someone who could build and fix engines. The man seemed to have many different talents which put his hands to good use. By his early twenties he caught the eye of a beautiful woman named Emily and they set up home together. Samuel turned his hand to anything and everything a young couple of the time could possibly need.

Emily was from the Cree people and wasn't used to the way of living that Samuel introduced her to, however, her husband was, by now, earning a good amount of money and was highly sought after for his skills.

Samuel continued to work hard and over the next twenty years, he employed many of Emily's family members from the Cree people to assist him in his work, training them in all the skills he had learnt from his father or those he taught himself. All he asked in return was for a token amount each week from the men he employed in lieu of the training they received. Over time he trained many men and before long he was able to live, if not a life of luxury, certainly one that was above average for his social standing.

Emily bore him many children. As was the time, not all survived but he lived long enough to see twenty grandchildren and even eight great-grandchildren. Four of his sons continued the business he had started, but in later life, Samuel, now a widower, found it increasingly difficult to come to terms with the wealth he was amassing and began to give away his money. Mathias, his youngest son, had taken over the running of the company. He seemed to have the best head for business and had taken the profits far and beyond what any of them could have imagined.

Samuel still had ownership and he took the decision to stop his sons from taking a payment from the people they trained, just as he had done when he first started employing them, but encouraged all of the men they trained, to use their skills learnt from the Hensley family, to empower others around them. To do this, he set up a fund, 'The Hensley Foundation', which was to be used for training men in all kinds of trades from engineering to carpentry and general building. The foundation lasted long after his death. He truly became a philanthropist to be proud of.

Mark sat back and thought. William Hensley had also started a business from almost nothing. He had made millions in his efforts and although he hadn't given away his wealth, his life cut short by the sadness that surrounded him, Mark could see similarities in the two men. He decided to research some more and see if there was a connection between William and Samuel.

This was the type of work that Mark loved best. Tracing family and constructing family trees is what brought him into this business and he was in his element as he started to construct the family tree of William Hensley. William was born in 1962, the second child born to parents Amanda and Jonathan Hensley. His older sibling was a girl named Anne. Jonathan had served in World War Two in the Royal Regina Rifles, as a member of the Allied army fighting Nazi Germany. Having signed up at the age of 18 he was one of the first men to land on Juno Beach, Courseulles-sur-Mer, France on June 6th, 1944, and therefore was in his forties before he became a father for the first time. Amanda his wife had met him when he returned home and needed nursing care for the many shrapnel wounds he had received. Mark's research meant he lost track of time and eventually took himself off to bed just before midnight.

After breakfast on Monday, Mark took his laptop into the public lounge of the hotel and opened it up. Sitting beside him was a steaming cup of coffee. Before he continued his research, he needed to call Sarah. She picked up on the second ring. "Hi Sarah, it is Mark. I wanted to see how yesterday went?"

"Hi Mark, it's definitely Alison. I knew it immediately I saw her!"

"Okay, that's great, how was she? When I saw her the other day, she was mightily confused and stressed."

"Definitely. It doesn't sound like she had a clue. One thing I'm pleased about is that she seems to have had a good childhood. Florence would have been happy to have known that much at least. What happens now; how do we go about the DNA test?"

"I'll take care of that, I don't know where it can be done yet, I need to make enquiries, leave that with me. Obviously, I will need your DNA too. Is that okay?"

"Naturally. Let me know what you need, I'll be there."

With that, Mark hung up and sent another email to Calgary. He'd just finished typing when a shadow fell across him, he looked up to see Reg standing there.

"Can I join you?" Reg indicated the seat across the table from Mark.

"Of course, be my guest. Would you like coffee?"

"I'd prefer tea, if there is one going?"

Mark motioned to the man behind the bar in the lounge, he came over and Mark ordered Reg a cup of tea. The man began to walk away when Reg asked if he could get a bacon sandwich with that also? The young man nodded and went to fetch the order. Mark brought Reg up to speed with the meeting between Sarah and Ava. Reg let out a long whistle.

"I'll have to keep the authorities up to speed. But if you can conduct an independent DNA test, it'll probably be quicker than trying to get one done via the police."

"Yes, I've just emailed my company to ask that same question. I'll hear back later, they will all be fast asleep right now.

"After seeing you, I want to pop in and see Guzeppi, I think they will have spoken to Lisa by now. I'm not sure how much he can tell me, but I'd like to know. I doubt there will be a forensic report yet on the car, but I'll ask the question."

The bacon sandwich and cup of tea arrived. Reg licked his lips, added the sachet of brown sauce that had come with it, and began to devour it. Mark had eaten Greek yogurt and fruit for breakfast, better for his digestion but he was very envious right now of the bacon sandwich that Reg was enjoying. Whilst Reg was eating, he started to tell him of his research and the article he had found on the Hensley family. Reg nodded with a certain amount of attention but Mark soon determined that Reg's interest lay in the cold case rather than any familial lines that Ava may or may not be part of. Obviously, his interest in all things ancestorial were not shared by everyone.

Reg's mobile rang and he answered it promptly. The part of the conversation Mark was hearing was not that enlightening.

"Haaallo!"

Mark smiled at the drawn-out use of the word.

"Sure, no problem."

"Right now? Okay. Ten minutes all right with you?"

"TTFN!" Reg ended the call.

"That was Guzeppi, his ears must have been burning, eh?"

Mark was a little confused by the statement, but he let it go and smiled in return.

"Wants to see me in ten, fancy coming along? Might be interesting to you too, since you're the one that has stirred up this case again."

Mark gathered up his belongings, took his room key to Reception, headed out the main door and down the steps to see that Reg had parked on the double yellow lines out the front and was waiting for him with the engine running. He got in the passenger seat and Reg was off before Mark fastened his seatbelt.

They arrived at the police station and the two men went inside. It was the same sergeant from the previous occasion and Reg delighted in using his Maltese to request to see Guzeppi. Minutes later, Guzeppi appeared and beckoned them through. He had a takeaway coffee cup in his hand and was spilling the contents as he was walking. He strode out at such a pace that Mark was almost trotting along behind the other two men. He felt a little foolish but needs must. Mark and Reg sat down on the two chairs in front of Guzeppi's desk. Mark asked if he was okay to join the conversation and Guzeppi nodded in approval. He got straight into it.

"Forensics have been carried out, no news as yet." He took a gulp of coffee, lifted the lid, and seemed to raise an eyebrow in curiosity. "I've been short-changed again!" he added.

Mark smiled to himself wondering how many times the contents of the coffee cups that Guzeppi had were sprinkled along the corridors of the police station. The cleaners must be wondering who was carelessly spilling their coffee each day. Guzeppi continued, "But we did visit Mrs Muscat, I won't go into details but we asked her a few questions about the car. It was an odd experience, as though she was expecting us."

Reg leant forward and rested his forearms on the desk in front. "We may have found Alison Hensley. Well, we are reasonably certain we have!"

Guzeppi looked over the top of his takeaway cup and stopped mid-slurp. "Are you certain? We have had many false leads in the past."

"Not one hundred percent," Mark intervened. "We need a DNA sample to be absolutely sure, but it's looking likely."

"Jesus!" Guzeppi exclaimed, then immediately made the sign of the cross over his chest and looked upwards, as if to apologise to the powers above for his blasphemy.

"She goes by the name of Ava Muscat," Mark continued, "she had no idea that she was abducted and if we put the pieces together, it appears that she has been living on Gozo with Stephen and Lisa Muscat all these years."

"Hang on, hang on…" Guzeppi opened the thick brown file on his desk, turned over the first dozen or so pages and jabbed his finger at a page. "See here, it says that the Muscats had a child called Ava. They even showed the birth certificate of the child to Ġakobb Farrugia when he went to check Stephen Muscat's car a week or so after her abduction. I'm not sure you have that right."

"I discovered that there are no medical records for Ava Muscat apart from her initial infant vaccinations, nothing whatsoever. I thought that was very odd. I don't think that is necessarily cause for alarm as there could be any number of reasons why that didn't happen but not one doctor's appointment or check-up. Basically, apart from her birth certificate, there is no medical trace of the child. It is almost as though she was being kept away from anyone in authority."

Guzeppi stared at Reg, seconds passed by and in the silent room you could almost hear the cogs whirring in Guzeppi's brain.

"Well, none of this is conclusive, there could be many reasons but… Jesus!" he said again, and once more signed the cross on his chest. Looked skywards and then shook his head in disbelief. "She could have been here all this time."

"Looks that way."

"Holy moly mother of God!" And again, Guzeppi signed his body with the cross.

Mark smiled to himself wondering how many times a day Guzeppi did this.

"I'm going to need to see Lisa Muscat again, I need to interview her urgently." Guzeppi stood and said no more. It was an indication for Reg and Mark to leave. "Thanks, I'll be in touch." With that, he closed the file on his desk and the two men got up and left. Mark carefully avoided stepping on the spilled coffee along the corridor, he didn't want to slip over.

Chapter Twenty-Five

Guzeppi called Lisa Muscat just before eight am and she answered the phone hesitantly. He enquired as to how she was feeling after her faint the other day and explained that he had some more questions to ask her. Giving her the option of either staying at home and they would visit or she could come to the station, Lisa chose to stay at home.

Sergeant Zeppa Gatt arrived at the station a little before eight fifteen and the two men headed towards the ferry terminal. Guzeppi was making more notes as they drove and had added in the comments he had received back from the Forensic Department. The sergeant pulled the vehicle up to the front door and they were both relieved to see that Lisa was able to answer the door herself this time.

"Can we come inside?" Guzeppi had already begun to walk forwards towards the house and Lisa stepped to one side to allow the men to enter.

"Would you care for coffee or tea?"

"Tea for me please," Zeppa answered "just black, no sugar"

"Coffee please, with a little milk."

Lisa showed the two men outside to the gazebo. The sun was washing the area with a delicate brush of morning glow, the garden was beginning to warm and it was a treat to sit there for a while rather than in the stuffy offices at the station. The two men thanked her and she returned to the kitchen to make the drinks. Returning shortly with three cups, Lisa gave each man theirs in turn and it didn't go unnoticed how much her hands were shaking as she did so.

"How can I help any further?" Lisa started the conversation hoping with all her heart that they were just needing more details on the car.

"I understand that you didn't drive your husband's car but has anyone else driven the vehicle other than the driver who collected it the other day?"

"Well, our daughter, Ava, learnt to drive in it and used it a few times after my husband died. But she didn't want the vehicle herself."

"Ah, okay, so just the three of you then?"

"Yes."

"Your daughter, Ava, how old would she be, approximately?"

Guzeppi noticed that Lisa's shoulders lifted towards her ears and her face froze. "She's mid-thirties."

"Ah yes, she probably wants a more modern vehicle then. Does she live here with you?" Guzeppi knew this wasn't the case but wanted to see Lisa's reaction to questions about Ava.

"No, she lives in Malta." Lisa was not giving much away.

"But she grew up here with you and your husband? Is this where you have always lived?" Guzeppi noticed that not once did Lisa query the reasons for his questions, and although obviously alarmed, she was answering them, albeit succinctly.

"Yes, that's right."

"You have a very pretty garden." Guzeppi watched Lisa's face relax a little as he changed the subject. "I particularly like that part over there, the small rose garden beyond the lawn." He held his gaze on her as she looked over to the back corner. Most of the garden was full of pots, and little brick walkways wandered between them. The pots draped their contents across the paths and the aroma from herbs, lavender and the olive trees that surrounded the garden was delightful. But the roses were planted in the ground and he noticed that they were all differing shades of pink.

"Um, yes, my favourite part of the garden too."

Guzeppi noticed a small change in the tone of her voice, although she still sounded very anxious.

"Tell me more about Ava?" He purposely left the question non-specific.

"Like what?"

"Oh, I don't know, where she went to school, what she liked to do?" he paused, then added, "Why she didn't have her booster vaccinations as a young child."

Lisa dropped the cup she was holding and it smashed on the floor, her tea spilling out in a large brown puddle. She pushed the chair back and dashed inside. Guzeppi nodded at Zeppa to follow her but she returned quickly with a dustpan and brush.

"Here, allow me." Zeppa took hold of the brush from her shaking hands and bent down to sweep the broken china into the dustpan. "Please sit." It was an instruction rather than a question.

"We couldn't find any medical records for Ava other than her infant vaccinations, nothing at all. No broken bones, no childhood illnesses and no booster vaccinations. Why is that, Lisa?"

Lisa was totally white, even her slightly pink lips had faded and she slumped back into her chair before answering him, "She was always a healthy child, no need to visit the doctor. I am not keen on doctors so I would help her with any colds she had with herbs." Lisa had her eyes closed the whole time she was speaking.

"And the boosters?"

"I thought Stephen had taken her."

"Really?"

Guzeppi lifted his cup and finished the contents before posing his last question to Lisa. "So, Lisa, can you explain to me, how the DNA of Alison Hensley was found in your husband's vehicle yesterday? We have samples on file from Alison's parents from thirty-three years ago, and those samples are a match to the DNA found in the vehicle." With that, Lisa fainted again.

Sergeant Zeppa went into the kitchen and brought out a glass of water. He offered it up to Lisa's lips and as the cool liquid touched them, she began to rouse. Guzeppi and Zeppa sat and watched her. The colour didn't return to her face but she was coming around from her faint.

"Lisa, I need to ask you again, are you aware how Alison Hensley's DNA could be present in your husband's car?"

"Perhaps the person he bought it from had something to do with her disappearance?" Lisa was clutching at straws—she knew it but so did Guzeppi.

"But there are only three sets of DNA in the vehicle. I need to take a DNA sample from you to make sure that one of them is a match to you and I also need to have something that belonged to Stephen, a comb maybe or something similar, so we can check his DNA too." Guzeppi handed her the glass of water and this time she took large gulps. "Can we take a look inside for something to use? I'd rather that we didn't require a search warrant to do this."

Lisa numbly nodded and Zeppa got up and went into the house to see what could be found. He came back shortly with a diary that he had found on Stephen's desk, a fountain pen and a small silver rotating perpetual calendar which showed an old date. Zeppa was hoping that Stephen was the last person to have changed the date on it. Hopefully, he would have coughed or sneezed on something, or licked his finger before turning a page in the diary. Zeppa had no idea if any of this would be useful but there were no personal items to be found of Stephen's, like a razor, comb or hairbrush.

"I need you to come to the station this afternoon, to give a DNA sample." Guzeppi hadn't brought anything with him to take a sample and was kicking himself for the oversight. "Are you able to make your own way to Malta or should we send a police car for you?"

Not wanting to draw any attention to herself in the neighbourhood, Lisa assured them she would find her own way there. With that, the two men made their departure, Guzeppi adding that she should arrive no later than four pm.

Once they had left, Lisa went into Stephen's study, sat in his chair and began to sob. This was not the first time in her life that everything was imploding in on her, the despair rising in her chest and the feelings of hopelessness filling her totally. Walking unsteadily, she went to the kitchen, poured herself a large glass of water and took two pills from a tatty-looking box. Swallowing them quickly, she went upstairs and lay down on the bed. She hadn't stopped sobbing before the pills took over and she was asleep.

Lisa woke just before two-thirty in the afternoon, glanced at the clock before calling for a taxi to take her to the ferry. She called Guzeppi to explain she had just woken and she was concerned that she might not make it to see him before four pm as she had promised. He agreed to wait for her. Lisa dragged a brush through her hair, put on a pair of cream linen trousers, a white blouse and went out to the front of her house to wait for the taxi. She was just able to get on to the last ferry as a foot passenger, she would pick up another taxi once on Malta.

The ferry got her to Malta just before four pm and she arrived at the police station not long after. Guzeppi met her quickly before taking her through to his office. He had arranged for a constable to take the necessary DNA swabs before he began the more formal part of the interviews which must now happen. Guzeppi had taken advice from his superior officer, he had explained the details of the case and had been instructed to arrest her upon arrival.

"Lisa, it has become apparent to us that we must formally charge you with the abduction of Alison Hensley on 24 April 1990, together with the charge of attempting to pervert the course of justice and assisting an offender. You will be arrested on these charges but I have already taken advice from the prosecution service and you may be released on bail following further enquiries. We will also be looking into the disappearance of the real Ava Muscat. Can you enlighten me any further in this regard?"

Lisa was already slumped down in her chair, her head fell forward into her hands which were on the table in front of her.

"She died." Lisa's words came forth with the tiniest of sound and Guzeppi had to ask for her to repeat them for the benefit of the tape.

"We have not been able to find any evidence to suggest this. Can you help us?"

"No." Lisa once more spoke in barely a whisper.

"Again, for the tape, please speak more clearly."

"No!" This time, Lisa yelled the word, her face pointing towards the offensive machine that was whirring upon the desk.

Guzeppi ignored the outburst but suggested they take a break. Lisa had already refused the offer of a solicitor to be present but Guzeppi was feeling uncomfortable. This woman looked to be at breaking point and having seen her faint twice already, he wasn't going to risk a third time. He left the room and called for the duty doctor to attend. It was over an hour before the doctor would arrive so Guzeppi took Lisa a sandwich and some coffee. He had left her with a female officer and had hoped that she would look slightly better when he went back in the interview room. He was mistaken.

"I have arranged for the duty doctor to see you and make sure you are fit to be interviewed," he advised Lisa. "Also, I will ask you again, if you would like a solicitor to be present?"

"Can I go now?" Lisa looked at him, her face strewn with tears. "I need to sleep."

"I'm afraid not, I need a written statement from you, but I'm not going to take that until you have been seen by a doctor."

Lisa laid her head on the table, put her hands over her ears as though to block out his words.

Guzeppi was not sure if she was being artful or was genuinely in need of medical help and willed the doctor to arrive as soon as possible. It took a little over forty minutes for them to get there but it was a female doctor for which Guzeppi was pleased, hoping Lisa would be more relaxed with a woman. The examination took place and the doctor gave her verdict.

"Mrs Muscat is mentally exhausted. I cannot recommend that you continue this interview at this time. She needs rest. I suspect she hasn't slept properly for some time. But apart from exhaustion, it is my opinion that at this point in time she is mentally competent. I have managed to find some old notes on her from early 1990 which say she was severely depressed and had been prescribed an anti-depressant for several months. But she did not follow up on the appointments as she was required to do, so was struck off from the medical practice and no further notes on her medical history are available.

"It is a shocking example of lack of care, but I can only assume that she has been functioning normally since then. She has told me that she is not taking any medication other than the occasional sleeping tablet. I believe that she would benefit from a brief stay in hospital, under light sedation, until she has recovered from her extreme exhaustion. At that point, I believe you will be able to continue your investigation."

Guzeppi asked the doctor to make the necessary arrangements and hoped that Lisa Muscat would go willingly. The formal statement would have to wait for another day.

Chapter Twenty-Six

Mark heard back from Calgary—they had arranged for Sarah and Ava to take a DNA test on Malta. There was a private clinic on the island that not only undertook this kind of work but were known to be exemplary. Mark contacted Sarah first and confirmed her availability before doing the same with Ava. Sarah asked if she could be the one to pick up Ava and take her.

"Of course, I will meet you both there." Mark wanted to make sure that he was present when the tests were done, plus, he had to pay for them.

They agreed to meet there in two days. Mark was eating into his two weeks so was hoping that the results would come back quickly. He would see if he could pay extra to expedite the results. In the meantime, he continued his research into the Hensley family.

Having established that Ava's grandfather was Jonathan Hensley a Canadian soldier, he then went to look for Jonathan's father. He soon found that Jonathan was born on 13 November 1924 in Quebec City to parents, Jonathan and Catherine Hensley née Gagnon.

They had run a florist shop in the centre of the city and had produced seven children. Jonathan was their eldest child. This couple were born in the late 1800s, Jonathan in 1895 and Catherine in 1897. It was becoming more difficult to find the records now, so Mark contacted a colleague in Calgary and asked him for assistance. It would be easier if he could visit Quebec City and do some research from there, but Mark would continue with his online pursuit and hopefully between them, they could trace the Hensley family back to the early 1800s.

Reg had dropped Mark back at his hotel after their meeting with Guzeppi. Mark promised to keep him informed of any developments. He realised that he didn't think he would have got this far if he hadn't walked into the library in Valletta and by chance spoken to Reg's brother. He was profoundly grateful and agreed to keep him informed of anything that was relevant to the abduction case. As to the inheritance, that was between him and Sarah and/or Ava and he would push on regardless in that respect. He got his office to email over the paperwork in preparation but asked them, for now, to leave the name of the heir blank.

Until the DNA results were back, no assumptions could be made, no matter how likely.

Mark made a reservation for dinner within the hotel and went back to his room to freshen up. He would have a proper meal this evening—he felt he had eaten too many snacks. Truthfully, they had all been delicious and he was fast becoming a pastizzi fanatic, but he felt it was time for a sit down meal with plenty of vegetables. He wasn't disappointed. The restaurant had an excellent menu and Mark was spoilt for choice. He deferred from having a starter and chose grain-fed beef tagliata. A Uruguayan beef steak, chimichurri with cherry tomatoes and an extra green salad on the side. He paired it with a glass of Maltese red wine which took his breath away with the taste and aroma—truly one to write home about, as they say.

Finishing his meal with a small glass of whisky and a teaspoon of water, he took his drink into the lounge where a keyboard player was entertaining the residents. Tonight, he would relax, tomorrow he had more work to do. The music was good and he sat back and enjoyed watching people having a fun time. One couple got up and danced a beautiful rumba to the music being played, another couple joined them. It was a great evening.

The next morning, Mark felt a little more relaxed after his evening spent in the lounge. He showered and dressed, made his way to the restaurant for breakfast and ate a plentiful supply of scrambled eggs, bacon and hash browns—not the most cholesterol friendly start to the day, but it was delicious. He settled down to do some more research into the Hensley family. He had another twenty-four hours before the DNA tests were to be done and was hoping to have a good amount of research complete by that time. He checked his emails and there was one from his colleague in Calgary who had been able to catch a last minute flight to Quebec. He had already been to the library and discovered more information on the Hensleys.

Jonathan, born 1895, was the youngest child of Mathias and Mabel Hensley née Ripnoté. Mabel's family were French but there was very little information on Mathias. Nothing about his employment nor where he was born. Not unusual for records from this time, but he had been able to find a record of birth for Mathias. He was born in 1853. His father had signed his birth record with an X, generally a sign of illiteracy, and there was no signature of his mother. He was just about able to determine the names of Mathias's parents. The handwriting was difficult to read and it was quite a blurred image of the original document. Whoever had written this out in the early 1800s had scribed the document with an ink pen that obviously leaked. A lot of the writing was covered in ink blots, but he was able to make out that Mathias was born to Samuel and Emily Hensley (deceased), presumably having died in childbirth. One further check and he found that Samuel Hensley was born in York, Canada. His birth date stated, 'About August' and his mother was listed as 'Woman, Cayuga', but sadly, the name of his father was illegible.

Mark was thrilled with the information, he was certain that Ava's three times great-grandfather was the philanthropist, Samuel Hensley. Her own father had mimicked his life without knowing, sadly cut short. Now Ava was due to inherit the wealth left by her father, DNA results permitting. He sent an email offering up huge thanks to his colleague. Whilst this amount of research wasn't necessary for his work, in this case he felt that this information might give Ava a true sense of where she came from. He hadn't researched Florence. Whether he would have time now, he was not sure, he was due to get to the laboratory for nine am tomorrow to meet Ava and Sarah—a big day for everyone.

Chapter Twenty-Seven

Ava had gone back to work for a few hours on Monday. She was exhausted after just one hour in the café but was determined that Indri would not realise. She started at eleven, worked through the midday rush and went home when Indri closed up for a couple of hours. Most people took a siesta and keeping the café open meant he had less time to prepare for the afternoon trade. Ava went home, fell asleep around three in the afternoon and didn't wake until gone five when she heard a knocking on her door. It was Christopher.

"Come in." Ava's hair was tousled from her sleep and it was quite obvious to Christopher that he had woken her.

"I won't stop, I just brought you this." He handed her a large round blue stoneware bowl, covered in brown paper. She peeked inside where there was a medley of fish and seafood, rice, courgettes, and black olives. She could see white flecks of garlic and her tummy audibly rumbled. "Sounds like you need it!" Christopher chuckled.

"Wow, this is amazing. I'm so sorry, but what with everything going on, I haven't been to see you and thank you for the fish the other day. Truly, you are a marvellous cook. I have told Indri all about you, and he wants to speak to you to see if you would like to earn some money, preparing some dishes for the lunchtime crowd at the café."

Christopher blushed. "I found a book of my mother's. Just a small notebook that had a few recipes written down." Christopher put the blue dish he was holding onto her kitchen countertop. "This is one of them, I hope you like it."

"When I feel a bit better, I will make you a prinjolata, one of my mother's recipes." She realised it was the first time that day that she had thought of her mother and just like before, the feeling of a stone plummeted into her stomach. She grasped the door frame, feeling a little wobbly.

"Hey, are you okay, come on, sit down." Christopher guided her to the couch, sat her down and fetched a glass of water.

"Sorry, yes, this whole business is just so bizarre, every now and again, it knocks the wind right out of me."

"Hardly surprising."

"I suppose so, but it is embarrassing. Thank you however, for the fish, it's really very kind of you. I cannot face shopping, never mind cooking currently. I have eaten quite a few pastizzi over the last couple of days." She laughed at her own comment. "Not exactly a healthy diet!" She then remembered her trip to Mosta with Sarah and told Christopher about her. "She was a great friend of your mother, she was really pleased to hear how well both you and Jack are getting on. I hope you don't think I was gossiping about you though."

"Not at all, how lovely to meet her." Christopher could see the colour returning to Ava's cheeks and was feeling less concerned. "So, does that make her your aunt?"

"It looks like it, we are both having a DNA test on Wednesday. We have to be certain as Sarah's sister has passed away and the man who appears to have started this all, has to have a DNA to finish his business with Sarah and me." She paused to see if he knew who she was talking about.

"The one looking for the dark-haired lady with green eyes?" Christopher gave her a big smile.

"Yes?" She looked at him quizzically.

"Oh, don't worry. I know Joe, one of the local car mechanics. He was convinced the man was looking for you. I think Joe has a soft spot for you. Ha! I keep telling him, he's too young for you. But… does that make Sarah's sister, your real mother?"

"Uh huh." Ava nodded. "That's too odd to think about right now. I have seen a photograph of her and I look much more like her, than I do my own mother." Ava realised that this was sounding peculiar but the only way she could think of the lady that had loved her all these years, cared for her and protected her, was as her mother. How could anyone take that place?

"Have you spoken to her?"

"No, and I know I need to. It's just I don't know what to say. I need to see her again, not just talk on the phone."

"Well, why don't I take you back tomorrow after you finish at the café?" Christopher was walking towards the door to leave. Ricco sprang across the floor and circled his legs. "I bet he can smell fish!"

"Would you really do that? I'd rather not go alone. I'm not sure how I will feel after talking to her and I definitely don't want to stay over or drive back here as some kind of emotional wreck."

"Of course, I like driving. I'll pick you up at two tomorrow. Now eat some of that fish tonight, promise me?"

Ava smiled, got up to see him out of the door. It was true, Elias had done an amazing job of bringing up two fabulous young men. Hopefully, he realises what a brilliant father he has been. Then the thought struck her. She had given no consideration as to her real father. She loved her dad as much as anyone ever could, but of course, she now knew he wasn't her actual dad. No one has mentioned him. Ava went back to the couch and dialled Sarah's number.

"Hey, it's Ava." Sarah had answered the phone so fast that Ava thought she must have already been holding it in her hand. "Have you got a minute?"

"Definitely."

"Well, I feel like I am being unfaithful to my father whom I loved dearly, but we haven't spoken about my real father. I don't suppose he is alive and wondering where I am."

"Oh gosh, I didn't realise that you were not aware. No, I'm so sorry to say that your real father passed away before my sister, your mother." Sarah felt awful telling her this over the telephone. "But he was a great man, a brilliant man in fact." Sarah was really hoping that the next question wasn't going to be about his death. She crossed her fingers. She knew that Ava needed to know everything, but not over the phone.

"That's sad, so neither of my parents are alive to know that I am here?"

"I'm so sorry, Ava." Sarah heard a sob down the phone line. "Would you like me to come over, I can be with you in an hour or so?" Another sob.

"It all seems so pointless, all this heartache, for what?" Ava knew that wasn't true, but at that precise moment in time, those were the words that came out of her mouth.

"Not pointless at all. I, for one, am overjoyed to have found you. You have been in my thoughts and prayers since the day we lost you. I understand how awful it must be. Actually, no I don't understand at all, how could I even begin to understand. But, Ava, they loved you so much. I have so many stories to tell you about them. I just wish they were still here to tell you themselves. Shall I come?"

"Please…" Another sob. "I need you."

156

"I'm on my way, I'll bring some more photographs. Hang in there, sweetie." Sarah hung up and then burst into tears.

The ferries were getting busy but Sarah was able to get the last place on the boat and was driving into Mellieħa just over an hour after their phone call. She had grabbed a bottle of wine from the fridge and left a quick note for Benny. She would fill him in later. He was thrilled for her to have found Alison after all these years and couldn't wait to meet her. Sarah had refused at the moment and he understood. She abandoned her car by the door to the flat, not caring that she was parked on double yellow lines and bounded up the stairs. The door was ajar, Ava had heard her pull up. Sarah walked into the room and flung her arms around Ava. This time Ava melted into them and let out an anguished sob. They stood there for quite some time, Sarah held her whilst the tears flowed, for both of them.

Eventually, it was Ava who pulled away, wiped her eyes, sniffed, and sat down on her couch. Sarah followed her and sat next to her. She pulled out the wine bottle from her bag, held it up towards Ava and raised an eyebrow instead of asking the question. Ava nodded. Sarah opened a couple of cupboards before finding two glasses. She filled one to the top. In hers, she added a little and topped it up with water. Taking the glasses back to the couch, placing them on the table in front, she asked, "What would you like to know?"

Ava took a big gulp, the cold wine hit the back of her throat and she let the pale golden liquid soothe her. She took another, just a sip this time, replaced the glass and looked at Sarah.

"Firstly, assuming I am who we think I am, what is my name?"

"Alison Hensley."

"Wow, okay." Ava sat back. "I'm not sure I can just change to Alison, I've only known my name as Ava."

"And… my mother, what was her name?"

"She was Florence and your father was called William."

Sarah didn't say anymore, this conversation needed to be led by Ava, not prompted by her. She would answer her questions but only when she wanted to know. There was a long pause. Ava took another sip, then another.

"Why did my father die?"

Sarah dreaded this question the most. It was only fair to tell her the truth. But firstly, she asked if she could tell Ava about him. Sarah thought that just maybe, that would soften the blow. Ava agreed, tucked her feet up under her and held her glass in her hand. Ricco had made his way to her lap and she stroked him gently. She often wondered if he had some kind of sixth sense, he seemed to appear beside her whenever she felt down.

Sarah flicked through the photographs to find one of William. She passed it to Ava explaining that this one was taken at the start of the holiday, just before she went missing. William was smiling and had a warm and endearing face. She could just see the top of a head, it was a child. Ava pointed to the head and Sarah nodded.

"Me?"

"Yes, you were quite the daddy's girl. But that was fine with your mum, they loved you so much."

"I think I was a daddy's girl with my dad," Ava drew in a sharp breath, "well, you know what I mean."

"Of course."

Sarah found another one, this was one of William and Florence together. He had a protective arm around her shoulders—they were both smiling, big beaming smiles, at the camera. The rest of the photos that Sarah had of her father were in his younger days. Obviously, they didn't take any more during the rest of the time they were on Malta back then.

Sarah began to tell Ava how they met in the hotel where they were both working. How they went on to build an empire of hotels but despite their obvious wealth, you couldn't find more down to earth people. When they became pregnant it was the icing on the cake, they truly had, at that point in time, the life that anyone would envy. Until it all fell apart. Sarah knew that Ava had some understanding of what happened after she was lost that fateful day. She had read Yvonne's letters and Elias had explained about the searches. But before she would tell her about her father's sad passing, she wanted to make sure she understood how he had built this magnificent worldwide business, in order to provide for her and her mother. She would drop the bombshell later.

Chapter Twenty-Eight

Sarah had left Ava's just after one in the morning and Ava had gone straight to bed. She had learnt so much about her father, how he had won a hotel in Dubai, playing cards and how he had amassed a swathe of other hotels all over the USA and Canada. She had sensed that Sarah was holding back on the reason for his death. Ava felt as though she was beginning to get to know him, as a live person, a man of great business acumen and she wasn't sure if she was ready to think of him in the past tense just yet.

Sarah had left a few photographs for her to keep, the one with both Florence and William grinning madly into the camera, a close up of Florence and another which showed the whole family sitting around a table enjoying a meal. There was Sarah, another man, who was presumably her first husband, William and Florence, though you could only see the back of William's head as he was bent forwards talking to a child, that child being Alison.

She had slept well and had arrived early for work in the café. Indri wasn't expecting her until eleven, but she walked into the kitchen a little after ten. May was busy at the sink, washing breakfast plates and Indri was preparing the ham which he would serve at lunch. "Good morning," she called as she entered the kitchen, "how are you both doing?"

Indri looked up from his carving and gave her a big smile. "You are looking refreshed this morning, how is your temperature?" He gave Ava a wink and inclined his head towards May at the sink.

"Yes, not too bad, thank you," Ava smiled, "I think I'm getting better each day."

"Well, scoot out of here, I don't want any germs in my kitchen," he teased, "go and sit beachside until I need you, I'll bring you coffee and a pastizzi."

Ava did as she was told, May wiped her hands on her apron and gave her a big smile too. "Good to see you looking better, love."

Ava settled onto one of the chairs facing the sea and waited for her coffee. She realised she was looking out at the very same beach from where she had been lost over thirty years ago—talk about coincidences. Indri brought out a tray, her coffee and pastizzi on one side and a large coffee for himself also.

"I've left May preparing some salads for lunch, that'll keep her busy for a while. How are you really doing?"

"Honestly? I have no idea. It is like watching a weird film play out in front of me and yet I appear to have the central role!" She let out a long sigh. "Christopher is taking me to Gozo this afternoon, to see my mother. I left her last week in a terrible state. I was so angry but I need to know more, I need to know what happened back then and how I came to be living with her and my father."

"This must be so hard for her too."

"I'm sure it is. I want to tell her that I am having a DNA test tomorrow. I need to be open with her about everything that is happening, I love her and I don't have any intention of losing her out of my life. She has been an amazing mum and I couldn't imagine a different childhood." Ava's thoughts swung back to the first few photographs in the album, she had seen such a sad little child up to the age of about four. Perhaps those days were not as good, but Ava couldn't recall them.

Just then, they heard May call out from the kitchen that Elias was outside, asleep at one of the tables. Indri got up and went to see if he was okay. Ava followed, taking her coffee cup and plate back inside. True enough he was slumped back in a chair; his head had lolled back against the wall of the café and his arms had fallen to his sides. Indri went out to him, checked he was okay, left him to sleep and went back inside to make him some tea. A few minutes passed before Elias woke and sat himself up.

"Sorry Indri, have I been here long?"

"Not at all, here, have some tea. There are some of yesterday's figolli biscuits that I made. They are still good enough to eat, I was just trying out a new recipe."

"Aren't these for Easter?" Elias looked confused. "How long was I sleeping?"

"Ha-ha, not that long, my friend. I know they are, but I had a bit of spare time yesterday so I thought I would experiment with walnuts and pistachios; tell me what you think."

Elias had eaten a plateful before he looked up, he lifted his thumb to Indri and mumbled something which was not so easy to hear.

"What's that you said?"

"Sorry Indri, my mouth was full. I was saying they are delicious, but I still prefer the prinjolata that Ava made!"

Indri laughed and left Elias to finish his tea.

It was just after two when Christopher turned up to collect Ava for their trip to Gozo. He had brought a paper bag with some pastry snacks, just in case she hadn't eaten anything. It was some flaky pastry that he had bought and had laid Ġbejniet on top, sprinkled with chopped basil from the garden, then he had cut the pastry into strips and twisted it into a corkscrew shape. Ava could smell them as soon as she got in the car. Once more, she marvelled at his skills in the kitchen.

The trip to Gozo didn't take long, Ava wished it had taken longer as she had no idea what to say to her mother. Her anxiety meant that her stomach was in knots and despite the pastries smelling wonderful, she couldn't face eating one. Christopher understood, at least he had them should she feel better later after talking to her mum. He parked the car in the shade of the olive trees and got out. Ava was sitting still so he walked around to her side of the car, opened the door and helped her out. He could feel her shaking. Together, arm in arm, they walked to the door. It took several loud knocks on the door before Lisa appeared, dishevelled. They had woken her by the looks of things and she looked stunned to see them standing there. Pulling open the door, she let them in. Ava didn't speak but Christopher said, 'good afternoon' and guided Ava through to the garden, sat her down and went back inside to make sure that it was okay for him to stay.

By the time he had got back inside, Lisa had pulled on a long kaftan and had quickly brushed her hair. She looked slightly less shocked but nonetheless, she looked like she hadn't slept in a week.

"Are you okay for us to be here?" Christopher was quite concerned. "It's just that Ava would like to talk to you more, if you are up to it?"

"Yes... of course... okay," Lisa stuttered. "How is she?"

"Let me make some drinks whilst you go and talk to her; I'll bring them out shortly."

Lisa made her way outside and sat at the table opposite Ava. They hadn't, as yet, exchanged glances. Christopher observed them from the kitchen. It was Ava who spoke first.

"I have met an aunt, her name is Sarah, tomorrow we are having DNA tests." Ava lifted her gaze towards her mother, hoping to see a reaction.

"I needed you," was all Lisa said in reply.

"Needed me!" Ava was incredulous. "What on earth do you mean by that!" She realised she had spat the words at her mother but she was so shocked.

"Please don't hate me, I couldn't bear it." Lisa was crying but Ava just stared in disbelief.

"Hate you? How could I possibly hate you? I love you, you are my mum, well, I thought you were. You have to tell me what happened though, I deserve to know."

Christopher brought out a tray of drinks but neither woman noticed he had appeared. For now, he would go back into the house and sit nearby, so he could be there in a moment, if he was needed.

Silence hung in the air. Ava had her face to the floor and Lisa was twisting her kaftan in her fingers. And then she began to talk.

"I had a baby, a beautiful baby girl. We called her Ava. Stephen and I doted on her, she was so precious and we loved her deeply. She was two and a half when she got meningitis. I didn't spot the signs. She died and it was all my fault. I didn't get her to the doctors in time. I was bereft and went into a deep depression."

Ava noticed that her mother had said 'Stephen' and not 'your father'. But, she thought, back then he wasn't her father, he was the real Ava's father.

Lisa took a deep breath and continued, "The hurt and pain inside me were awful and I blamed myself for it all. Stephen just wanted to help, wanted to get back to how we were before Ava died. I was taking some tablets from the doctor and most days I didn't get out of bed, just lay there wishing it was me that had caught it and not Ava. I lost all track of time, I still don't know how long I was in that state, no idea what was going on in the outside world and I didn't care. All I felt was the pain of losing my child."

Ava was looking at her mother. The tears her mother cried now were slow and steady, these were tears that had been there for over thirty years, tears for the loss of her baby. Ava wanted to reach across and take her mother's hands but she couldn't do that—she sat still and waited for more.

"Stephen travelled over to Malta frequently. He would buy cars, bring them back here, tinker with them until they were in a better state and then sell them on. So, it was not unusual for him to have three or more vehicles out the front, all in varying states of repair. It used to annoy me a little that he had so many vehicles spoiling the way the house looked. I would say it looked like a scrapyard—that hurt his feelings I'm sure, but it did. There were bits of old rusty metal everywhere. One car could be up on bricks another would have no door. It was a mess. That's when he built the garage on the side of the house, so he could at least keep some of them in there. That's where he spent a lot of time after Ava died. I would be in bed and he would be working in his garage. Times were not good." Lisa took a sip from the iced water that Christopher had left beside them. She looked at the glass as if wondering where it had come from.

"Go on," was all Ava could say.

"I didn't know he had gone to Malta that day. He didn't tell me much about what he was doing but, I wouldn't have remembered anyway. He was late back, I remember that. He had taken a taxi to the ferry, then a bus to Valletta where he was picking up a car. It was on his way back that he thought to stop and take some photographs to show me. He thought that it might interest me and he stopped at Mellieħa Bay. He knew how beautiful it was as we had spent a few days with Ava there, not long before she died. It was then that he saw you.

"At first, he thought he was seeing our Ava, the same dark hair, the same smiling face. He went to talk to you and you smiled at him. He just offered his hand to you and you took it. He walked back to the car and sat you inside. He always said in later years, he had no idea why you didn't cry out, but you didn't and he believed that you were our Ava that the angels had returned from heaven."

"Did he not for one second, think logically. Think that someone would be looking for this child, looking for me?"

"Not then." Lisa wiped the back of her hand over her eyes. "He had set you beside him on the front seat and you thought that was fantastic. He thought that maybe you weren't used to sitting in the front of a car and you were enjoying it. Then it hit him what he had done. He drove away from Mellieħa, took a dirt track away from the main roads and stopped once he thought it was safe and no one would see him. He chatted to you and showed you that silly trick that he did with his thumb, the one where it looks like he is removing his thumb and then putting it back again. He said you loved it.

"He didn't know how long he sat there, he told you some stories and you fell asleep. By now, he was getting frightened and realised that he had to return you, but how? If he did, he thought he would get caught by the police. He panicked. So, he lifted you gently, wrapped you in a blanket that he found on the back seat, laid you in the boot and headed home. All the time thinking that at any moment you would wake and scream, but you didn't." Lisa had stopped crying and she now looked at Ava. "He was not acting rationally, he was hurting as much as me, but he had been hiding it."

Christopher had been listening this whole time. The story was astonishing and yet he had a little sympathy for the two grieving parents. Without Lisa or Ava realising, he had joined them at the table. He wanted to hear this, be witness to what was being said. Whether Ava was taking this all in, he wasn't so sure but he knew that this needed to be heard.

"Then he joined a queue of traffic. It turned out that the police were stopping every car in the area. He froze as he drew closer and closer to the policeman that was talking to the drivers. Then he saw it was Ġakobb Farrugia, he had repaired his car on more than one occasion. He relaxed a little but was on his guard. As he approached Ġakobb, he rolled down his window and held his breath. He told me he was so terrified that he made the sign of the cross and asked Mary, holy mother of God, for help and forgiveness. He chatted to Ġakobb about cars, asked if his were running okay, and Ġakobb waved him through. Because he had managed to get through the police roadblock without being discovered, he truly felt that he had been given a gift from the angels and he brought you home to me."

Ava now reached over and took her mother's hands in hers, as extraordinary as it all sounded, she was beginning to understand. It was obviously so terribly wrong, what her father had done. She could see that he was trying to help, it was an awful way to do it, but he had the best of intentions.

"What happened when I woke up? Surely, I was frightened."

"You were, but it was not until the next morning. The sea air must have made you so tired. He laid you in Ava's bed and when you were sleeping, it was as though she had returned to us. My heart leapt for joy, my baby was back. We stayed up all night, trying to decide what to do, what to say. Living out here, no one sees us unless they are coming to visit. My depression had meant that I wasn't going out and we didn't have friends that would just drop in. We felt we could keep you.

"The next day, when you woke, you called out for your mummy but it was me that held you. I comforted you and explained that your mummy had asked for us to take care of you for a while. I know that it was wrong, I know that, and whilst it is no excuse, I was depressed and not thinking straight. I decided I would cut your hair to match the photographs we had of Ava before she died. I had always cut her hair too so I encouraged you to sit, bribing you with an apple

164

pastizzi, so I could trim your fringe and cut a lot off the length. Now, apart from your eyes, you were our Ava once more. I called you Ava from the start and you never questioned it."

Ava let out a huge sigh, she flopped back into the chair and gazed upwards. "Did the authorities not realise? The doctor, anyone?"

"No, I changed doctors to one in Victoria. I had Ava's birth certificate so I was able to enrol you in school when you were five and you were such a healthy child that you didn't see the doctor. Before long, the whole episode of Ava dying seemed to fade into the back of my mind; after all, you were back with me. Just as though you had never left. I didn't hide you, I treated you like normal, we went shopping, we went on holiday and before long, a few months maybe, you began to call me Mummy. I always referred to Stephen and myself as 'Daddy and Mummy' to you and before long it seemed second nature to you too."

"I don't know how much more there is to hear, but I need to absorb all this. I need to go home now."

Lisa looked crestfallen, but she understood. She followed Christopher and Ava to the door and waved them off, went back inside and collapsed into a chair, sobbing.

Chapter Twenty-Nine

Sarah picked Ava up just before nine the next morning. Ava hadn't slept at all well and Sarah could see that her eyes were bloodshot. They were due to meet Mark for coffee in half an hour, before they went to the clinic for their tests. Mark had called her the evening before and explained that he had researched Ava's father's family and had found her ancestry most interesting. Both he and Sarah felt the DNA was just a formality, they were certain Ava was Alison. He had called the clinic and they had said that if Mark was prepared to pay extra, they would agree to expedite the tests, but it was going to cost a lot. Mark agreed.

Mark had arranged to meet Sarah and Ava at the hotel in St Julian's Bay, where he had first met Ava, (if you didn't include the accidental meeting at the café). He had arrived first and had managed to get a table with a wonderful view of the bay. The day was glorious already and there was only one tiny wispy cloud in the sky. This case was one he would never forget. He had put all the information he had found onto a USB stick for Ava and had even drawn up a family tree for her as well, taking that side of her tree all the way back to Samuel Hensley. He saw the ladies arrive, held up his arm and waved. Mark went to the bar and ordered coffees and iced water for everyone.

Ava had decided not to mention too much about her trip to see her mother yesterday. She knew now that she was Alison. The DNA test was irrelevant as far as she was concerned, but Mark had told her at their last meeting, that without that his company would not sign off on the inheritance. She didn't feel she should have an inheritance anyway, she thought that should go to Sarah, but for now, she would go through the formalities. How much there was to inherit, she didn't know. She realised too, earlier that morning, that she didn't know the circumstances of her real mother's death either, but like her real father, she wanted to know her first as a live person. She would make sure that Sarah knew this.

"I saw my mother yesterday."

"How did that go?" Mark enquired.

"Well, if what she tells me is true, then I am convinced that I am Alison."

Mark looked up from his coffee. Sarah stopped still, her cup halfway to her mouth. Ava looked away.

"I need to process what she has told me. However, unless you believe that angels return babies from heaven, then I think it is safe to say that I am not Ava. Though for now, I'm sticking with that name. I can't change after all these years. That would be too odd."

Mark and Sarah continued to stare at Ava. They had both believed that she was Alison, but it now sounded like Ava also knew who she was. She had facts. The three of them sat for a while, no one knowing what to say.

Mark spoke first, "I have done some research for you, into the Hensley side of your family." He slid the USB stick towards her. "For when you are ready to know more. I imagine Sarah can help you with your mother's side of the family, but I had time to kill and some interesting things turned up."

"Thank you, that is so kind." Ava put the stick into her bag. She was not ready for that yet but she was grateful regardless.

"All being well, we should have your DNA results back by the end of Friday. I have arranged for the tests to be expedited as I am supposed to be leaving at the end of next week and I would like to get this all sorted for you as soon as I can."

"I don't think it is right for me to inherit," Ava looked at Sarah, "it should be you."

Sarah smiled gently at Ava. "My sister would have wanted you to have every penny, so would your father."

"Well, we can share then, that seems fair to me."

Mark looked at Ava and took the plunge. "There is quite some inheritance to come to you. It is the only reason that I am here. We don't travel all around the world for a few thousand dollars."

"How much do you mean?" Ava was looking terrified. It had never occurred to her that there would be anything significant. Even when she learnt about the hotels. It was not something she had given any thought to.

"Sarah knows this already." Mark looked at Sarah for confirmation to continue, she nodded her head and smiled in affirmation. "Originally, I thought Sarah was the only remaining relative of your mother, she is the person I came to find. Only, when we met, she told me that you had been lost, in fact, you were presumed drowned. There is a death certificate for you in Canada."

Ava went white. She slumped forward and took several deep breaths. "Oh, my dear God! Dead!"

"I'm afraid so," Sarah picked up the story. "We searched for you for years. After quite some time, the police here said it was their belief that you had walked into the sea and drowned. Your mother was never convinced. After seven years, the Canadian Court issued a death certificate."

"That's awful, poor woman. And now, she will never know!"

"The sum, your inheritance, after our fees…" Mark was speaking slowly, he could see that Ava looked pale still, "will be a little over twenty-six million Canadian dollars." With that, Ava collapsed to the floor.

Chapter Thirty

The next week flew by in a blur. The tests came back from the laboratory and it was confirmed that Sarah and Ava had a twenty-five percent match to each other, which is what was to be expected, but Sarah had also taken a hairbrush that belonged to Florence and the clinic had been able to extract DNA from some hairs. To those, Ava and Florence matched at fifty-three percent. In other words, it was confirmed, Florence was her mother and Sarah was her aunt. There was no doubt whatsoever. Mark had to fly back to Calgary. Indri insisted that Ava take at least two weeks off work and Sarah invited her to Gozo to stay with her and Benny. To start with, Ava refused, she couldn't leave Ricco. But Christopher and Jack agreed to take turns in visiting Ricco, so she accepted and packed a small bag for her stay.

Ava had spoken to her mother just once more since her last visit. She rang her to tell her the DNA results. Lisa was quiet but agreed that it had to be true. Not much more of a conversation took place, but Ava finished the call by telling her mother how much she loved her. She knew she was loved and she didn't believe she could feel anything other than love for her mother in return, despite what had happened. Ava agreed to speak to her in a week, she didn't mention her trip to Gozo.

With full instructions left for Ricco's care, Ava gave him a long squeeze, kissed him several times on the head and left him snoozing on the balcony. Sarah picked her up first thing on Saturday morning as agreed the night before. They had both gone to the airport to see Mark off. He was reluctantly leaving the island but he told them both he was leaving a piece of his heart there. He knew he would be back. He hadn't had much time to do any sightseeing and that was something he definitely wanted.

Reg had gone to the airport too. The two men had a formal farewell, a stiff handshake. Whereas, with both Ava and Sarah, Mark hugged them close and made them promise to keep in touch. Officially, he would be in contact as soon as he got back but he meant on a more personal level. He had arrived in Malta only a few weeks ago. In that time, he had made a brief visit to the UK, enabled the help of a retired police officer, and between them they had tracked down the vehicle which had taken young Alison from Malta to Gozo. For all these years, she had been hiding in plain sight. But despite all that, it was meeting Ava and discovering that she was part of the legacy left by Samuel Hensley and now an extremely wealthy young lady, that gave him the warmest feeling. It was his job to track down the inheritors but, in this case, it had given him such pleasure. There was sadness in all this too. A lot of sadness, and for that, he felt sorry for pulling on that needle and thread in the haystack.

Ava and Sarah took the ferry to Gozo and arrived in Gharb late morning. Benny was at work and Sarah was secretly pleased. She was able to settle Ava in without Benny asking too many questions. The girl was still very fragile and she needed to speak with him and make sure he understood that he was not to probe her for information.

Ava thought it was a pretty house and she could see why Sarah liked it there. It fronted the street but had a beautiful courtyard garden surrounded by pots of all descriptions, full to the brim with various plants and herbs. It reminded her of Elias's garden and Ava wondered if Sarah had taken her inspiration from the way Yvonne had kept her courtyard garden. The house had three levels, a sitting room full of overstuffed sofas and a basic kitchen on the lower level. Two bedrooms and a bathroom which contained the deepest bath Ava had ever seen, and then a top floor with its own bathroom and a Juliet balcony with views over Gozo that were breathtaking. It was this room that Ava had for the next two weeks and she marvelled at the space around her.

Later in the afternoon, once Ava had unpacked, she and Sarah sat in the garden amongst all the pots at a small wrought iron table and chairs that had been painted lime green.

"How are you feeling, Ava?" Sarah showed every concern any aunt would do, but she now felt she needed to be both aunt and mother, though there was no way she would say that to Ava, especially as she was still referring to Lisa as her mother. That did stick in Sarah's chest a little, but she understood.

"Still dazed. I'd like to say that I'm getting used to the whole thing, but truthfully, I'm not. I wish with all my heart though, that Florence and William were alive. I would have loved to meet them."

"They would have been so proud of you, Ava. And the fact that you had a loving upbringing was all your mother hoped for you. She would say to me, each time she visited over the years, that if she could believe that you had been taken into a loving home, then despite her heartache, she would be glad."

"I'd like to know more about her, well, more about both my parents. But as they were before they died. Sarah, can we leave that bit for now? I need to get to know them first."

Over the next few days, when Benny was at work or making himself scarce so the ladies could talk easily, Sarah drew a mental picture for Ava of her parents. She began, as they say, in the beginning. How they met. How they fell in love, even adding in how she was jealous of their closeness at first. Then she told her about the business that they grew from sheer hard work and determination. Sarah had kept all the letters that Florence had sent her, and Ava sat in the sunshine, under a gazebo that was draped with delicately scented, climbing roses, and read all about the work they had put into every hotel. How, unbelievably to them, each hotel grew and prospered.

She talked about her favourite one. A small twelve-bedroomed hotel in Quebec City that sat in a side street just a few minutes' walk from Place Royale, being the birthplace of the city, where Samuel De Champlain established the first settlement in the early 1600s. She recounted a story of how they had stumbled across a small restaurant in a corner of a square and how she and William had enjoyed the food and atmosphere so much that they had visited it again and again on their first trip to the city. Some of the hotels which they owned were vast with hundreds of bedrooms, but to Florence, that one in particular, held a special place in her heart. Ava decided that, one day, she would visit it.

Ava had been with Sarah for almost a week. Whilst they were having a morning coffee together with a plateful of fresh berries from the garden, Ava asked about how her father had died. She knew he had passed away first, and, wanting to take it one step at a time, she wanted to know what happened to him. Sarah's heart sank. She knew she needed to tell her, but in her own mind this would be the harder of the two to hear.

"I'm so sorry to tell you, Ava, that he took his own life."

Ava's hand flew up to her mouth, her eyes wide open in shock. She hadn't expected that at all.

"But he had such a successful business empire, why would he do such a thing?" Sarah looked over towards Ava, leant forward and took her hands in hers.

"They say that he never got over losing you, blamed himself for turning his back for a minute whilst he removed his shoes. They both stayed with me for almost nine months after we lost you. We tried everything we possibly could to find you. They were both heartbroken but William blamed himself. Less than a year from the day you went missing, he was found. He had taken an overdose. It was too late to save him."

"Dear God!" Ava sank down into the chair, she felt like she needed to root herself into its frame, let it support her. "All because I walked away."

"Now, never blame yourself for this, never, do you hear me!" Sarah had raised her voice a little too much and she could see she was upsetting Ava. "I'm sorry, Ava, I didn't mean to sound cross. But heavens above, you were only three, you cannot possibly take any blame for this."

"No, I know. It's just that I seem to have a trail of heartache at my feet. First William and now my mother. I haven't caused any of it, but it is streaming behind me nonetheless."

"Just remember what a great man he was. What he achieved to provide for Florence and you, building his empire from the ground up. He was highly thought of. Florence told me that he expected a high standard of craftmanship from his employees. After a while he was able to gather around him a team of men and they had to be good at their job. No 'corner cutting' or 'making do'. In return he paid them over the going rate. He was highly respected. That is the man you should remember. And don't forget you have that information from Mark about William's family. That may tell you a bit more. When you are ready, obviously."

Ava sat in silence for a while. She knew that Sarah was right. She wasn't to blame, but she was at the centre of it all, yet she hadn't the faintest notion about any of it for thirty-three years. Ava went to her room, came back with the USB stick.

"Do you have any means of me seeing what is on here?" Ava laughed. It hadn't occurred to her when Mark gave her the stick, she didn't have a way to read it. Under her arm, she also had a file of papers.

"I don't, but I'll call Benny and get him to bring a laptop home from his café tonight."

Ava tucked the USB into her pocket and opened the file up on the garden table. On top was a family tree, it had been drawn out with precision and there were little notes next to some of the names.

The Hensley Family

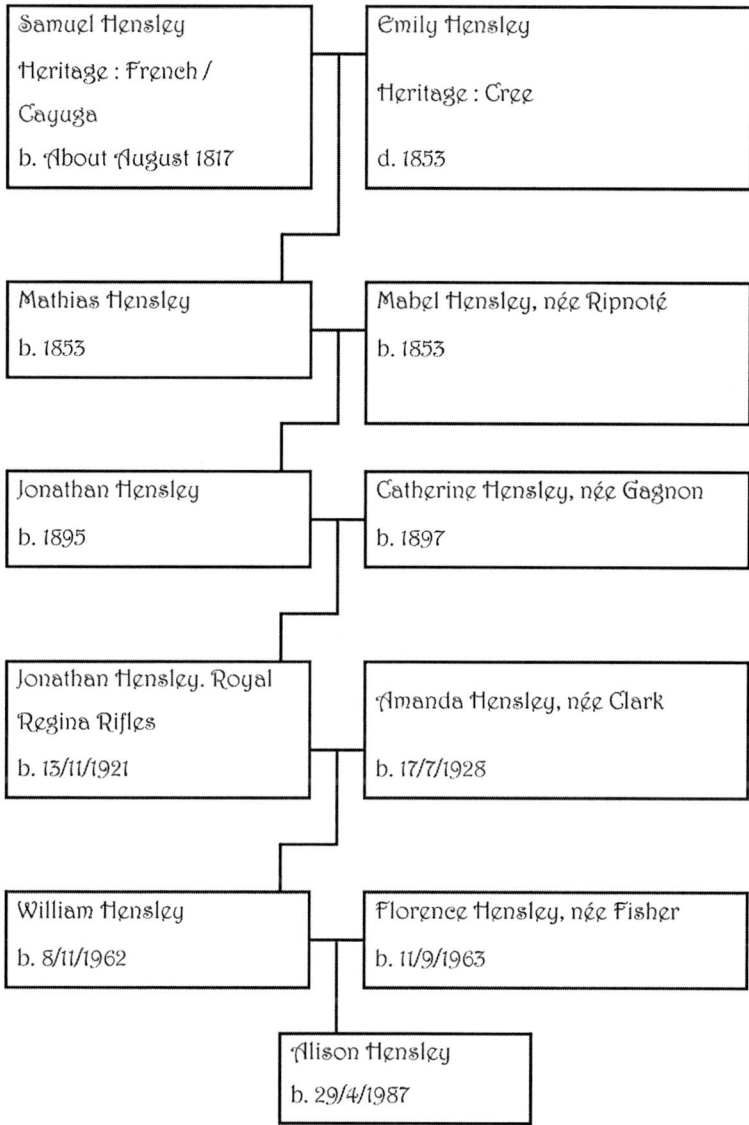

Samuel Hensley
Heritage : French / Cayuga
b. About August 1817

Emily Hensley
Heritage : Cree
d. 1853

Mathias Hensley
b. 1853

Mabel Hensley, née Ripnoté
b. 1853

Jonathan Hensley
b. 1895

Catherine Hensley, née Gagnon
b. 1897

Jonathan Hensley. Royal Regina Rifles
b. 13/11/1921

Amanda Hensley, née Clark
b. 17/7/1928

William Hensley
b. 8/11/1962

Florence Hensley, née Fisher
b. 11/9/1963

Alison Hensley
b. 29/4/1987

Ava read about William's father, Jonathan, her grandfather, who had fought in the war against Germany—how he was one of the first men to land on the beaches in the D-Day landings. That was something to feel proud of and gave Ava a warm feeling. Then she read about her great-grandfather, also called Jonathan and his father too. That would be her great-great-grandfather. He was called Mathias. It was his father, Samuel, her three times great-grandfather who had signed Mathias's record of birth with an X, who held her attention the most. He was born in York in Canada and, like her father, had built up a business from scratch, in order to provide for his wife and family.

There were connections to the people of Canada, the First Nations. The Cayuga and the Cree people. Ava touched her hair, her long dark straight hair. In Malta a lot of people had dark hair, but hers was different. Whilst Sarah and Florence had similar hair, she wondered how much of hers was a throwback to her ancestors. Her interest was piqued. She already knew that she wanted to visit the little hotel in Quebec, well now she also wanted to know more about her heritage.

That evening, on the laptop that Benny brought back from the café, she was able to read the Hensley Legacy, the article that Mark had found, and she learnt about the Hensley Foundation too. What a wonderful man he was. Self-made and yet he gave it all back to his family and to those that had helped him make his money. She was genuinely proud of him also. They had just finished eating dinner, it was a little after eight in the evening and Ava poured them all a glass of red wine. The three of them were sitting in the lounge, their stomachs full of delicious fresh fish, salad and potatoes. She sat forward and proposed her idea.

"Sarah, how do you like the sound of a trip to Canada? I'd like to learn more about my ancestors and I'd like to go to Quebec City where Florence's favourite hotel was."

"Gosh, well..." Sarah looked at Benny. He smiled and nodded silently.

"I'd prefer it if you came with me. I'm sure there is more for us to learn about each other and I know there is more I need to know about my mother. We could take the trip together and learn on the way."

"What about your job? And Ricco?"

"I know, I need to talk to Indri. I don't want to let him down." Her mind was whirring now. Different things were dropping into place. Sarah saw a spark in her eyes that she hadn't seen since they first met.

"I have an idea, but I want to keep things to myself for now—don't be offended, but it concerns others. Please think about it though, a proper trip, not just a couple of weeks. I'm not sure how long, we could catch up with Mark too." Ava was very animated.

"I'd love to go," Sarah enthused. The idea of a trip to Canada, with the niece that she thought had been lost forever, was a wonderful idea. Hopefully, they could take in a visit to the place where Florence's ashes had been scattered. As yet, Ava was unaware of how Florence had died, but that was something for another day.

The next morning, Sarah could hear Ava in the garden on the telephone. She was pacing up and down and using her arms to express her words. Sarah held back, giving Ava all the space that she needed.

"My mother," Ava said as she walked back into the house. "Not too happy about the idea of my visit to Canada. Cheek of the woman! I've promised to call but all I got in return were selfish whinges of how she would be lonely. It was so hard to stay calm."

"You still want to go?"

"Damn right I do. I want to get planning as soon as I've spoken with Indri."

"Well, I have no plans that we need to be concerned about; just tell me when, for how long and how much!"

Ava burst out laughing. "I don't think we will make too much of a dent into our money."

"Your money, remember."

"Our money, Sarah, we are family now. Would you be offended if I went back home today? I want to talk to Indri; now I have the idea, I can't wait to share it."

"Of course, you get packed and I will fetch the car."

Chapter Thirty-One

Ava got back home late in the afternoon on the Sunday. Sarah helped her upstairs with her bags. There was no need but she wasn't ready to part yet, plus she wanted to hear more about Ava's ideas for the trip. They sat on the couch, Ricco curled up on Ava's lap, and discussed possible places to visit. Really, apart from flying into Toronto, Ava was happy to wing it, but Sarah needed a little more planning. She had got a postcard which Florence had sent her, picturing the hotel in Quebec, and she would call and make a reservation for a few nights there first. They would stay overnight in Toronto and then fly to Quebec as soon as they could. For Ava, this was the part she was most looking forward to.

After Sarah had left, she called Mark. She had calculated that he was six or seven hours behind so it would be early afternoon for him. He answered quickly, "Ava?"

"Hey, good, you haven't forgotten my name!" She laughed.

Mark was thrilled to hear the laughter down the end of the phone line.

"Believe it or not, I was just sending an email through to you. I have the final figures for your inheritance and need you to tell me where I am to send it. A bank account I mean. You can talk to one of our investors here if you like, but I am sure there is someone in Malta that can help you."

"Well, I have news. I will want some of it sent to me. But I will think about how much, then please could you invest the remainder in Canada? Sarah and I are going to visit and we will come and see you. Then I can tell you my plans."

"That is fabulous, I look forward to seeing you both again. When will that be?"

"We will visit Quebec City first, then I am not sure after that. But I think we will be around for a month or two, so I will be in touch." With that, Ava finished the call and went to bed.

For once, her mind was whirring in a good way. She slept well.

Waking early the next morning, she fed Ricco and went down to see Elias and the boys. Christopher and Elias were out on the boat but Jack was sitting in the courtyard drinking coffee. Ava explained that she was back and wouldn't need them for a few days, but would they like to look after Ricco for a couple of months as she wanted to go away. Jack readily agreed. He had become quite fond of Ricco in the last few days.

"It might be easier if he came and stayed here, if that is okay with your dad."

"Of course it will be, he is a great cat. We will take good care of him."

"Brilliant, though do let me know later, once you have spoken to him. I don't want to presume. I will pay for all his food obviously." Jack began to chuckle.

"With all the fish heads and guts that we have, we could feed him forever." Ava laughed too and left him to his coffee. Tick, first job off the list.

She was too early to see Indri. She wanted to catch him during the morning lull and he wasn't expecting her to be at work, so she went for a walk along the beach. She took off her flip-flops and held them in one hand, walking down to the water's edge. The cold water on her feet was chilling to say the least, but it was a lovely feeling. She walked for some distance before sitting on a large rock at the top of the beach. She pulled her knees up under her chin and stared out to sea.

The crashing of the waves on the shore and the call of the gulls above was idyllic. She always loved the sounds of the sea as well as its salty spray that seemed to permeate her clothes. Her hair was tied back at the nape of her neck but the wind was whipping it to one side. She reached across her shoulder, turning her head to grab her ponytail when it caught her eye. Carved into the rocks behind her was just one word. 'ALISON', and a small heart.

Ava scrambled across the rocks, it was quite high up but she managed to perch onto a large rock set to one side. She ran her fingers over the words, knowing who had carved them. Her eyes filled and she began to cry. She had walked this beach, time and again over the past few years, even sat on the same stone, but she had never noticed the carving before today. She touched it again as if she was touching her mother's hand, cold rock, and yet it appeared to feel warm to the touch.

Back at the café, she waved to Indri as she noticed him. He was carrying a tray piled high with white crockery and one large green mug, so he couldn't wave back. Ava went in through the doors facing the beach and on into the kitchen.

"No May today?" she queried.

"No, I have finally managed to get her to take the day off. I think I'd have had to deal with her collapsing on me if she didn't rest up soon." Indri put the tray down into the sink and began to run the water. "You're back early."

"Yes and no." Ava began to shuffle Indri out of the way, it was the least she could do, to wash the crockery from the early breakfasts. He didn't refuse. "I might need you to sit down though, I have a lot to tell you."

Indri poked his head out of the kitchen, the café was empty. Ava was pleased. Whilst she continued to wash the china, Indri listened agog to all that had been happening. He knew some of it but she filled in the gaps, leaving to the end the piece that concerned him. She explained that she now had quite a large inheritance, most of which she didn't really want, so she wanted to do good things with it. Starting with the café. Firstly, she wanted to see if he would employ Christopher in the kitchen to cook his incredible fish dishes. That would mean opening up in the evenings, this all being subject to Christopher agreeing of course.

Secondly, and this was the big one, she wanted to buy the café off Indri, if he would let her.

She would keep him there as if he still owned it but pay him favourably for his time. Just like William had done, good workers should be paid above and beyond, and she knew that Indri often didn't pay himself. She had spotted him eating the leftovers many a time so she knew that things were tight. Thirdly, she wanted to set up a foundation, using the upstairs rooms in the café, to help not only Indri and Christopher, but lots of young people in the area. To give them the funds to acquire a good trade, one that would help them through their lives.

Indri didn't speak, he walked to the door, turned the sign from open to closed and sat down. Ava was worried. She thought she had upset him and having dried her hands on her apron, she followed him into the café.

"Indri?"

He went from sitting on a chair to kneeling in front of her, his hands clasped together. "You have answered my prayers."

"What do you mean?"

"I have been praying for a miracle to keep the café going. I knew that we needed to open in the evenings as well, to keep us afloat. But it felt too much for me. If Christopher is happy to join us, then all I can say, Ava, is…" He stood up, put his hands on her shoulders and kissed her on each cheek. "Welcome to Ava's café!"

"We haven't talked price, Indri. What do you want for your business?"

"No idea. You give me a fair price and it is yours."

"Here is the next bit though," Ava hesitated, "as soon as possible, Sarah and I are leaving to spend some time in Canada. I won't be here to do my shifts."

"Well, if Christopher is on board, we will be fine. I'm not sure that May wants to carry on much longer. We might need a bit more help—well, let's be honest, we will definitely need more help. At least one more person."

"How many people would it take to make it successful yet not stressful?"

"Two."

"Then two we will get, plus Christopher. We can start to advertise straight away."

Ava hugged Indri, this was the first stage in her plan. So far, it seemed to be working. She flipped the café sign back to open, went into the kitchen to finish washing up and asked Indri for an espresso. Soon they were sitting, like usual, facing the sea. Ava told him about the carving.

Once the lunch rush subsided, they shut for the siesta. She had already put in a call to a solicitor who would draw up the exchange of ownership for the business. Indri looked as if she had removed the weight of the world from his shoulders. But it was a price that she was stumbling over. Then she remembered something else.

"Indri," Ava sat up and turned herself to face him, "you have trained me in this business, I knew nothing about working in a café when I came to you and you taught me everything I know. So, I have a proposition."

Indri was intrigued. He never felt he had taught her anything, she worked hard and was happy to turn her hand to whatever was required. He thanked God for the day she walked into his life.

"Well, what if I pay you a good wage for the hours you work here? Not a minimum wage, but a good comfortable wage? Then I double it! Each week I will be paying you back for the business. At whatever age you decide you wish to retire, you continue to receive your wages, up until the day you pass." Ava raised an eyebrow as though looking for an answer, none was forthcoming. "Or I could pay you outright, your decision."

"That sounds far too generous to me." Indri was flabbergasted.

"Good." Ava was feeling the best she had in weeks. "Then do we have a deal?"

With that, Indri got up, slowly put down his coffee cup and went running down the beach. He kicked off his shoes as he ran and dived headfirst into the sea! Ava stood and watched, first in shock, then in absolute joy!

Chapter Thirty-Two

She found Christopher, later that day, out at the front of the family home. He looked like he was just going out, dressed very smart.

"I'm glad I caught you."

"Jack said you were back. You'd like us to look after Ricco whilst you go away, is that right?"

"Yes, a month or two maybe. I want to go to Canada, Sarah will come with me. But there is something else."

Ava explained in less detail than she had to Indri, how she was going to buy the café and how they were looking to open for the evening trade. She wanted him to join the team. Put his cooking skills to good use, and in addition, to pay him and Elias for fresh fish each day, to serve in the café. Furthermore, as many fresh herbs, tomatoes and vegetables as they could provide. She explained that she would pay him for any extra training which he would require. She touched a little on the need for a couple more members of staff as well as wanting to open a foundation to help other young people obtain skills, using the café premises as a base. Christopher listened intently and quietly. He was silent a little too long for Ava's liking but she let him process the information.

"When do I start?"

Ava laughed. She asked him to come and see her tomorrow in the café to show him around the kitchen. She was so relieved. His food was incredible and she knew that he would make a success of the evening meals. Tick, that was the second job done.

Later that evening, Ava called Sarah and told her about her day. She knew that she wanted to honour her family by using this money for good. Just as Samuel had, and then her father too. She might not have known them, but she wanted to do as they did. Sarah thought that was an amazing idea and she was thrilled that Ava sounded so positive.

Ava explained that this was only a part of her plans and she would explicate more when they next met up. She knew she had to try and arrange staff to help Indri so she wasn't certain if that would be soon. Perhaps it could wait for the long aeroplane journey. Sarah too had been busy, she had arranged their flights and their stay in the Hotel Florence. It appeared that William had changed the name of Florence's favourite hotel in her honour.

The next week or so was filled with meeting prospective staff. The first person that both Indri and Ava agreed on was Gino's daughter, Sofia. May had decided it was too much for her to carry on, but would happily fill in, as and when needed. She popped an advert in the boutique where Francisca worked and before long, they were inundated with people wanting to work there. They whittled down a short list to four people and asked them to work for free for a day to see how they got on. One refused immediately, two reluctantly but were okay at the job, the last one, a girl named Marie, was perfect.

She worked hard, did anything that was asked of her from cleaning to washing up. Ava and Indri offered her the job straight away. Then they paid her for her day's work. It had been a great idea, all those years back for Ava, so it had been a good test and it had worked. Feeling relieved that she could now leave Indri with Christopher, Marie and Sofia, she called Sarah to ask her out to dinner, to celebrate.

Sarah turned up a little before seven in the evening and Ava rushed down the stairs to meet her. She hadn't seen her for a few days and she realised she had missed her. Just then she saw Christopher on the other side of the road, arm in arm with his girlfriend. They crossed the road to meet Ava and Sarah. Ava smiled intently.

"Well, I hope you two can work together, I had no idea that you were Christopher's girlfriend!"

"Going anywhere nice?" Christopher asked.

"Not sure yet, we are going to find a restaurant to eat and celebrate my purchase of the café. Any suggestions?"

"As a matter of fact, I do." Christopher turned to Sofia and grinned. "Two more for Chez Elias. Your table will be ready shortly."

Sarah and Ava readily agreed and walked the short distance to Elias's. Elias was thrilled to see Sarah again after so many years and welcomed her like an old friend. Sofia set the table for the six of them and Jack handed around glasses of wine. There was a beautiful salty tomato and basil bruschetta to start. They had all finished when Elias stood up to clear the plates away.

"You can't beat a bit of tomatoes on toast!" Everyone laughed, but he was right.

Their next course was the gilthead bream with courgettes. This time, Christopher had added chopped aubergines and chillies. It was just as delicious as Ava remembered from the first time she had tasted it. He had added some fresh homemade bread to the table, crusty and dusted with flour and black pepper.

"When do you have time to prepare all this?" Ava was so impressed.

"Well, we are normally back from the sea by about ten. Jack tends to help Dad these days with the fish, prepping them for sale. I like to be in the kitchen, I learnt from Mum's notebook but I like to try new things."

"This has been one of the best fish dishes I have ever eaten." Sarah sat back, her empty plate testament to what she had said. "You are a genius, I can't wait to come and eat in the café when we are back from our trip."

There was even a dessert. A glazed flaky pastry tart with apples and raisins, sprinkled with chopped hazelnuts and a spoonful of thick cream with flecks of vanilla. Sumptuous. Ava already knew she had made the best decision employing him. She knew he would need food safety training and made a mental note to get Indri to look into that first thing in the morning. Tonight, she would enjoy the meal and the company. Elias nodded off after dessert. No one knew if he was just full of the delicious food or he had slipped into a narcoleptic snooze. But it didn't matter either way.

Ava asked Christopher to join her in the garden—she wanted to know what kind of money he would expect for working in the kitchen. He said he had researched what the minimum wage was and, as he had no official training to speak of, he would be more than happy to accept that. After all, he would be out fishing with his dad in the morning, have a siesta and then start working in the café in the afternoon. Plus, there would be the income for the fish. He thought that was fair. Ava disagreed.

"You can cook some of the finest food I have ever tasted. I have eaten far worse in high class restaurants where all they do is put a fancy bit of food in the middle of the plate, on top of a sauce and give it a weird name." Ava was determined he should realise his worth. "Now let's start again." They spent the next few minutes discussing the wage until they were both happy. Ava offering more and Christopher asking for less. It was a strange conversation. In the end, they agreed on a one month trial at twice minimum wage and as long as the takings proved that they could continue, Ava would increase it to four times. She had no concerns that the café wouldn't be able to support it. Once word got around about his cooking, she was sure they would be turning people away. Thrilled with how the conversation had gone, they went back to join everyone else.

Ava went to see Indri the next morning, explained about Sofia being Christopher's girlfriend and also about the amazing meal to which he had treated her and Sarah the night before.

"The tomatoes on toast were incredible!" She chuckled and then explained how Elias had described Christopher's bruschetta. They then came up with names for the rest of the food that Ava had sampled the night before. Bream and courgettes with peppered bread, much better than some fancy title that every customer would either need explaining or having to accompany it with a photo. Then apple and raisin tart with cream. Again simple.

"Not one fancy name," said Ava. "Nothing that needs explaining or photographing. If we stick to that, good simple honest food, we can't go wrong." Ava was happy. She knew this was going to work and be successful—all because of William and Samuel Hensley.

There were only two more days to go before Ava and Sarah would be on their way across the Atlantic Ocean. Ricco was now happily ensconced with Elias and the boys, stretching out in the sunshine of their courtyard garden and being spoilt with fresh fish. Ava was happy to leave him in their care but she knew she would miss him terribly. Marie, one of the new café employees, was going to stay in Ava's flat whilst she was away. It saved on travel time for her and gave her a taste of independence. She was just nineteen, but ready to find a little place of her own. Ava could have left Ricco in the flat with Marie, but Jack would have been so upset, and it meant that she didn't need to worry about leaving food for him. Everything was sorted apart from a last visit to her mother.

Going alone this time, Ava borrowed Indri's car and took the mid-morning ferry to Gozo. She had called ahead to let her mother know she was on her way. She had sounded distracted but Ava needed to visit so didn't enquire if there was anything wrong. She arrived in Munxar to see the doors to the garage wide open. Her father's car was missing, which was a surprise. She got out of the car and walked over to the garage. Lisa was standing at the back looking through the contents of the freezer. She hadn't heard Ava arrive and as she turned around, she was startled to see her standing there. Lisa looked pale and dishevelled. Her hair was unkempt and her clothes looked like she had been sleeping in them. Ava was shocked. "Where is the car?"

"I scrapped it."

"But why? You always said you couldn't part with it."

"I… I… I thought it best." Lisa brushed past Ava on her way back to the house. There was something very wrong and Ava followed her. Obviously, these past few weeks had been a shock to her and upsetting to her mother, but this seemed far more serious. Ava thought she must be ill. She followed her into the house and to the kitchen to find Lisa holding onto the sink, her head down, taking deep breaths.

"You go and sit down, I'll put the kettle on. Tea or coffee?" Lisa didn't answer but moved away from the sink and collapsed in a heap on the sofa. Ava made coffee in a tall ceramic pot, put some milk in the bottom of a cup for her mother, added a cube of sugar and then took the coffee and cups to the coffee table near to where her mother was sitting. Ava poured the coffee and stirred her mother's cup to dissolve the sugar. She touched her gently on the knee and offered her the cup. Lisa shuffled into a sitting position and took the cup into both hands. Ava noticed her eyes were rimmed with black circles, it was obvious she wasn't sleeping.

"Are you okay? Is there something wrong?"

Lisa sipped her coffee and put the cup back on the table.

"The police are involved," Lisa began. "They have the car, the man at the scrapyard called them."

"How would he know to do that and why would he think it necessary?" Ava looked at her mother whose eyes had glazed over. "Oh no! Don't tell me that is the car that I was carried in from Malta? He kept it all this time!" Ava was stunned. That car could prove her father had taken her. Until then, in Ava's mind, this was a private matter, and seeing as her actual parent's had now passed away, why would anyone need to know? She was wrong, it seemed.

"It was silver originally," Lisa was recounting the story with her eyes closed, "Stephen painted it dark green and swopped the number plate from another car which he already had. Then it took him a week or so to find another Fiat Panda in silver. He had to pay the owner more than it was worth to buy it from him, as he didn't really want to sell it. But with extra money in his hand, he gave it up. Stephen then scrapped that one, with the number plates on it from the car in which he had been stopped in at the roadblock." Lisa was shaking her head, almost in disbelief of her own story. "He spent all that money getting the car and within hours it was at the scrapyard."

"Did the police come here at the beginning? Did they come and see if I was here?" Ava couldn't believe what she was hearing. How much more was there to discover?

"Yes, the day after Stephen scrapped the car he'd just bought. The timing was perfect. We were asked to look after a neighbour's dog for the week and all you wanted to do was be in the garden with it. You would spend all day out there, throwing a ball and giggling in delight when he brought it back to you. When the police came, Stephen was able to tell them he had scrapped the car, knowing that if they went to find it, it would either have been crushed or if not, there would be nothing to find belonging to you. A little evidence that he had been in the car maybe, but that would be expected. I'm sure they noticed you, but we had photographs around of our Ava, you looked so similar. I had even cut your hair to match hers, and once we showed them Ava's birth certificate, they went away. We never heard from them again."

Ava flopped back into the chair in amazement. She had noticed that her mother kept referring to her father as 'Stephen' now, that was new and a little odd to hear.

"I'm not sleeping, barely eating. I'm so frightened, Ava." Lisa let out a howl, it was awful to hear. Then she clutched a cushion from beside her and buried her face into the fabric. Ava had come to tell her mother about her trip, she wasn't sure she could leave her like this.

"But it was Dad that took me, not you. You told me yourself that you were depressed from losing your Ava. Surely you won't be held accountable for his actions, will you?"

"I have been released on bail, I will have to appear in court at some point. They have charged me with child abduction, attempting to pervert the course of justice and assisting an offender. But the police have said they have to gather further evidence and only then will I hear more."

"Good God!"

"Listen, I might not have been part of your abduction but once I was feeling better and the antidepressants had helped me return to my normal state of mind, in my head I knew what Stephen had done was wrong but, in my heart, I felt it was also the right thing. He had found you on the beach, no one watching over you. He assured me that you were alone and we would take care of you. Besides, at which point could I have owned up and told someone? It was too late."

Lisa seemed almost to be reassuring herself, whether that was to do with the original abduction and how she had processed it over the years or if it was to do with more recent events, Ava wasn't sure, but she noticed how Lisa was beginning to relax and sound more like herself once more.

Chapter Thirty-Three

They arrived at the airport a little over two hours before their scheduled flight. Sarah had arranged for Benny to collect Ava en-route and drop them both at the airport. Ava travelled quite light, but Sarah seemed to have enough luggage for the two of them. They checked in the majority of their bags and went through security. Ava was still feeling anxious leaving her mother, but she was not going to miss out on this trip. She wanted to fill in so many missing blanks from her history and it was only for a couple of months. Lisa would have to manage without her, besides, she had promised to call her occasionally.

The flight was on time and Sarah and Ava settled back into their seats for the long trip. Ava still had lots of questions for Sarah, some of which were, to her, more pressing than others.

She wanted to know more about Florence, what she was like as a young girl and a teenager. What their relationship was like, and then she wanted to hear all about the wedding between Florence and William. The cabin crew brought around a drinks trolley, Sarah opted for black tea with lemon but Ava thought she would have something stronger, she was hoping that she would sleep, at least for some of the journey. She had a gin and tonic, a double.

Sarah recounted tales of childhood, the usual illnesses and details of their friends. What games they played and how they spent Thanksgiving and Christmas. It sounded like the Fisher family was a normal Canadian family that enjoyed the pleasures of life. Not grand but not poor either. Sarah described the bedroom the two young girls shared, the posters that they stuck to the walls with tape, which annoyed their father a little. The music they listened to and the clothes they wore. It seemed like they got on really well.

Ava already knew how William and Florence had met. Sarah recounted the proposal, which by all accounts was not particularly romantic. They had been dating a while when William, out of the blue, just said, 'Shall we do it then, get married?' Sarah said that Florence was taken aback, she had thought that he would at least have got down on one knee, but no. They were sitting in the front of his car eating fish and chips! This story was one that the family would laugh about and tease William for his lack of romance. But that hadn't mattered, they had a wonderful marriage, albeit a short one.

Sarah had been their bridesmaid, she hadn't really liked the dress but Florence had chosen it and she wore it and tried not to look too glum. It was too childlike for her but she accepted it and was still happy to be beside her sister on her big day. It was a little church that was made of grey stone, the front of which was surrounded by a low stone wall. There was a path leading up to a small arched doorway with big wooden doors, adorned with decorative black metal studs. Sarah said Florence looked beautiful—she had photographs back home in Gozo that she would show to Ava on their return.

"I'd like that very much." Ava was trying her best to picture the church and the scene that Sarah had painted for her, even down to the proposal in the front of William's car. That bit made her smile.

Sarah told her that even after William had died, Florence returned time and again to Malta. She would visit Mellieħa Bay every evening and would be heard calling out for Alison. Sarah had gone with her many times and she would hold her sister close and let the tears flow as her words floated away, out to sea.

"I found a carving the other day, in the rocks at the top of the beach."

"Ah, I remember that. One day, Florence had gone to the beach whilst I was out shopping. She seemed to be a long time so I went to find her. She had taken a hammer and chisel from my husband's toolbox, and was carving out your name—well, carving out the name 'Alison'. She was crying when I found her. I added a heart to the end, it was always Florence's hope that one day you would see it and know that you were loved."

That was enough for now, Ava told Sarah she wanted to sleep. She put on an eye-mask and laid her head against the head rest. She did sleep eventually, dreaming of the little church where her parents had married. In the dream she was there, wearing a little yellow and red check dress. It had white buttons down the front and she was proudly holding a tiny bag in front of her. She was sitting on the small stone wall, watching the wedding guests go by and the wedding ceremony taking place around her. It was a good dream.

A while later, Ava was jolted awake by turbulence. It didn't last long but that was all the sleep she would get for the rest of the flight. The two ladies sat back and flicked through the films that were on offer. Sarah opted for a nineteenth century drama but Ava needed something funny and found a comedy, Mr Bean. She had never seen such a silly film before but it made her laugh and that was what she needed right now.

Taking a taxi from the airport, they went to a hotel only a few minutes away, to spend the night before heading to Quebec. That meant another flight and they wanted to rest a little beforehand. The hotel Sarah had booked was quite stunning. It had a glass core which was open to the sky and what appeared to be a tropical garden at the base. A dramatic waterfall fell into a deep pool of waterlilies and it was surrounded by magnificent plants which you would not expect to see in this climate. The thick pile carpet that covered the lobby floor seemed to give a little beneath their feet—this was luxury that Ava was not accustomed to.

"This night is at my expense," Sarah insisted. "I thought we deserved a little treat after such a long flight. But we are sharing a room, I hope that is okay with you?"

"I wouldn't want it any other way," Ava reassured her.

Long into the night, they chatted more about their lives as they were now—well, as they were before all this happened. Ava learnt more about Benny. She had not yet visited his café and had assured him, that she would do just that, once they returned from their trip.

Ava told Sarah about the regular customers that visited the café each day, the mechanics, and how they had exactly the same order of drinks and breakfast every day of the week. Then there was Ġorġ and his big green tea mug. How he would sit outside most days with his bag of fresh fish beside him. He too, would have the same breakfast. Ava went on to explain how Ricco came into her life, and how she couldn't imagine life without him.

"He seems to know when I'm sad—he will appear from wherever he had been soaking up the sun and wriggle his way onto my lap. Usually turning in circles and sometimes pummelling his paws into my lap, before making himself comfortable. I love him dearly."

Both ladies were content to talk about these things, leaving the family to one side, just for now.

They woke to the sound of the telephone in the room ringing out quite loudly. Ava leapt out of bed in fright, but Sarah reassured her that she had asked for an alarm call, so that they would have time for breakfast before heading back to the airport, and their onward journey to Quebec. The breakfast didn't disappoint and

Ava hungrily tucked into scrambled eggs and toast, followed by a bowl of fresh fruit and yogurt. Sarah was feeling a little tired still and just opted for an espresso coffee and a plate of cold ham and cheese. After checking out, they made their way to the airport again and then took their short flight to Quebec.

It was only when they were onboard, and the announcements were made in both English and French, Ava recalled that Quebec was part of the French speaking area of Canada. This reminded her of how Samuel was part French and part Cayuga. She had researched the latter part a little before they left Malta. It was interesting to find that this was a First Nation Tribe that still existed today in parts of Canada—although it originated in the area that today, is New York state, before they were forced to disperse. The name means 'People of the Great Swamp, or Great Lake' and it was made up of several clans, all of which had an animal as their figurehead. They originally lived in longhouses with in excess of fifty people in each one. Ava was fascinated and really hoped that she could learn more about her ancestors during the trip.

It was only much later in the day, once they had unpacked in the Hotel Florence, that Ava told Sarah how she wanted to find out more about Samuel Hensley and the foundation he had left behind.

"That sounds fascinating," Sarah said. "Any idea how we start?"

"Not really, but I'm going to call Mark and see if he can help us." Ava had already pre-empted this with an email to him before they left. She was hoping that he would have found out some more information on Samuel before they met up with him in a week or so. "I really want to emulate him, back home in Malta. This is how I want to use part of the money." Ava realised that she was making decisions about spending the money without checking with Sarah first. "That's if you don't mind?" she added.

"I've told you, it is yours to spend." Sarah was adamant that all the money should go to Ava.

"Well, I am going to give you a large portion of it. I have other plans for some of the rest, but I want you and Benny to have a comfortable life, spend it how you will, but please accept it. I couldn't bear it if you refused."

"On one condition."

"Name it."

"That it is used to buy out Benny's café, make his life a little easier and you can be the silent partner. Then he won't need to worry so much about running the café and can relax more. So, in essence, it is still yours, but Benny will run it. Oh, one more thing, I will leave everything in my will to you." Sarah paused. "Those are my terms."

"Phew, it sounds to me like you had this all worked out."

"I have, I knew you had talked about sharing the money with me. But I really feel that it is yours however, this will make life easier for us, and in the end, it will all come back to you anyway. Agreed?"

Ava laughed. "Agreed," she said.

Ava realised that she would then have two café businesses in her ownership. She would do the same with that one, as she had planned with Indri—bring in extra staff to take the pressure off Benny; make sure that everyone was paid a good wage and made to feel valued. She had never understood why a business would try and obtain the best employees possible for their work and yet, hold back when it came to paying them. Surely, treat your staff with respect and pay them well, and you will receive loyalty by the bucketful in return.

It seemed obvious to Ava, but she knew from past experience that this was not the norm. This was how William had run his business and Ava would make sure that she followed in his footsteps.

That night, Ava and Sarah set off to find a small restaurant tucked into a corner of a square, not far from the hotel. They first passed by an amazing wall mural that seemed to depict the Old Town of Quebec City. They stared at it for quite some time, each time they looked, they saw something new. There were two nuns looking out of a top window, a couple embracing on a bridge and a small dog, seemingly alone, walking under the old stone bridge going into the city. It was magnificent.

They walked towards a small church that stood centred in the square ahead of them. There was a restaurant set to the right-hand side. It had a few tables outside, but Florence had definitely described one, tucked into a corner, with a small wooden deck out the front. Sarah had turned around before Ava. She reached out to grab Ava's hand and steady herself. There it was. Just as Florence had described. Small tables sat neatly on the decking. There were blankets over the back of the chairs and simple candles in the top of wine bottles on each table, the wax gently flowing like semi-molten lava over the top of the previous evening's cascade. You could pick out the different colour candles that had been used, and the bottles were embraced by a rainbow of wax, adorning their shoulders like a magnificent cape. This had to be the one.

Ava and Sarah took a small table inside the restaurant. The walls were whitewashed over the stone construction and just like outside, small wooden tables sat with a varied selection of chairs around them. They too, had candles sitting in wine bottles and Ava decided that she would replicate this back in Malta. The wine bottles would be re-used and she loved the way the layers of the wax seemed to add their own story to the ambience. No wonder Florence loved this place.

The food was delicious and made even more special to Ava, knowing her parents could have sat at this same table. As though to make a connection, she touched the wall beside her, stroked the table in front of her and gazed all around, wanting to make certain that her eyes rested on the same places as Florence and William had done all those years ago. The food was exquisite too. Just as she hoped to do with her cafés, nothing too fancy, simple food cooked well and served with local wine. She made a mental note to research more about Maltese wine on her return. It was an evening to remember. Tonight, she sat back and enjoyed Sarah's company, tomorrow she decided, she wanted to know more about how Florence had died. She was ready.

They were staying at the Hotel Florence for a couple more nights. Ava wanted to explore more of the old town and to talk to the staff to see if anyone had worked there long enough to remember William. It was asking a lot seeing that he had passed away over thirty-two years ago. Not surprisingly there wasn't anyone who had, but they all knew of him and his legacy. He had made provision that all the staff employed would be valued. She noticed a document that was framed and proudly displayed on the wall in Reception, signed by her father. It was written in beautiful calligraphy and Ava was enthralled. It merely read:

Employees who feel valued are more productive and always do more than what is expected.

I promise to make sure that all my employees feel valued.

William Hensley

Ava's eyes filled to the brim with tears which overflowed onto her cheeks. The lady behind Reception was concerned.

"William Hensley was my father—sadly, I never knew him."

"Wait here." The receptionist disappeared and came back with two other colleagues. One of them held a package under his arm and another held out a photograph frame. "These are for you. We have kept them safe for a long time. We didn't think we would ever get to meet you. Are you really Alison Hensley?"

Ava paused, looked up at the words on the wall in front of her and felt proud. "I am."

"Then please accept these, with love from all of us who work here. If it wasn't for your father, we would not feel so valued. Thank you."

Ava didn't know what to say. The photograph was of William and Florence cutting a ribbon outside the doors to the hotel, smiling proudly with the staff standing around them. The young man who had given it to her explained that this was the day that the name changed to the Hotel Florence. The package, so carefully wrapped with green and white string, had her name in beautiful handwriting, 'Miss Alison Hensley. To be kept in hope that one day, she learns about her family and visits this hotel.' Inside was the same document as the one hanging on the wall. Framed in a simple black frame, but this one appeared to be the original, she could see the strokes of the ink pen as it had formed the words on the page. This meant so much to her, she would treasure it for life.

The man who had held the package approached her next. He held out another document. It had been folded carefully and closed with a wax seal. Ava opened it gently, read it slowly, then read it twice more.

"This says that this hotel is held in trust for me. I own this hotel?"

"Yes, that is right. I am the general manager. It is owned by the William Hensley Foundation. William set up a trust that the ownership would pass to you one day; until then, it remains under the management of his foundation. If ever you came forward then the ownership documents would pass to you. If after one hundred years from 29 April 1987, you are not identified, then it remains part of the foundation."

Ava hadn't realised that Sarah had appeared at her side. She stood quietly listening to what was being said.

"I wonder why that date?" Ava was confused.

"Your birthdate," Sarah spoke and as she did, Ava turned to face her.

"But my birthday is in June, 25 June 1987."

"Alison Hensley was born on 29 April 1987."

"Crikey! Not only a different name to learn, but a different birthday too! This is so confusing."

"You could always have two!" Sarah laughed. "One for Alison and one for Ava!" Ava joined in the laughter.

Ava called Mark a little while later to see if he knew anything about the hotel and how she was the owner. It appeared that this hotel had not been passed to Florence on William's death. All of the others had, but as this was part of the William Hensley Foundation, then it hadn't formed part of Florence's estate. It was only her estate that he had worked on. She asked Mark to recommend a lawyer to go through the paperwork with her and she also wanted to speak to the William Hensley Foundation. She wanted to know more about them.

Chapter Thirty-Four

Ava and Sarah left the Hotel Florence having arranged for the framed document to be shipped to Indri. It was to go by a special service that insured valuable items for the journey. However, to Ava, it was priceless. They reassured her that it would arrive in less than a week and would be taken by a courier to the address in Malta. Ava phoned Indri and explained that he should expect a package for her and to keep it safe. She would explain about it upon her return.

They had to take two flights but they were soon landing in Calgary and Mark met them out at the front of the airport, ready to take them to their chosen hotel in Banff. Ava's jaw hit the floor when they approached the outskirts—the most beautiful town, framed by mountains and delicately topped with snow despite the temperature being in the high twenties. He promised to give them a guided tour the next day, but for now, he took them straight to their hotel, offloaded their luggage and left them to enjoy their evening. The hotel was stunning. This time it was not one that belonged to the William Hensley Foundation, for which Ava was relieved. It was enormous, high above the town with stunning views both towards the mountains and down to the town of Banff below.

Ava and Sarah's room had a magnificent view and the next morning, Sarah sat in the window, taking in the vista, when Ava awoke.

"Have you been awake long?"

"A while, I couldn't sleep. I was so excited to tell Benny of your proposal so went down to the lobby and called him. He is already deciding on who he would like to help him in the café and, with your permission, he will start to call them to talk about his ideas."

"No permissions needed, the café is his to run and manage as he sees fit. Just make sure he understands that I want all staff recompensed properly, no minimum wages, that is my only insistence."

"Yes, I explained that to him. He couldn't believe our fortune in finding you and the stress lifted from his voice as we spoke. Ava, you are a true inspiration, I'm so proud to be your aunt."

Ava and Sarah went down to the dining room for breakfast. It was a sumptuous room with grand round tables covered in pristine white tablecloths. They were shown to a window overlooking the valley beneath them. The sun shone through the window and despite the outlying snow, they couldn't get over the warmth. It was almost like being back home in Malta. Following a delicious breakfast of Eggs Benedict for Sarah and more modest yogurt, fruit and pastries for Ava, they went to the lobby to wait for Mark.

It was a little after nine am when Mark called to say he was on his way. He had arranged for a few days holiday from work so would be able to show them around the area as well as to help Ava with contacting the William Hensley Foundation. Ava and Sarah ordered coffees for them all and sat waiting for Mark in the lobby area. It had a beautiful open fireplace, surrounded by leather armchairs more usually found in a 'Gentleman's Club'. The carpet was almost oriental in design and the room was flanked with rich wooden panelling. It was a stunning location and an equally stunning hotel. The coffee arrived just a few moments before Mark walked into the hotel lobby. He waved towards them then spoke briefly to the man at the reception desk before joining them.

"Ladies," Mark had barely sat down before he began, "are you up for a little adventure this morning?"

Ava looked at Sarah, who was mid-slurp with her coffee.

"I'm game if you are, Sarah? Though I'd love to know what kind of adventure you are talking about before I fully commit."

Sarah was already nodding, she had seen some leaflets in the reception area earlier and had a good idea what Mark was intending. She also knew that Ava had decided that she wanted a bit more information on why Florence had died, and despite feeling a certain amount of trepidation as to what she believed Mark was going to suggest, she readily agreed. Any distraction to put off the conversation was good for her.

"Well, despite the magnificent views of Banff and the Rocky Mountains which you have from here, just a quick walk up the hill and we can take a gondola ride even further up the mountains and from there, I can assure you, the view will take your breath away."

From where, she did not know, but Ava felt a surge of bravery that was not usual for her. "Absolutely! Sarah?"

"Let's do it!" Sarah added.

"Before we go, I have news about the William Hensley Foundation. We have a video call booked with the managing director for later this afternoon. His name is Trevor, Trevor Barnes. He has held the position since William passed. Trevor was just a young man at that time, but William apparently saw great potential within him and having left instructions for him to have the appropriate and necessary training. He took over from William and has run the foundation ever since. He has been a great asset and has managed not only the properties that are still part of the foundation but the various monies and investments that it also holds.

"Since taking over, when the value of the foundation was approximately nineteen million Canadian dollars, it is now worth a staggering sixty-eight million Canadian dollars today! It may have been thirty-three years in the making but Trevor has not only successfully driven the business forward, but he has helped hundreds of people start new businesses, get training and for some, to become millionaires in their own right. Many of these people now help fund the foundation with the same work ethic and sense of philanthropy and altruism that has been handed down since your great-great-great-grandfather, Samuel Hensley, began doing the same thing all those years ago."

"I can't wait to talk to him, thank you, Mark, that is amazing. I have decided that I will continue in the same vein with the money which my parents have left me. I will set up trusts over here in Canada but also back home in Malta, to make sure that the money is used to the same end as William, and Samuel before him, had intended. I will honour the legacy of my ancestors."

"Ah, talking of which, we have a meeting arranged for next Monday with the head of the Cayuga. So, we must think carefully about an appropriate gift."

"Is it crass to offer part of the inheritance? Or set in place trusts in the same way which I want to set up in Malta, to help their members in business or training, that kind of thing?"

"That is very generous, Ava, if that is what you would like to do, I will call ahead and make certain that this does not cause offence, but perhaps also, we could take something personal along too. I know it is cheeky to ask but would you make prinjolata to take to the meeting? You are most welcome to use my kitchen."

"Excellent idea." Ava raised her coffee cup in salute and Mark and Sarah followed suit. "To the Hensley Legacy!"

With that, Mark stood up.

"This deserves a proper toast," he raised his coffee cup once more, Ava and Sarah stood also, and once more they toasted.

"The Hensley Legacy!" they said in unison.

The gondola ride was truly magnificent, just as Mark had promised. The glass capsules were hung like Christmas lights, draped up the mountain side as far as you could see. Ava's knees buckled slightly as they entered the building ready to board their particular gondola. Mark faced inwards towards the mountain, assuring them both that the view looking outwards would take their breath away, and with it, any fear they may have of being so high up above the ground. The gondola drifted gently over the tops of exceptionally tall trees that clung to the side of the mountain, appearing like miniature nursery saplings below them. Sarah and Ava were in awe and gasped in delight at the views beneath.

On landing at the top, they opted to go to the fourth level of the mountain building that not only hosted a restaurant with stunning views, but in addition a linked pathway which would take you even higher should you so wish. The sun was now high in the sky and was beating down an amazing twenty-six degrees Celsius despite a thick carpet of snow all around them. They found some seats that overlooked the view and Mark took their photographs with a backdrop of the stunning Rocky Mountains. This was one adventure Ava would never have dreamt of, but one she would commit to memory for the rest of her life.

Taking the gondola back down, Ava remembered that she wanted to ask Sarah about her mother. Sarah was looking out of the gondola, a wistful look on her face.

"Mark? Sarah? Will you tell me what happened to my mother?"

The question surprised both of them, they were just beginning their descent and neither had expected the question at this time. Mark looked over to Sarah and nodded to her, indicating that he would take over this difficult part of the conversation. He explained how Florence had struggled with her mental health since she and William had lost Alison that fateful day. Not surprisingly she was racked with sadness, and depression took hold of her soul. When William could take no more, Florence was burdened with carrying the loss of her husband too. He explained how she had needed to go into special mental health facilities from time to time, and then, on that last night, she had lost her life in a most tragic accident.

Ava sat silently for the rest of the journey back down the mountain. She had experienced such a high at the top, overlooking an amazing view and now she felt that stone hit the bottom of her stomach once more. The stone which had done the very same, all those weeks ago, when she first began to learn of her true ancestry. They left the gondola building and walked back to the hotel, still in silence, neither Mark nor Sarah feeling it appropriate to speak. Back inside the lobby, Ava stopped, turned to face Mark and he could see how her eyes were brim-full of tears.

"The facility, where Florence was staying before she died," Ava began, "can I visit?"

"I'll make enquiries." Mark left it at that, no more words were needed.

Ava made her excuses and went for a lie-down in their room. This was so much more for her to take in, she felt like she would either burst or melt and she knew not which.

Ava didn't resurface from their room until well after lunch. She hadn't been hungry and after waking had decided to take a long bath and allow the warm bubbly water to envelop her in a womb-like hug. Sarah had taken a bus ride down into Banff and had found an upstairs bar with views over the street below. She too had not felt hungry but after an initial coffee, she threw caution to the wind with a large glass of Canadian Lakeview Cellars, Viognier 2020. She was no wine connoisseur but the taste reminded her of peaches and apricots with a refreshing citric hit of lemon and lime. It was truly delicious and although very expensive, she could understand why it commanded such a high price.

Walking towards the bus stop, Sarah went into a small tourist shop to choose something small and quirky to take back home for Benny. She settled on a beer bottle opener fashioned into a bear. She had yet to see one on their travels but had hoped to encounter the elusive animal and hopefully photograph the same. Back in the hotel, Sarah sat in one of the large leather arm chairs, ordered a pot of coffee and was about to start drinking it when Ava appeared.

"Hi."

"Hey, did you manage to rest?"

"Sort of, I took a bath as well. I feel drained though. Is there enough in that pot for me too?" Sarah asked for a second cup and the two ladies had almost finished the pot when Mark appeared with his laptop.

"I've arranged for us to use a small side room to have our chat with Trevor. Are you ready now or would you like some more time?"

Ava stood and Sarah followed suit. They walked behind Mark as he headed down a small set of stairs and on into a meeting room which really was far too large for their needs. Nonetheless, it was flawless. It held stunning views over the mountains, there was a high gloss table surrounded by large leather chairs and places set for each of them, small green glass bottles of water with crystal glasses and a sumptuous looking basket of fruit for them to share. Mark took out his laptop, connected it to a nearby power source and clicked on his Skype app to contact Trevor. Ava opened up a bottle of water and without realising what she was doing, took a small bunch of grapes and began to nibble on them. Sarah sat to Mark's left hand side and Ava to his right. He made the connection and Trevor's image appeared on the screen in front of them.

"Hey Mark, great to see you again."

"Hi Trevor, let me introduce you to Ava, William Hensley's daughter, and to Sarah, his sister-in-law."

Formal greetings were made, but they soon relaxed into a more informal chat about their trip so far. Ava listened intently as Trevor explained how the foundation worked today and how it was continuing in the footsteps of William's vision to help finance, educate and train young people or those in need of development. He described one particular young person who only recently had been referred to the foundation. A girl in her late twenties who had always held a penchant for photography but had not been able to forge a career path for herself within the field. Her black and white images were some to behold, and Trevor had arranged for a local gallery to display her artwork. She had received multiple offers for her photographs and with it, recognition for her skills as a photographer. On this occasion, the amount of funding had been small but the result had been great, with the girl receiving a nomination for a wildlife photography award.

Ava explained how she had already started to use her inheritance to fund two cafés back home on Malta and how she intended to set up a similar facility as the foundation, for the young people there. But she also took the opportunity to quiz Trevor about her father. She knew that he had known him, albeit briefly, but she wanted to glean as much information on him as she could. She drank in his description of William, his work ethics, his likes and dislikes, as well as how he would hold a large banquet each year for everyone within the foundation and those that it had helped. This, Ava decided, she would replicate back home. It might start small with only a handful of guests, but she knew in her heart that this would just be the start of something much grander.

They made their farewells to Trevor with a promise to invite him to Malta soon to see how the Hensley Legacy developed. In turn, Trevor would be available to Ava for help and advice. It was, in a small way, a simple link to her father by way of his work. Ava felt a warm glow of pride.

Chapter Thirty-Five

Ava and Sarah took the next few days to truly unwind and enjoy all the facilities of the spa within the hotel. Several times they took the local bus into town and would wander amongst the gift shops and marvel at the scenery around. They took an evening wildlife safari tour and were lucky enough to spot an elk quietly wandering across a clearing, plus a couple of grazing bighorn sheep but sadly they didn't see any bears. They drank local wine, enjoyed some wonderful food and bonded over stories of Florence and William. There was laughter and there were tears, they were getting to know each other as friends as well as aunt and niece.

Mark collected them on Monday morning for their onward journey to meet up with one of the Cayuga nation tribal council, Rodney Cuttingtree. The Cayuga homeland lies in the Finger Lakes region along Cayuga Lake and Mark had been able to arrange for Ava and Sarah to meet him at a harbour front hotel. A few years ago, Mark had located Rodney as a partial heir and he was looking forward to meeting him again. The previous day, Ava had prepared a prinjolata to take to the meeting and had laid it upon an intricately carved cedar platter. Mark had sourced the platter explaining that cedar is one of the sacred "medicines" or symbols of earth, the others being sage, tobacco and sweetgrass, and how this was a polite way to acknowledge the Cayuga culture. He also helped them to attempt a greeting in Cayuga. Ava had never mastered more than a few basic greetings in Maltese having always struggled with languages but Sarah was able to speak Maltese fluently and with Mark's help, they were able to pronounce the greeting with confidence.

Ava was quite nervous of the meeting and although Mark had spoken with Rodney on the telephone and explained the reason for their visit, Ava was acutely aware of the delicate nature of respect that was due to all First Nations and did not want to embarrass or offend in any way. The hotel had a stunning view over the harbour, the small room which he had arranged for the meeting faced the waterfront. They arrived with an hour or more to spare before the meeting. Ava had laid the prinjolata on a table in the centre of the room and Mark requested glasses of iced water for them all. Ava sat in a window seat and fidgeted with her hands, she wanted to honour her ancestors with this meeting and her nerves were frayed. The door opened and a tall thick set man entered, he beamed at them all before approaching Mark with a held out hand.

"We come with respect for this land that we are on today, and for the people who have, and do reside here." Mark took Rodney's offered hand in his as he spoke.

Ava and Sarah gave their best attempt at the native greeting.

Rodney smiled warmly and then let out a small chuckle, he was grateful that they had tried but totally understood how difficult it was to pronounce his mother tongue. They all sat overlooking the harbour and after Mark made the introductions, they fell into an amiable chatter about the beautiful surroundings.

Ava had printed a copy of the family tree which Mark had drawn up for her and she proudly showed Rodney her connection to the tribe and to Samuel Hensley.

"Well, that makes you Cayuga too." Rodney held her hand in his and patted the back gently. "I see that you are also part Cree which is the same as my own mother. So, our heritage is not dissimilar."

"Are you aware of the Hensley Legacy?"

"Mark gave me the information during our telephone call last week and I have managed to find out about your ancestor. However, it is also William that I hoped to talk with you about as he was an important man in my brother's young life and I wish to give my thanks to you, as his daughter, for the help and opportunities which William opened up for him. Before meeting William, my brother was on a wrong path. He had succumbed to alcohol and the family were concerned for his well-being. He was drinking heavily and passed many hours in bars and hotels spending every cent he had earned."

Ava had had no idea that the connection to Rodney would be so close and she looked across at Mark for reassurance that this was all real. Mark smiled and inclined his head. He had been amazed himself when he had spoken to him about their visit but had decided to let Ava hear about it directly from Rodney.

"It was one of his worst days—he had been drinking for several hours in one of the hotels owned by William. My brother was never aggressive or abusive with his drinking but it was costing him his livelihood and the more it cost him, the more depressed he became. He would work as a labourer for a low wage and spend it all on alcohol. William approached him on this day, sat beside him and talked to him for hours. By the end of the conversation, William had gained his trust and arranged for my brother to work for him the next day instead. He gave him a bed for the night and the next morning a free breakfast too.

"My brother was very grateful for the food and room to sleep and he worked extremely hard the next day, working for the builders within the hotel who were constructing a large extension to the rear of the property. William paid him well for his work and gave him a hearty meal. My brother did not stop drinking at that point—that would have been impossible for him—but the food which William gave him, absorbed some of the alcohol, and the time he took over the meal meant there was less drinking time. This continued for several weeks, William fed him and gave him a bed each night; he paid him well which encouraged my brother to work hard in return. It began to show after a month or two that he was not drinking so much, he was becoming sociable with his workmates and was growing in confidence.

"William arranged for training on different aspects of building work and my brother showed a definite flair for plumbing. This was encouraged by William and before long, he had acquired enough experience and training to set up his own plumbing business. The day he began working for himself, he told me and the family that he had stopped drinking completely and to this day he has not fallen for the liquor again. My gratitude to your father goes beyond words Ava. My family and I owe the life of my brother solely to him, and you are forever in the hearts of the Cayuga, in name and with affection."

"I don't know what to say." Ava was overwhelmed by the story she had just heard but it reinforced the feelings of love that she now had for her father, and for that she was extremely pleased. "I may not have known my father in life, but his honour and his work ethic will be something I hold dear and will do my utmost to replicate it by using the money he has left me."

Rodney stood to embrace Ava; the gratitude he felt was so sincere and Ava would take this from him and pass it forward. They tucked into the prinjolata, with Ava promising to send the recipe to Rodney's wife, and he gratefully accepted the cedar platter too. This had been a wonderful meeting for both parties and one which neither would ever forget.

Ava proposed her idea of continuing in her father's footsteps by funding training for young members of the Cayuga, to help them on their way in employment and within life. To do this, she would set up a trust for the Cayuga people and would ask the manager of the William Hensley Foundation, Trevor, to manage this on her behalf. Now it was Rodney's turn to be overwhelmed, he took Ava's hands within his own and clasped them tightly and closed his eyes in prayer.

"We have been given the duty to live in balance and harmony with each other and all living things. We bring our minds together as one as we give greetings and thanks to each other as people. We are all thankful to our Mother, the Earth, for she gives us all that we need for life."

Rodney then kissed the top of Ava's head before making his farewell to the group. Ava sank into a chair after he had left, shaking her head in disbelief from what she had learnt. She had a new path in life and where that would lead, she was not sure, but she was certain that she would try and make the Cayuga proud. They had each made promises to keep in touch and Ava had assured him that she would return soon, to spend more time with Rodney and his wife but also, hopefully, to meet up with his brother.

Chapter Thirty-Six

Ava and Sarah decided to take one last stop at Niagara Falls before they headed home. This time their trip was just about the two of them. Mark had gone back to work and Ava had accomplished all that she set out to do. She had met with her ancestorial roots, she had learnt more about the William Hensley Foundation and had visited the mental health facility where Florence had spent her last few months. She had set up a trust fund to support anyone in need of the facility but unable to pay the fees. It was a small way in which she could remain connected to the facility and also to her mother.

Her ashes had been interred in the beautiful gardens there, and Ava knelt before them, laying a hand on the soil and saying a goodbye to the mother she couldn't remember but one she would also never forget. She had learnt more about her parents and would honour, not only their legacy but also that of her forefathers. She was full of sadness for not knowing them in the physical sense but she would hopefully make them proud of the daughter they had brought into the world.

Ava and Sarah had taken a room overlooking the falls. The view was spectacular and they looked out at the thundering water as it plunged to the depths below. There were small boats which took tourists close to the falls and seemed to immerse them in a cloud of spray so intense that the boats almost disappeared to the naked eye. A day or two after their arrival, they were sitting enjoying breakfast in their room when the telephone interrupted their meal. Sarah stood to take the call but waved Ava over to take the handset from her. It was Lisa.

"I am to appear in court in two days' time. I thought you would like to know." Lisa's voice was quiet and subdued.

"Oh my." Ava sat down quickly onto the bed beside her. "I will try and get back to be there."

"That's not necessary, don't cut your trip short. I just want you to know, whatever happens to me, that I love you. I have always loved you."

Ava didn't respond.

"I hope to see you soon."

With that, the call ended, Lisa didn't give her any more chance to talk but Ava had already decided that she would do all she could to get back home and be in the courtroom to support her. She still had loving feelings for her, but they were definitely muddied now and that emotion was so difficult to admit to herself.

Ava and Sarah spent the day exploring more of Niagara whilst the reception at the hotel arranged for their return flights. There was a quietness between them since the phone call. Sarah knew why Ava wanted to return. Despite having a wonderful time, not only getting to know her niece more but also learning about the foundation and how Ava would mimic its ethics, she too was looking forward to returning home to Benny.

Their flight arrived a little after four in the afternoon. It was the earliest one available but Ava knew that Lisa would already be in the court room. She took a taxi straight there whilst Sarah waited at the airport for Benny to pick her up. Ava called Guzeppi on the way from the airport to see if she would still be allowed in.

"There is no need to rush, Ava," Guzeppi began, "Lisa has admitted her guilt. She has been charged with child abduction, attempting to pervert the course of justice and assisting an offender. For this alone, we are expecting she will serve quite a lengthy jail term. The judge is deliberating and will reconvene in an hour, but I imagine it will be in excess of eight years."

"Oh, that is awful! Poor Lisa."

Guzeppi waited on the front steps to the Courts of Justice building in Valletta for Ava to arrive. He had something else to talk to Ava about before they went inside.

"I want to find out where the real Ava's body is. Now that Lisa knows she will be convicted, I am hoping that she will give up this last bit of information."

"What will happen to her?"

"She will be taken to prison after sentencing. She has admitted her part in all of this and whilst, at the time of your abduction, she wasn't of sound mind, it has been decided that she will go to prison for these offences. Will you come with me to talk to her? I want to see if she will give us anything that will lead us to Ava."

"It's so weird hearing you talk about the real Ava and then refer to me in the same breath. But yes, if I am allowed, I will come with you."

Guzeppi and Ava were taken to the holding cells where Lisa was sitting on a bench, her feet up in front of her and her knees under her chin. The officer-in-charge opened the door and they went inside. Lisa looked up, only noticing Ava, and leapt to her feet.

"Oh, thank goodness you have come, I thought you weren't going to." Lisa reached out to embrace Ava. She wanted to hug her, hold her close, to turn back time before anyone knew of the deception. In the end it had all felt so real. She had never forgotten about her first born, but over time, the memories of her had morphed into a dreamlike state. This Ava, the one stood before her, had become one and the same as her real Ava.

"I've heard that you have admitted about the abduction." Ava was holding Lisa at arm's length, she wanted to look into her face, see her expression. "Just remember, you gave me a wonderful and loving home and for that, I am grateful. I cannot begin to understand the pain you caused my true parents, but I am told they wished that whoever had taken me would treat me with love and kindness. You did."

"Please forgive me, please forgive your father?"

"I don't know if that is within me as yet. I am only just beginning to discover the lives of my parents and who they were. But I don't hate you. I am saddened that this is happening but I am also glad that the truth has come out."

With that, Guzeppi stepped forward. "Lisa, it is important that we find out what happened to Ava. We know she died, but what happened to her body? There are no records to show her death."

Lisa looked shocked to hear him speak—she hadn't realised that he was in the room. She lowered her head and shook it violently from side to side.

"Ava deserves a real grave, not something makeshift, can you let me arrange that for her?" Guzeppi was using a softly-softly approach, trying to appeal to her maternal instinct.

Lisa lifted her face towards him, her eyes cold and staring. She had on a smart pencil skirt with a pinstripe blouse. Her face was becoming damp with sweat, she looked away and began to roll up her sleeves. Guzeppi thought she might faint again and requested a cup of cold water for her. Lisa said nothing. The water arrived and Ava handed her the cup; Lisa took it and gulped frantically.

"Would you tell me?" Ava spoke very softly, not because she didn't want Guzeppi to hear but because she wanted Lisa to feel comforted. "Let me do this for you, let me give Ava a proper resting place."

Lisa finished the water, handed the cup back to Ava and asked the officer to let them out of the cell. Guzeppi and Ava were taken back to the public area. They had tried their best but Lisa wasn't budging.

Ava spoke first, "I'll miss her garden, I loved being there and her olive trees were fabulous. She cared so much for all her plants, it was her happy place."

Guzeppi nodded in agreement, his mother had been the same. If not in the kitchen rustling up fresh bread or beautiful colourful salads, she could be found tending the plants and fruiting trees outside.

"What has happened to the house?"

"Nothing so far, but I would suggest you arrange for it to be boarded up if you don't mind. Unless you wish to live there whilst Lisa is interned."

"Gosh, no. I want to stay in my own place. I'm not sure I can go back. It doesn't feel right somehow."

Guzeppi received a tap on the shoulder from the prosecution barrister who said that the judge was returning. Lisa was refusing to leave her cell but the judge would pass sentence regardless of whether she was in the courtroom or not. Ava went into the courtroom with Guzeppi, sat beside him and gripped her own hands tightly in her lap. She looked across the room and noticed Reg was sitting in the public gallery. He gave her a half-hearted smile. Ava raised her hand to acknowledge him but lowered it quickly as the judge came into the room and everyone was asked to stand.

It took a few minutes—no longer—and the sentencing was over. Ava had held her breath and once he passed sentence, she gasped for air. Ten years. She was to be taken immediately to Corradino Prison at Paola.

Guzeppi held Ava by the elbow and escorted her out of the building. He wanted to make sure she was okay, but he also wanted to talk to her further. He had an idea and he wanted to share it with her. They crossed the street and walked towards the Cathedral. He knew of a small restaurant serving Maltese food just behind the imposing building. He found the restaurant and took a small table outside. The waiter came over and he ordered himself a coffee and a large brandy for Ava. She was visibly shaken and hadn't spoken since the judge had passed sentence. The drinks arrived and Guzeppi put the brandy glass into Ava's hand instructing her to drink. Ava lifted her gaze to meet his, took the glass and emptied its contents. Guzeppi signalled to the waiter for a second glass for her.

"Ava, will you have something to eat with me?"

Ava put the glass on the table and picked up the small dish of olives that the waiter had left alongside their drinks.

"The garden."

Guzeppi didn't quite catch what she had said and asked her to repeat.

"The garden, the rose garden. It's the only part of the garden where I was not allowed to go near."

Guzeppi had been thinking along the same lines. Not the rose garden specifically but following their conversation earlier about how Lisa had loved the garden, it had stirred a feeling inside him. If that was her happy place, then surely there was a chance that Ava was buried there.

"I was allowed to play in and around the olive trees." Ava popped an olive into her mouth, then another. "But only once did I venture near the rose garden. I would have been about five or six I suppose. I wanted to retrieve my ball that had landed there. I stood between the roses so carefully, I didn't want to get pricked by the thorns. Lisa ran down the garden, shouting at me to get off. I had made her so mad. I tried to tell her that I was just getting the ball and I hadn't damaged anything, but she wouldn't listen. I remember crying but she gave me no comfort." Ava looked down at the small dish of olives, now empty. Her stomach grumbled and she realised she hadn't eaten since the meal that had been served on the aeroplane earlier that day. "I'm hungry, shall we order?"

Guzeppi patted her hand in acknowledgement, he knew what his next day at work would now be. He would arrange for a forensics team to begin work at the Muscat house first thing, but for now he would make sure that Ava had a good meal inside her, take her back to Mellieħa and then tomorrow he hoped this sorry story would have a proper ending.

Chapter Thirty-Seven

Ava was late back to her flat but she had called Marie from Canada to warn her that she was returning. It would be great to sleep in her own bed once more. As wonderful as it had been to spend the time in Canada, there was nothing quite like returning to your own bed again. Marie had been happy to hear from her. The job at the café was working out great and she had already found herself a place to live nearby. She had promised to flat-sit for Ava so was waiting for her return before moving out. Marie went out and made sure that there was food in the fridge, fresh flowers on the table and had arranged for Jack to deliver Ricco back before Ava returned. It would be a lovely surprise for her. It was the least she could do—she felt she owed Ava so much for everything she had done for her.

Ava turned the key in the door and was met by Ricco twisting himself around her legs and purring contentedly. She bent down, picked him up and took him to the couch where she flopped down with exhaustion. Nuzzling into her neck, he purred once more before curling up in her lap. It was as though she had never left. She fell asleep moments later. Ava woke a little before four am, her neck was aching badly from the way she had fallen asleep. She padded over to the bed, undressed and climbed into it. The sheets smelt freshly laundered and she lifted them to her face and inhaled. Once again, it was a matter of moments before she drifted back into a deep sleep. Ricco had followed her and curled into a ball between her legs.

The sun came streaming through the window and roused her from her sleep a little after nine. She couldn't believe how late she had slept, but she had definitely needed it. Throwing back the covers, she went for a shower, made Ricco some breakfast, dressed in her denim shorts with a white vest top and headed across the road. Ġorġ had been and gone—the telltale being the large green mug still sitting on the table outside. Ava picked it up and headed inside to the kitchen. She could hear conversation before she got there, she knocked on the door frame and waited for Indri and Marie to notice her arrival.

Indri stopped washing plates and embraced her with his wet hands dripping down her back. "Marie said you were back, how are you doing? How was Canada? What did you learn?"

"Oh wow! One question at a time please." Ava laughed.

The café was quiet, the midday rush hadn't begun so Ava and Indri took a coffee outside to the beach. Marie was happily busying herself inside and said she would call if she needed help. Ava told him, as succinctly as she could, all about her trip, starting with the hotel in Quebec City. Indri had got the parcel and he fetched it for her to open. True to their word, the frame had arrived in perfect condition. Ava explained to Indri about the hotel and how she was the owner. That was just the start. They sat there for over an hour whilst Ava regaled him with more details.

In turn, Indri explained how the new regime of evening meals were working out; how Christopher was gaining a fabulous reputation and that they were booked up weeks in advance. He explained how Sofia and Marie worked so hard and that the takings had already exceeded their expectations. Ava was thrilled to hear the news. Indri had cleared the upstairs room above the café and had arranged for some furniture to be delivered in preparation for Ava's new workspace. On one hand, she wanted to stay waiting tables and working in the kitchen with Indri, but she was not needed there now. However, just knowing that she was going to be upstairs was all she needed to feel heartened.

Shortly after lunch, Sarah called. Word had spread fast about Lisa's sentence and she wanted to see how Ava was coping. They chatted a while with Ava filling Sarah in on how they had tried to get Lisa to tell them where her child had been buried. She didn't elaborate on her theory; Guzeppi said he would call if there was news. Ava was invited to visit at the weekend and would also go to see Benny at the restaurant and meet his new team. It was all beginning to work nicely. Ava had decided that she wanted some help in the office, not necessarily to work alongside her in the building but to assist her in administering the work.

She offered the role to Sarah who leapt at the chance. Sarah would work from home, they could Skype if they needed to do so but they both knew they would see plenty of each other from this point forward. They may have spent the last few weeks together, but they had thirty-three years to catch up on.

Finding Ava

Guzeppi had called Reg first thing. Well, strictly speaking, it was after he had arranged for the forensic team to go to the Muscat residence and start checking the garden for the remains of Ava Muscat. Reg had not been surprised at the sentence which Lisa had received but was interested to hear Guzeppi's gut feeling about locating the child.

"Any chance I could be an observer?" Reg enquired. "I'll keep in the background."

"Sure, after all, you got us this far, you and that heir hunter from Canada." Guzeppi agreed to meet Reg out at the front of the police station just before midday. There was no news from Gozo as yet, so he didn't see the need to rush there. They would get lunch on the way and enjoy the calm before, what he felt, was yet another inevitable storm.

The hands on Reg's watch just ticked over to one minute after twelve when Guzeppi appeared. He climbed into the car and they set off for the ferry. Then, just as Mark and Reg had done previously, the two men headed for Victoria and The Grapes. Reg recommended the bolognaise ragu and the two men tucked in with gusto. The warm midday sun had caused them to take a table inside to stay cool and it was only just as they were finishing their meal that Guzeppi realised that he didn't have any phone signal. He stepped outside and his phone pinged immediately.

"We have found a body." The voice on the other end of the phone line told him when he called back. "How soon can you get here?"

"I'm on my way now."

Reg had settled the bill and the two men set off sharpish for the Muscat house. They pulled up outside amidst several vehicles. There was a police car, two small vans and, what Guzeppi guessed to be, a mortuary transport vehicle. The back garden was a sea of people and it took a few minutes for Guzeppi to locate the man in charge. There were three police officers, two with spades and another with a small trowel standing around a large hole. The roses had been uprooted and moved to one side.

"So, you have found her then?" Guzeppi stepped forward and he peered down the hole.

There was what appeared to be a pink blanket showing at the bottom. It was mostly rotted away but you could clearly see that it was once wrapped around the body. At one end, there was the top of a skull—a very small skull.

"We are just going to erect a canopy over the area. Whilst we don't think we will be affected by the weather, we have already had to move along a couple of onlookers hoping to catch a glimpse of what we are doing."

"Mind your backs!"

Two policemen came through and began to erect the shelter. Guzeppi and the others stood back and waited. Just then, his phone rang and Guzeppi moved further back up the garden to take the call.

"Hi, it's Ava, is there any news?"

Guzeppi told her that they had found skeletal remains but they were taking the process very slowly. They wanted to make sure they kept it as intact as possible and to do this, they would dig further around the area and gently tease away the soil.

"Can I come over? I don't know if I am allowed, or do you think that is too gruesome of me?"

"Of course, after all, this is a significant occasion. And as the only kind of family that Lisa has, we would ask that you make the arrangements for the child to be properly cared for."

"I'm so pleased you said that, as I'm already at the ferry terminal and about to head over."

Guzeppi finished the call and asked Reg to wait out at the front of the property for Ava to arrive. In the meantime, he could make himself useful and pour some cold water for the team. Reg went inside the kitchen. The doors had been unlocked when they arrived and Guzeppi had made a mental note to ensure that the building was secure before they left later that day.

It was a little over an hour before Ava arrived and, dutifully, Reg was waiting out at the front for her. They walked around the side of the building and headed to the shade of the gazebo. The child's remains were being gently scraped free of the soil. Ava and Reg watched as small amounts were carefully lifted and deposited to one side of the hole. The hole must have been a metre-deep at least as there was now a man, from the forensics team, only showing above hip height each time that he stood up.

A large black sheet of plastic was laid on the floor by the hole and, firstly, parts of the pink blanket were laid upon it. Then, in total silence, a tiny complete skeleton was lifted from its hiding place. Ava stood to allow herself a better view but there were so many people standing around, she only got the briefest of glances. Without realising, she had taken Reg's hand and he was gently squeezing it for reassurance. They stood and waited as the team began to gently fold over the plastic, covering up the perfectly laid out bones of the child. Ava felt a sense of relief flood over her, she sank back down onto the seat beneath her and a single tear escaped her eye.

The officer in the hole began to lift himself out when part of the soil gave way and he stumbled backwards. His superior officer let out an exasperated groan and offered him a hand to help him out.

"Oh, Christ Almighty!"

Everyone turned to see the officer had dropped his hand, leaving the man still standing in the hole, and had leapt down himself. He took the trowel from the hand of the other man and began to scrape at the soil. Gently, he scraped and teased away at the ground, lifting small amounts up out of the hole. Guzeppi moved closer, knelt down on his haunches and peered in.

Slowly, the trowel moved, flicking one way then the other, the sound of scraping being the only noise to be heard. It was as though they were all holding their breath. Deftly, the officer-in-charge moved the last piece of soil away—to reveal another tiny child's skeleton.